The Grip Of Desire
The Story Of A Parish-Priest

by

Hector France

Double 9
BOOKS

The Grip Of Desire
The Story Of A Parish-Priest
by Hector France

ISBN: 978-93-62204-87-5

Published by

DOUBLE 9 BOOKS

2/13-B, Ansari Road
Daryaganj, New Delhi – 110002
info@double9books.com
www.double9books.com
Tel. 011-40042856

ABOUT THE AUTHOR

Hector France is a celebrated author renowned for his gripping narrative style and insightful portrayal of human emotions and societal dynamics. His masterpiece, "The Grip of Desire: The Story of a Parish-Priest," delves into the intricate journey of a parish-priest navigating the complexities of desire, duty, and morality. Set against the backdrop of a small parish community, France's novel offers a poignant exploration of the human condition, delving deep into the inner conflicts and external pressures faced by the protagonist. As the parish-priest grapples with his own desires and the expectations of his congregation, France skillfully weaves together themes of faith, temptation, and redemption, inviting readers to contemplate the nature of sin and virtue. With lyrical prose and nuanced characterizations, France captures the essence of the human experience, eliciting empathy and introspection from his audience. "The Grip of Desire" stands as a testament to France's literary prowess and his ability to engage readers with thought-provoking narratives that resonate on a deeply emotional level. Through this captivating tale, France invites readers on a journey of self-discovery and moral reckoning, ultimately leaving them with a profound understanding of the complexities of human nature and the enduring power of faith and forgiveness.

CONTENTS

I
THE CURÉ

"I will sing thy praises on the harp, oh Lord. But, my soul, whence cometh thy sadness, and wherefore art thou troubled."

(The *Introito* of the Mass).

The Curé of Althausen was reputed to be chaste. Was he so really? To tell the truth, I never believed him so; at thirty men are not chaste; they may try to be so; they rarely succeed. However that might be, he was a singular man.

He had a profound reverence for common sense, and it was said that he taught a strange doctrine to his flock; for example, that a day of work was more pleasing to God than a day of prayer; that the temples were for those who labour not, and that a good action was well worth a mass.

He maintained too that we purchase nothing with money in the other world, and that the coins, so appreciated among ourselves, have no currency beyond the grave, and a hundred other oddities of this kind, which in the good old times would have brought him to the stake. The Bishop had severely reprimanded him for all these heresies; but he seemed to pay no attention to it. Every Sunday, from the height of his pulpit, he continued to brave shamelessly the thunders of his Bishop and the thunders of heaven.

I went one day to hear him. His voice was sweet, persuasive, with a clear and harmonious tone. He said simply: "Love one another. That is the true religion of Christ. Love one another! everything is there: religion, philosophy and morality. Charity, properly understood, that which comes from the heart, is more pleasing to God than all the prayers. There are people who in order to pray neglect their home duties, their duties as wife and as mother. To them, I say of a truth, God remains deaf. He wills, before aught else, that you should fulfil your duties to your own. Every prayer which causes another to suffer is an impiety." Such was pretty near the essence of his sermons: they were short and simple. No great sonorous words, no pompous digressions, no Latin quotations which no one would have understood, no declamations on Our Lady of Lourdes or of La Salotte, on the miracle of Roses or the Immaculate Conception.

Thus he placed himself on a level with the simple souls who heard him, addressed himself only to their good sense and to their heart, and did not waste their time. He thought that after having worked hard throughout the week, it was well to spend the Sunday in rest and not in fresh fatigue.

But that which struck me most in him was his intelligent and expressive countenance, and I was astonished that a man hall-marked with such originality, should consent to vegetate, obscure and future-less, in the care of a poor village.

They said he was chaste. In truth that must be a task more arduous for him than for any other, for he bore on his face the impress of ardent passions. A disciple of Lavater would doubtless have sought for and found the secret of hidden dramas in the fine pale face. From his looks, now full of feverish ardour, now laden with sweet caresses, like the limpid eyes of a bride, the desires of the flesh in rebellion against deadly duty, seemed to burst forth with bold prolific thoughts.

One saw at times that his thoughts escaped in moments of forgetfulness from the clerical fetter.

Wild, wandering and licentious, they plunged with delight into the ocean of reverie. They left far behind them on the misty shore our conventions, our prejudices and our follies, and all those toils of spider-web which beset and catch and destroy so well the silly crowd, and which we call social rules, opinion and propriety.

Then the priest was gone; the man alone remained, the man of thirty, robust and full of life and yearning for all the joys of life. And beneath his gold-embroidered chasuble, near that altar laden with lustres and with flowers, amidst the floods of light and the floods of perfume, in that atmosphere saturated with the intoxicating waves of incense and the breath of maidens; surrounded by all those women, by all these girls on their knees before him or hanging on his lips; before all these modest or burning looks fixed upon his gaze, a strange sensation rose to his brain; the perspiration stood upon his forehead, he blushed and grew pale by turns; a shiver ran through his frame, and trying to subdue the ardour of his gaze, he turned towards the crowd of young girls, and said to them in a trembling voice:

—*Dominus vobiscum.*

—*Et cum spiritu tuo*, answered the choir of maidens. Oh, how willingly instead of the name of God would he have cast to them his heart.

II
THE CONFESSIONAL

"In the course of the holy missions to which I have consecrated a great portion of my life, I have often come across upright souls, disposed to make great progress in perfection, if they had found a skilful director."

THE REV. FATHER J.B. SCAROMELLI (*The Spiritual Guide*).

However, almost in spite of myself, I was interested in this young priest, and although disposed to believe that he was a knave like the rest, I was sensible of something in him so upright and so loyal that I was, from the very first, prejudiced in his favour.

And besides, these flashes of fiery passion which at times betrayed him, could they serve as an accusation against him? Could one take offence at his not having completely stifled at thirty years the fierce passions of youth and his violent desires? Was it not a proof on the contrary of his victorious struggles and of his energy?

And even though he should succumb before the imperious needs of potent nature, which would be the more culpable, he or the women who surrounded him, enveloped him with their gaze, encompassed him with their seductions; he or the husbands and fathers who seemed tacitly to say to him: "You are young, ardent, fall of passion and vigour, there is my daughter, there is my wife, I hand them to you, receive their confessions, dive into their looks, read in their soul, listen month to month to their most secret confidences, but beware of touching their lips."

Fools! And when the priest succumbs and their shame is noised abroad, they make a great uproar and complain to all the echoes, instead of bowing their head and humbly saying: *mea culpa.*

What? silly fool, you cast the modesty of your young wife and the virginity of your daughter as food for that envious celibate, you leave them alone in the mysterious tête-à-tête of the confessional, with no obstacle between his burning lust and the object of that lost, between those mouths which speak so low![1]

What will stop them? Duty? Virtue? His duty to himself? Laughable obstacles. Fragile plank on which you place your honour.

Her own virtue? Trust not to it overmuch, for he will know how to lead her to the will of his appetite. He will form her in such a way that she will pass by all the roads by which he will wish to guide her. It is a gate which he will contrive sooner or later to force, however it may be bolted, however it may be guarded by those sleepy gaolers which we call Principles.

The Confessional! Marvellous invention of greedy curiosity, satanic work of some hoary sinner! Hallowed goad of concupiscence, blessed antechamber which leads to the alcove, mysterious retreat where the priest sits between husband and wife, listens to their private talk and stands by, panting at all their excesses. Refuge more secret than the best padded boudoir. Formidable entrenchment sacred to all! What jealous lover would dare to lift that curtain of serge behind which are murmured so many secret confidences?

It is there that the artless virgin utters her first confessions; there, that the plighted maid reveals the beatings of her heart; there, that the blushing bride unveils the secrets of the nuptial couch.

He, the man of God, he listens … he collects all their voluptuous nothings and out of them creates worlds. Do you see him give ear? His face has kept its sanctimonious expression, but the fire gleams forth beneath his drooping eye-lid. He is leaning near, as near as possible to those stammering lips…. The penitent is silent. What! already? everything said already? Oh! that is not enough. She has passed too quickly over certain faults the remembrance of which covers her forehead with a blush. He is not satisfied. He wishes to know further. He reproves gently, "Why hesitate? God is full of pity; but in order that the pardon may be complete, the confession must be complete," and anew he questions, he presses … his temples throb, his blood boils, his hands burn, the demon of the flesh completely embraces him.

Come, incautious girl, speak, explain, give details, and by the confession of your pleasant faults, plunge into ecstasy the ruttish confessor.

[Footnote 1: In the confessionals of the Church of St. Gudule at Brussels and in those of the majority of Belgian churches an opening may be seen contrived in the screen, through which it is easy for mouths to meet.]

III
THE PARSONAGE

"The pretty parsonage encircled with verdure,
With its white pigeons cooing on the roof,
Assumes to the sun a saucy air of sanctity
And permits a smell of cooking to go forth."

CAMILLE DELTHIL (*Les Rustiques*).

The parsonage is seated on the summit of the hill and overlooks a part of the village and of the plain. The traveller perceives from far its white outline in the midst of a nest of verdure, and feels delighted at the view. Nothing more simple than this peaceful house. A single story above the ground-floor, with four windows from which the panes shine cheerfully in the first rays of the sun, and upon the red-tiled roof two attics with pointed gable. The door, which one reaches by a broad stone stair, is framed by two vines, their vigorous branches stretching up to the side of the windows, yielding to the hand, when September is come, their velvety, ruby bunches. Behind the house, a little garden surrounded by a hedge of green, at once an orchard, flower and kitchen garden.

In front, two hundred paces away, the old church with its stained walls on which the ivy clings, and its pointed belfry. The distance between is partly filled by several rows of lime-trees, which, seen from a distance, give to the parsonage the calm and cheerful look of those peaceful retreats where we sometimes dream of burying our existence. "Is not this the harbour!" says the tempest-beaten way-farer. "Oh! how happy must be the dweller in this calm abode!"

He might enter; he was welcome. The door was open to all, and this house, like that of the wise man, seemed to be of glass.

And all the women, young or old, knew hour by hour how their Curé spent his time, and in spite of all the perseverance which, according to principle, they had applied to discover some mystery in his life or the knot of a secret intrigue, they acknowledged unanimously that no one could give less hold for scandal than he.

Every day, when he had said mass, pruned his trees, watered his flowers, visited some poor or sick person, he shut himself up with his books and lived with them till the evening, until his servant came and said to him, "It is time for supper." Then he rose, ate his supper in silence, after putting aside the portion for the poor, and then returned to his books. That was all his life.

On Sunday, if the weather was fine, he took his breviary, and walked with slow steps along the high-road.

The children would stop their games and run forward to meet him in order to receive a caress from him, while the young girls whispered together and seemed to avoid him. The bolder ones met his gaze with a blush: perhaps they too would have liked, just as the little children, to receive a caress from the handsome Curé of Althausen. But he passed on without ever stopping, answering their timid salutations with an almost frigid gravity.

He acted wisely. He was full of distrust of himself, and kept himself in prudent reserve in face of the enemy. For he knew full well that the enemy was there, in these sweet woman's eyes and those smiles which wished him welcome.

Then the pagan intoxications of the Catholic rites were no more surrounding him to over-excite him and betray the trouble of his heart and the straying of his thoughts, and if he felt affected before the smiles of these marriageable girls, he armed himself with force sufficient to thrust back carefully to his inmost being his boldness and his desires.

It was no more the ardent passionate man who disclosed himself sometimes in rapid moments of forgetfulness, it was the priest austere and calm, the functionary salaried by the State to teach the religion of the State.

IV
EXPECTATION

"And the days and the hours glided on, and withdrawn within itself, affected by sorrows and joys unknown, the soul stretched its mysterious wing over a new life soon to dawn."

LAMENNAIS (*Une voix de prison*).

One of his greatest pleasures was to plunge into the woods which surround the village. He sought silence and solitude there, and when he heard the steps of a keeper or of some pedestrian, or even the happy voices of young couples calling one another, he concealed himself behind the masses of foliage, and hid himself with a kind of shame like a criminal. He wished to be alone, completely alone, so as to dream at his ease. Then he stretched himself in the sun on the warm grass, opened his breviary, the discreet confidant of all wandering thoughts, the screen for the priest's looks and thoughts, and listened to the insects' hum.

He followed the goings and comings of an ant or the capricious flight of a bumble-bee; then with his eyes lost in space, immersed in the profundity of nature, he dreamed....

One could have seen by his smile that he was wandering in spirit in the laughing and limit-less garden of hope, pausing here and there on rosy illusions and fair chimeras like a butterfly on flowers.

They were delicious hours which he passed thus, full of forgetfulness and indolence. He enjoyed the present moment, the present, poor, humble and obscure, but which held neither disquietude nor care.

Sometimes regrets for a past of which no one was aware came and knocked at the door of his dreams, but he drove them for away, saying like Werther:

"The past is past."

The hand of time revolved without his giving heed, and often night surprised him in his fantastic reveries. The good country-folk bad been sorely puzzled by these solitary walks in the depths of the woods.

They talked at first of some scandalous intrigue, and the Curé had no difficulty in discovering that he was followed and watched by rigid parishioners, anxious about his morality and his virtue. More than once through the foliage he believed he saw vigilant sentinels who watched him carefully.

Lost labour! Never did those who tried with such unwearied perseverance to detect his secret amours, have the pleasure of beholding *that mistress* whom they would have been so happy to cover with shame and scorn.

They were obliged to renounce it, for his mistress then was that admirable fairy, invisible and dumb to the common herd, who displays her beauties to the gaze of a chosen race alone, as she murmurs her divine and chaste sonnets in their ear.

It was nature all radiant, which caressed his brow with the breeze, which sang by his ear with the mysterious harmony of the woods, which gladdened his sight with the flower of the fields, the verdant meadow, the golden harvest. His loves were the hollow path which is lost in the mountain, the old willow which leans over the edge of the pool, the sparrow which chatters among the leaves, the splendours of the starry sky, the magic mirages of the evening.

They were all the melodies which poets have made to vibrate on the strings of lyres, and in those moments of delicious ecstasy he forgot the vexations, the littlenesses and the miseries of the world, and if anyone had asked him what was the aim of his life, he would have replied like Anaxagoras:

"To love Nature, and to contemplate the sky."

But among his uncouth surroundings, who would have been capable of understanding these sweet pleasures and that over-excitement of soul and brain, by means of which he sought to benumb his senses and to change the current of his heart, that heart which like the body has its imperious needs.

He had reached that fatal epoch when man experiences an insatiable hunger for love, and for want of a woman will nourish some monstrous fantasy, or even, like the prisoner of Saintine, become enamoured of a flower.

V
THE MEETING

"Skilled physicians have remarked that an emanation of infinitely projectile forces continually takes place from the eyes of impassioned persons, of lovers or of lascivious women, which communicates insensibly to those who listen to or behold them, the same agitation by which they are affected."

RESTIF DE LA BRETONNE (*Le Paysan perverte*).

One afternoon, while returning to the village, the Curé chanced to meet a young girl who was unknown to him. She was but poorly dressed, and her shoes were white with dust; but youth and gaiety shone forth beneath the glow of her cheeks, her blue eye sparkled under the dark arch of her eyebrows, and the voluptuous opulence of her shape made one forget the poverty of her dress. From her straw hat with its faded ribbons escaped heavy tresses which shone like gold.

Bending over his breviary, the Curé passed, casting a sidelong look, one of those priestly looks which see without being seen; but the stranger compelled him to raise his head. She had stood still and was fixing on him smiling a bright and confident look.

On seeing this, the Curé stood still also.

Certainly, in the white flock of his congregation he counted just as lovely creatures every Sunday, he encountered just as provoking smiles. Nevertheless, he was troubled; he felt a secret flame course through his veins; a kind of charm emanated front this girl. He remembered reading that magnetic currents flow forth from certain women which inflame the senses, and he took a step backwards; but the charm operated in spite of himself, his eyes remained fixed on the seductive outlines of the figure of the unknown. She enquired of him politely the way to the *Mairie*. In pointing it out to her the Curé perhaps displayed more earnestness than was necessary, he even took a few steps with her as far as the entrance to the village, then he returned home, thinking of this pretty girl.

During supper his servant told him that some mountebanks had arrived in the village, and that they were going to give a performance the same evening in the market-place. In fact a drum was heard beating the call, and the hoarse voice of the clown announcing "a grand acrobatic spectacle, accompanied with dances and followed by a pantomime."

Involuntarily the Curé's thought turned to the stranger; he went upstairs into his study and behind his half-closed shutters he could take part in the spectacle.

As he expected, the pretty girl was there, and seen from this distance in the night, half-lighted by a few smoky lamps, with her little bodice of velvet, her gauze skirt spangled with gold, her flesh-coloured tights, she was really charming. At that moment she was dancing, with wonderful lightness and grace, some lascivious fandango, while she accompanied herself with the castanets.

She was smiling at the crowd, delighting in the effect which she knew how to produce with her sparkling eye and her white teeth and her rosy lips, and the Curé was intoxicated by that smile. Then he cast his eyes over the rough crowd, and ha was grieved at so much cost for such an audience: *Margaritas ante porcos*, he murmured, *Margaritas ante porcos*.

In order to admire her better, he had taken a field-glass and lost none of her gestures.

Her bosom was boldly bared, and he feasted his eyes upon the sweet furrow of her breasts, he followed the delicious outline of her leg, and found his heart melting before the undulating movements of her graceful bust and her sturdy hips.

He abruptly left the window, took up a book at random and tried to read.

But this was in vain; his eyes only were reading, his thoughts were elsewhere; they were in the market-place which was in frolic with the dancer.

He wished to stop this libertine thought; he read aloud: "The fall is great after great efforts. The soul risen so high in heroism and holiness falls very heavily to the earth.... Sick and embittered it plunges into evil with a savage hunger, as though to avenge itself for having believed."

At another time, he would have said: "It is a warning." But he saw not the warning, he only saw the dancer, and he murmured: "How beautiful is she!"

He took the hundred paces round his table; but his body only was there, his thoughts always were hovering on the market-place round the spangled petticoat.

He returned to the window. All was over; the lamps were put out, the crowd was slowly dispersing; five or six inquisitive ones were standing round the heavy carriage of the company, from which some gleam of light escaped.

He remained a long time leaning on his elbow at his window, looking at the stars and listening mechanically to all the noises outside. The market-place became empty. Only the stamping of the horses was to be heard fastened near by, in the thick shade of the old lime-trees. A slender thread of light again filtered up to hint.

VI
THE LOOK

"His pupils glowed in the dim twilight, like burning coals."

LÉON CLAUDEL (*Les Va-nu-pieds*).

It was like a lover attracting him, a magic thread which fastened yonder was unwinding itself to his eye. He could not withdraw it thence, and armed with his glass he tried to reach the bottom of the mysterious light. Two or three times he saw a figure which he thought he recognized, pass and repass in the lighted square.

Then the devil tempted him, like Jesus on the mountain. He did not show him the kingdoms of the earth, but he gave him a glimpse of the mountebank undressed. "Go not there," his good angel cried to him. But the Curé turned a deaf ear; he went down noiselessly from his room and ventured into the market-place.

In order to approach the carriage, he displayed all the strategy of a skilful general; he first walked the length of the parsonage, then crossed the market-place, then little by little, artfully, disappeared beneath the lime-trees.

[PLATE I: THE LOOK. No one could have detected him plunging his burning gaze into the depth of the little room where the fair dancer, stripped of her tights, appeared to him half-naked.]

The house on wheels was only a few paces away, silent, motionless, crammed up. Within those ten feet of planks was perceptible an excess of lives, passions, miseries, joys, of comedies and dramas; quite a world in miniature.

Breathings and rustlings issued now and then from this living coffin. It wan the heavy slumber of fatigue, of fever, or of drink.

One window was lighted still, and the half-drawn curtain allowed a room to be seen the size of a sentry-box.

He passed slowly by, and gave a look.

A strange emotion seized him: he would have wished not to have seen, and he felt full of a delicious trouble at having seen.

He looked round him with alarm; he was quite alone. No one had detected him, no one could have detected him, plunging his burning gaze into the depth of the little room where the fair dancer, stripped of her tights, appeared to him half-naked and dazzling like a goddess of Rubens.

VII
THE SALUTE

"She is fair, she is white, and her golden hair
Sweetly frames her rosy face:
The limpid look of her azure eyes
Beguiles near as much as her half-closed lip."

N. CHANNARD (*Poésies inédites*).

The next day, from break of dawn, the strolling players were already making their preparations for departure.

He saw the fair dancer again.

No longer had she on her gauze dress with golden spangles, nor the tights which displayed her shape, nor her glittering diadem, nor the imitation pearls in her hair. She had resumed her poor dress of printed cotton, her darned stockings and her coarse shoes; but there was still her blue eye with its strange light, her pleasant face, her silky hair falling in thick tresses on her sunburnt neck, and beneath her cotton bodice the figure of an empress was outlined with the same opulence.

A knot of women was there, laughing and talking scandal. What were these stupid peasants laughing at?

At length the heavy vehicle began to move, drawn by two broken-winded horses.

The fair girl is at the little window and watches, inquisitive and smiling, the silly scoffing crowd.

"Pass on, daughter of Bohemia, and despise these men who jest at your poverty, these women who cast a look of scorn and hate. They scorn and hate you, because they have not your splendid hair, nor the brightness of your eyes, nor your white teeth, nor your fresh smile, nor your suppleness, grace and vigour, nor your bewitching shape; despise them in your turn, but envy them not, them who despise and envy you."

Thus the Curé murmured to himself as the carriage was passing by.

She is there still at her little window, like a youthfull picture by Greuze. She lifts her eyes and recognizes the priest, and bows with that smile which has already so affected him. What grace in that simple gesture! What promises in those gentle eyes! In the midst of the hostile scornful looks of that foolish crowd she has met a friendly face; she has read sympathy and perhaps a secret admiration on the intelligent countenance of the priest.

The Curé replied to her salute, and for a long while his gaze pursued the carriage.

Meanwhile the good ladies whispered among themselves, and said to one another with a scandalized air: "Did you see? He bowed to the mountebank!"

VIII
THE FEVER

"Who has not had those troubled nights, when the storm rages within, when the soul, miserably oppressed with shameful desires, floats in the mud of a swamp?"

MICHELET (*L'Amour*).

He was quite aware of his imprudence, but was unable to withdraw his eyes from the road, and his thoughts still followed the carriage long after it had disappeared behind the tall poplars. It seemed to him that it was a portion of himself which was going away for ever.

What! was the madman then beginning to cast his heart thus on the roads, and could he feel smitten by this creature whom he had scarcely met?

No, it was not she whom he loved, but she had just made the over-full cup run over. She or another, it was indifferent to him. His altered feelings of desire needed at length to drink freely. He was thirsty, what signified to him the vessel?

Hitherto he had only felt that ordinary confusion which the chaste man experiences in presence of the woman, for hitherto his sight bad only paused complacently upon pretty fresh faces, and if his thought wandered beyond, he drove it back with care to his very inmost being; but now that he had seen the naked breast of a pretty girl, that he had relished it with his gaze, embraced it with his desire, that he had yielded to a fatal forgetfulness, his flesh, so long subdued and humiliated, profited by that moment of error, and subdued him in its turn.

A kind of frenzy had taken possession of his being in a moment, and in the sleepless night which he had just passed, he had given himself up to an absolute orgy in his over-excited imagination.

That wandering girl who had just disappeared, had carried away his modesty.

He felt his heart beating for her; but he felt that his heart was beating for all alike; girls or women, he wanted them all, he defiled them all with his thoughts.

And so, after ten years of struggles, the virtue of the Curé of Althausen dissolved one evening before the naked breast of a rope-dancer, like snow before the sun.

That day was a Sunday, and, as he did not come downstairs, his servant came to warn him that the time for Mass was drawing near.

She stood struck with the strange look on his countenance, at the fatigue displayed on his features, and anxiously enquired of him the cause.

The Curé assured her that she was mistaken, that he bad never felt better; but at the same time he gave a glance at his mirror.

He was frightened at his face and he remained a long time thoughtful, contemplating the gloomy fire of his own look.

That sinister countenance seemed to him to presage some approaching calamity.

Thus, there are men whom fate has marked on the forehead with a fatal stamp. The mysterious sign is not displayed at every time and before all; but at certain epochs of life, when the unknown breath caresses the predestinated or cursed head, the mark all at once appeals, like a tawny light in the depth of night.

A curse! Fatality has moulded that man's brain, it has left its potent impress on his skull.

—With what seal then am I marked? he cried. Is it that of reprobation which God has stamped upon my face?

No, simpleton that thou art, it is the phosphorus of thy brain, which catches fire from time to time.

IX
DURING VESPERS

"There is a beautiful girl of sixteen, white as milk, rosy as a rose-bud, fresh as a spring morning,—and chaste as Vesta."

A. DELVAU (*Le Fumier d'Ennius*).

He went up into the pulpit, and preached a sermon on this text: "Blessed are the pure in heart." He had prepared it the day before, previous to the arrival of that enchanting player, and his thoughts had been since then too occupied with very different subjects for him to search for another theme.

Bitter mockery! What could he say to these good people about hearts pure and chaste? He tried, all the same, and said some excellent things. He spoke above all about temptation, which, following the expression of a Father of the Church, "is only, to commence with, an ant which tickles, and finishes by becoming a devouring lion."

"Alas," he said, "how many, without meaning it, have been thus devoured, beginning perhaps with this pious individual."

His sermon took great effect. An old woman wept, and several members of the congregation appeared to sigh and think that it was a long time since they had been devoured thus.

He had an inclination to laugh, as he came down from the pulpit, at the words which he had just uttered on purity of heart, and he wondered that he had been able to bring so much conviction and warmth to bear upon a subject to which he was henceforth completely a stranger.

His own scepticism terrified him, and he saw that he had taken a long step into evil Nevertheless he did concern himself at that, and from his place near the pulpit he turned his impassioned gaze with more assurance on the group of young girls.

Passion is a brutal level which equalizes us all. There remained in him nothing more of the priest, there only remained the man full of desires, and he flung his desires in riot upon that gyneceum which he thought belonged to him.

In certain village churches, all the young girls are placed apart, near the choir, sometimes even in the choir itself, under the eyes of the priest, as if they wished to leave the most convenient choice to that never satiated Priapus.

The handsome Curé of Althausen made his choice therefore at his ease and without the least shame.

This one was fair and pale, that other dark and high in colour; this one was thin and delicate, that one fat and plump; this one was prettier, that other more graceful. He knew not upon which to stop. He would have wished for them all, for they all had that provoking beauty which pleases the devil so much: exuberant youth.

And he could not grow weary of contemplating all these fresh faces; his look, more than once, encountered sweet looks, and then he experienced a delicious shock which stirred his heart.

It was not only the faces which excited his longings. In spite of himself, the opulent breast of the fair player entered his imagination and his thoughts seemed to search each one's neckerchief, seeking this powerful nourishment for his appetite. He bad tried to drive away these abominable desires, but it was in vain: the forbidden fruit was there and something seemed to tell him that he had only to stretch out his hand to seize it.

As he tried to escape from this diabolical hallucination, he remarked all at once in the gallery set apart for the wives of the principal inhabitants, a young girl, a stranger, whose beauty struck him.

She was pale and dark, and her full lips, of a brilliant red, were lightly pencilled with a black down.

Her deep, burning eyes darted flames, and were fixed on the priest with a persistency which made him blush.

The erotic fever which had possessed him disappeared at once. He was ashamed of himself and of his secret thoughts, for it seemed to him that this stranger read to the bottom of his soul.

This flaming look which he had caught sight of, weighed upon him like remorse.

In the evening, at the *Salut* he saw again the same face and the same burning eyes, fastened on his own; but be thought he discovered that there was nothing terrible about them, and that what in his trouble he had taken for inquisition and wrath, might in reality be nothing but tenderness and sweetness.

He made skilful enquiries regarding the stranger; she was Mademoiselle Suzanne Durand, who had just completed her education at Saint-Denis, the daughter of Captain Durand, "a bad parishioner," his servant told him, "who paid little regard to the service and treated the priests as humbugs."

X
IN PARENTHESIS

"Is it meet for you to be among such vicious people? Envy, anger and avarice reign among some; modesty is banished among others; these abandon themselves to intemperance and sloth, and the pride of these rises to insolence. It is all over; I will dwell no longer among the seven deadly sins."

LE SAGE (*Gil-Blas*).

I must take my courage with both hands to continue to unfold before you the events however simple of this simple tale. Already I hear the eternal flock of hypocrites and fools protesting and crying out at outraged morality. I know them, these indignant voices of the defenders of morality. They arise every time that we unveil the vilenesses, that we expose the gangrenes of our institutions; corrupt magistracy, vicious clergy, rotten army; tottering tripod which holds up that worm-eaten scaffolding which is called *social order*.

But the sages of the present day and a great number of those of former times have always made me laugh, particularly where beneath the mask of the venerable philosopher or the hood of the austere monk, I discovered the grin of the rogue.

I shall stop my ears then to their clamours and I shall continue the task I have undertaken.

Nevertheless, some sincere persons may object: "What sort then is this cynical priest which you display to us? Is there nothing then remaining to him, and in default of modesty and morality, in default of his energy, which has foundered thus all at once, could he not still lay hold of the wrecks of faith?"

Faith? It had fled away long ago, since the day when he had laid aside his dress of catechumen, and, initiated in the secrets of the sanctuary, he had laid hand on the priestly jugglings.

Then he had been filled with an infinite sorrow. But he had prudently repressed it deep within, and in this centre of devout hypocrisy and holy intrigue, he had covered himself again, like all the rest, with a varnish of sanctity.

Faith! What priest is he who, amidst the religious pageants, the public falsehoods and the private apostacies, the burlesque scenes behind the stage preceding the solemn performance, what priest is he who has preserved his faith?

What priest is he, upright and wishing to remain upright—there are such lost in obscure positions—who has not said quietly to himself, in his inmost being, all alone with his conscience, what the Curé of Althausen often repeated to himself:

"Faith, bitter mockery! to believe by order, without examination and without reply!

"Annihilation of the individual, murder of the thought, criminal denial of the intelligence, the most sublime of man's gifts!

"Oh miseries of the soul! filth of the body! vileness of the spirit! unfathomable depths of human folly! What am I and what are we, and whom do we wish to deceive?

"What are we, we who say to others, 'Be just, humble, chaste, pitiful? Have faith.' Oh! priests, my brethren, and you, my masters, you have tried to close my soul as we close a book, to extinguish my thought like a too lively flame and to bend my rebellious reason; but my soul unfolds in spite of you; the book swollen with doubts, bursts under the clasp, my thought rekindles at the first spark, and my reason rises to its full height to protest from the deeps of darkness where you would bury it.

"For I have followed you step by step in the tortuous ways of your dark lives. I have listened to your words and I have seen your deeds, and the deeds gave the lie to your words.

"Then I said to myself: Perhaps we are living in an evil period. The curse is upon this age. And I have sought to relieve my thoughts in less gloomy pictures. I have ransacked history to find there the golden age of Catholicism. But the pages of Catholic history are stained with mire and blood. The dealers of the temple, more powerful than Christ, have in their turn driven him out of the sanctuary. Humanity, imprisoned in the round of hypocritical conventions and nefarious laws, revolves unceasingly on itself, the eternal Ixion fastened to the eternal wheel.

"Whither are we going? Whither are we going in the ocean of social tempests, of political knaveries, of religious falsehoods? Centuries pass, empires fall, nations disappear, religions, at first blazing torches, then smoky harmful lamps, die out one by one, generations succeed generations with hands stretched out towards the future whence the new light must spring, and the future, gloomy gulf, will swallow up all, men and things, worlds and gods.

"I have ransacked history and I have discovered that yesterday as to-day, there were among those men who call themselves shepherds of souls, pride, falsehood, injustice, thirst of riches, hatred and luxury, but neither belief, nor truth, nor faith."

Do not cry out, saintly souls, virtuous prelates, gentle apostles, frank and rosy curates, but let him among you who is without any of his sins, rise up and cast the first stone at the Curé of Althausen.

XI
THE FLESH

"The man tries in vain, he must yield to his nature:
A woman excites him untying her girdle."

VICTOR HUGO.

Eight days had passed away.

Eight days, during which he had tried with supreme efforts to silence his senses, and to chain down his wild thoughts.

He had become calmer and more master of himself.

The species of vertigo which had seized him is an accident frequent enough among young priests, who in spite of all the seductions which surround them and the occasions of falling, wish to remain steadfast in duty.

"For we do not deny ourselves the inclinations of nature with impunity, it is an age at which the physical delights of love become necessary to every well organized being, and it is never but at the expense of health, and of the repose of the whole life, that we can he faithful to the vows of perpetual chastity."[1]

The crisis, according to the temperament of the *subject*, is more or less violent, and occurs again several times, until he finally yields to the temptation, or again until madness seizes him.

Then everybody is terrified to learn one day in the *Gazette des Tribunaux* the horrible details of some crime so abominable that one would believe it sprung from the horrors of a nightmare.

Let them not be astonished! the wretch who has committed it was in reality overcome by hallucination. In the struggles of the will against the appetites, the reason expires.

Madness has clasped the brain, too feeble to strive against the flesh in revolt, and the latter has avenged itself as the brute avenge itself by the act of a brute.

"The torch of reason completely extinguished, the victim of senseless vows has brought the piece to an end by a catastrophe which alarms modesty, astonishes nature and disconcerts religion."[2]

Meanwhile, I repeat, the Curé seemed calmer: to the crisis had succeeded a kind of depression and languor.

He resumed his studies with more eagerness, and only went out in order to go from the parsonage to the church, conscientiously occupying himself in his profession.

His senses were slumbering again.

But the mischievous devil was at his heels and did not lose sight of him.

The old serpent, says the apostle, finds the means of tempting by the very virtues which we possess, even to making them the occasions of sin to us; how would he not tempt us when it is sin itself which dwells in our heart?

[Footnote 1: *Dictionnaire des Sciences Médicales*. Vol. VI.]

[Footnote 2: The inconveniences of compulsory chastity are more or less grave according to different cases: with youthful subjects, vigorous, and fed on succulent foods, mental derangement under the most horrible forms, such as Satyriasis, Priapism, Erotomania, Nymphomania and even death may quickly result from it. Instances are numerous. (Sciences médicales).]

XII
THE TEMPTATION

"Alas! to return alone to our deserted home
With no open window to herald our approach,
If, when from the horizon we behold our roof,
We cannot say, 'My return gladdens my home'."

LAMARTINE (*Jocelin*).

It was at Sunday's Mass, in the sanctuary itself, that he waited for his prey. The priest had scarcely reached the steps of the altar, his hands laden with the holy vessels, when, lifting his eyes to the gallery, he encountered the look he dreaded.

Suzanne Durand was there, fixing on him her eyes, filled with magnetic force.

He returned once again full of trouble.

His servant, surprised at his agitation, overwhelmed him with inquisitive questions; he escaped from her and hastened towards the woods. He cast himself on the moss at the foot of an old oak and began to reflect. The dark eyes followed him everywhere.

"Whither am I going?" he said to himself. "Why does the sight of this young girl agitate my heart in this way?" And he examined his heart and found it saturated with bitterness, disgust, weariness and regret, and in the midst of all that, something unknown was springing up. It was like a germ of hope which all at once had risen out of nothingness, a fleeting light which flickered in the dense gloom of his life.

He heard the sound of a voice at some distance, a fresh, gay, melodious voice, to which a deeper note was answering. Spring, youth and love were mingling their accents together. Between the foliage he saw them slowly passing. They did not see him. Absorbed in the contemplation of themselves, arm in arm, with joined hands, their faces together, they passed along with bright looks, and open hearts, rejoicing in the seventh heaven.

Now and again they stopped, and he all in play, took hold of her thick knot of hair, drew her head backwards and gave her a long kiss on the lips.

He did not tire of it, but she pushed him back with all her strength, putting her hand on his mouth and saying to him, "That's enough, naughty boy, that's enough." The Curé knew them well. She was the best and prettiest girl in his congregation, and he, the happy rogue, sang in the choir. And he began to envy the happiness of this rustic; he would have wished to be for a moment this rude ignorant peasant, and who knows, for a moment? why not always? Would he not be happier going each morning to till the fruitful soil, to sow the furrow, and then to cut the sheaves of the golden harvest, than to vegetate as he was, casting his sterile grain upon arid souls.

After the hard toil of the day, when he returned in the evening to his roof of thatch, he would meet with a smile of welcome, the smile of a loved wife, which would compensate him for his fatigues.

He followed them with his eyes, full of envy and bitterness at heart, and when they had buried themselves behind the young underwood, when he no longer heard the sound of steps, or fresh bursts of laughter, he rose and sadly resumed his way to the village.

Evening had come. The twilight was stretching its dark veil over all. The peasants dressed in their Sunday clothes were chatting on their door-steps while they waited for supper. Near the inns there rose the confused sound of gamblers' voices and drunkards' songs; but here and there through the windows he saw the bright fire of vine-twigs blazing merrily on the hearth, while the mother or the eldest daughter poured the steaming soup into the large blue-flowered plates ranged on the white wood table.

He saw it all, and he walked with slow steps to his solitary abode.

He thought of his life wasted, of the years of his prime which were passing away, without leaving any more traces than the skimming of the swallow's wing leaves upon the verdant brook.

Oh! the fleeting time which carries all away, the hour which glides away dull and empty, the barren youth which flies, and the white hairs which come with disillusion, discouragement and despair. "Stay, stay, oh youth; stay but another day!"

But what matters his youth to him? What joys has it brought him; what pleasures has he tasted? has he breathed the burning breath of life, of that fair life at twenty which unfolds like a ripe pomegranate, and casts to the warm sun its treasures and its perfumes?

XIII
THE RESOLUTION

"My life was blighted, my universe was changed; I had entangled myself without knowing it in an inextricable drama. I must get out of it at any cost, and I had no way of unravelling it. I resolved by all means to find one."

J. JANIN (L'Ans morte).

He sat by his desolate hearth and began to think with terror of the eternal solitude of that hearth. Alone! always alone! Already he had said to himself very often that he had chosen the wrong road, that this arid and desolate path was not the one needful to his ardent soul, that the hopes with which he had formerly been deluded, were falsehoods in reality, and that the God whom they had made him believe that he loved with such ardour, left his soul empty and barren.

To love God! The love of God! High-sounding, hollow words which enable hypocrites to take advantage of the common people; fantastic passion kindled in the heart of fools for the amazement of the simple!

Ah! how willingly would he have replaced the worn-out vision of this chimerical phantom with the likeness of some young girl, with sweet look and smile, full of promise.

And the burning memory of the wanton player came and blended with the fresh and radiant memory of the charming pupil of Saint-Denis.

"But why, priest, dost thou permit thy fevered guilty imagination to wander thus? Pursue thy course, pursue it without stopping, without looking back; henceforth it is too late to retrace thy path; anyhow be chaste, be chaste under pain of shame and infamy.

"Thou must not be chaste in view of recompense like a slave, thou must be chaste without expectance."[1]

He took up a book, his sovereign remedy in hours of temptation. It was the life of St. Antony, written by his companion, St. Athanasius.

"The demons presented to his mind thoughts of impurity, but Antony repulsed them by prayer. The devil excited his senses, but Antony blushed with shame, as though the fault were his own, and strengthened his body by faith, by prayer and by vigil. The devil, seeing himself vanquished thus, took the shape of a young and lovely woman and imitated the most lascivious actions in order to beguile him, but Antony raising his thoughts towards heaven and considering the loftiness and excellence of the soul which is given to us, extinguished these burning coals by which the devil hoped to inflame his heart through this deception, and drove away the devilish creature."

Marcel shrugged his shoulders and closed the book. How many times already he had tried all those means without success.

He leant his burning forehead on his hands and, in self-contemplation, tried to see to the bottom of his soul.

Chaste! always chaste! What! Was the flower of his youth wasted away thus, in incessant, barren struggles? If only peace of heart, and a quiet conscience remained to him; if quietude sat by his hearth, as his masters many a time had promised him! But no, alone with himself, he felt himself to be with an enemy.

For many years, it had been so, and a lying voice had cried to him without ceasing: "Wait for happiness, for sweet pure joys, wait for it till to-morrow: to-morrow all this fury will have passed away, these raging blasts which rise to thy brain will have vanished; thy vanquished senses will leave thee in peace, and calm and strong, thou shalt rejoice over an untroubled conscience and over the satisfaction of duty fulfilled."

And he had waited in vain. Now he had reached ripe age, and the future is visible ever more gloomy; to-morrow has come, as sad, as empty, and as desolate as yesterday.

He was tired at last of waiting, patiently, humbly, resigned like the beast of burden which awaits the slaughterhouse. Beasts of burden! Are we not that, all we who with brow bent under humiliation, injustice, thankless toil; with the heart embittered by tedious deception and tedious despair, miseries of heart and miseries of body, wait, wait ever, wait vainly for a more brilliant sun to shine at last, until at the end of the day there rises before us the only guest we have never expected, on whom we counted not,—the solution of the great problem, the radical cure for all our ills— DEATH.

Death, which with its brutal hand, seizes us at the moment when perhaps at last we are going to rest ourselves and rejoice.

No, that shall not be. He will not continue to vegetate without happiness in these dull, common-place surroundings; to walk at random in this road bristling with thorns; to pursue his disheartening career, enclosed by miserable vices.

Nothing around him but stupid, vulgar prosiness, foolish moral annihilation. No poetry, no golden ray, no rainbow! Everything most low, unsightly, pitiful. Such was his lot as priest.

Complaints of the soul, wandering flashes of the imagination, criminal aspirations of the heart, sinful desires … these … that was all.

Was this then life?

Was it for this that God had created him, that his mother had drawn him painfully forth from her entrails, that nature had one day counted one intelligent being the more?

Ah! he felt full well it was not so. He felt full well it was not so by his thirst for emotions and enjoyment, by his altered lips, by his aspirations for an unknown world. He was in haste to strip off for once at least this old man's shell which enveloped him, this black, hideous, hardened covering of the bad priest, beneath which he felt his vitality, his youth, his strength, his heart of thirty, bounding, boiling, roaring, like burning lava.

The next day be remembered that though it was nearly six months since he had taken possession of his cure, his pastoral visits were not yet completed.

In fact, he had gone everywhere, even to Captain Durand's. Only, he had found the door closed and, after the information he received, he had fully resolved not to go there again.

[Footnote 1: The Antigone of Soto.]

XIV
THE CAPTAIN

"The disposition of a man of sixty is nearly always the happy or sad reflection of his life. Young people are such as Nature has made them; old men have been fashioned by the often awkward hands of society."

ED. ABOUT (*Trente et Quarante*).

The old Captain was in fact a bad parishioner, as his servant had told him, and had only one good quality in the eyes of that careful housekeeper, "that he was always shining like a new halfpenny."

Durand, in fact, was what is called in a regiment "a smart soldier," which means to say "a clean soldier." And still, one of his most important occupations was to brush his things. The son of peasants, without patronage, fortune or backstairs influence, he had raised himself, a rare and difficult thing nowadays; therefore he was proud of himself, and would say to anyone who would listen to him: "I am the son of my own deeds."

He had been one of those serious-minded officers of whom Jules Noriac speaks, who instead of dividing their many spare hours between the goddess of play and the goddess of the bar, employ themselves in regimental reforms.

The dimensions of a spur-rowel, the length and thickness of a trouser-strap, the improvement of a whitening for belts which does not fall off, were questions which had more importance and interest for him than a question of State.

The slave of his duties, he was excessively severe in the service, and this stiffness and severity he had brought, it was said, into his household.

With these military qualities; passive obedience, scrupulous cleanliness and the vulgar courage necessary for a son of Mars, Durand, with a good reputation and full of zeal, had had when very young, a rapid advance. At one moment he had foreseen a brilliant future, but his ambitious hopes had been quickly deceived. He saw the Baron de Chipotier, the Comte de Boisflottant, and the son of Pillardin, the lucky millionaire, successively come into the regiment, and these sprigs of lofty lineage, full of brilliancy and loquacity, naturally eclipsed the modest qualities of the obscure upstart soldier. Spending their life in cafés, overwhelmed with debt, loved by the women, they laughed among themselves at all the *minutiae* of the service, which they treated as beneath their notice, ridiculed their superiors, and especially the serious-minded officers. Everything was forgiven them, they were rich. Durand was filled with indignation; he saw everything he had respected become an object of sarcasm to these young men, and his most cherished convictions turned into ridicule. He was like those devout persons who, when they hear an unseemly oath or an impious word, tremble and pray heaven not to cast its avenging lightning; he asked himself if social order was not overthrown, if the army was not marching to its ruin. He began to talk of his apprehensions, of this pitiable state of things, and they laughed in his face. But when these frivolous, turbulent, incapable officers became his chiefs, chiefs over him, the studious, model officer, the upright man, the slave to the regulations, he began to mistrust everything, society, France, the empire, the justice of God, and himself. It was from this period that the crabbed character dated, by which he was known.

He passed a long season thus, full of anger and jealousy: then the time for his retirement arrived, that time to which all the forgotten, the obscure, the pariahs of the army look forward during long years, and which casts them forth into the social world, ignorant and strangers.

Then he had retired to his own village, dividing his time between the tending of his garden, and the cares which were occasioned him by his daughter Suzanne.

XV
MEMORIES

"Often risen from humble origin, he has gained the respect of all and the public esteem; but this cannot prevent his having a restless spirit; he misses the duty which has called him for so long at the appointed hour. Around him are scattered the memorials of his regiment, his eye catches them and a mist comes over it."

ERNEST BILLAUDEL (*Les Hommes d'épée*).

He was up by dawn, and the villagers on their way to their fields sometimes stopped to cast an inquisitive look over his garden palings. They saw him dressed in a linen jacket, with the glorious ribbon adorning his button-hole, weeding his flower-garden, turning up his walks, pruning his trees, clearing his flowers of caterpillars, watering his borders, with great drops of sweat pouring down, bending over his labour like a negro under the lash.

"What a pity!" they said, "for a rich man to give himself so much trouble! If it only repaid him!" And they shouted to him: "Good-morning, Captain Durand, how are you to-day?" — "Pretty well, thank you," replied Durand, in a peevish tone. — "Still warm to-day, Captain; but you had it warmer in Africa, didn't you?" At the word Africa, the old soldier's eyes brightened, his forehead lost its wrinkles, and a smile came to his lips. All his past rose before him. Africa, the Bedouins, the gunshots, the razzias, the bare desert, the fresh oases, the life in camp, the glasses of absinthe, the days of rain and sun, the ostrich chases, the watch for the jackal and the races over the plain. All this, helter-skelter, in crowds, crossing, following, multiplying, like the sheaves of sparks which burst forth from a rocket.

Ah! Ah! that was the happy time. And then he would stop and forget his work, his flowers, his grafts, and his espaliers; he would forget the peasants who were there, laughing quietly and nudging one another, and saying: "The old man is gone in the head."

For they understood nothing of the tear, which all at once trickled from the corner of his eye-lid, a bitter drop which overflowed from the too full cup of his heart.

Ah! youth has but one time, and they do well, who when the sun gilds their brow, cast their sap to its warm caresses. The winter, gloomy shadow, will come but too soon to freeze their slowly opened buds, leaving only a trunk, dry and bare.

Then, when nothing more than a few warm cinders remain at the bottom of the human engine, we try to warm ourselves again at this cold hearth, and to search among those dying sparks which we call memories.

And these memories of a time for ever fled, these lights which gladden or stir again your old heart sad and cold, these are the simple and fruitful beliefs, the transports of the soul, the insane devotions, the ardent passions, and all those orgies of heart and sense, all those frenzies of imagination, and all those follies of youth, which cause the wise to cry out so loudly, and which are the only feast-days of life.

Hasten then, young man, hasten; take the good which comes to thee, and be not decoyed by idle fancies; wait not till to-morrow to be glad. To-morrow is the age of ripeness, of the falling fruit, the wrinkled brow, the faded flower; it is the vanished locks; it is the blood which grows cold, the smile which comes not back; it is in fine the worm of deceptions, which is ever growing larger and gnawing what may be left of thy heart.

XVI
THE EPAULET

"Really, yes! I love my calling. This active adventurous life is amusing, do you see? there is something as regards discipline itself which has its charm; it is wholesome and relieves the spirit to have one's life ordered in advance with no possible dispute, and consequently with no irresolution or regret. Thence comes lightness of heart and gaiety. We know what we must do, we do it, and we are content."

EMILE AUGIER et JULES SANDEAU (*Le Gendre de M. Poirier*).

And Durand threw down his rake or his spade.

—Well! here you are already, cried the old housekeeper; breakfast is not ready.

—My paper? he said shortly.

Sometimes the paper had not yet arrived; then he sat down near the window and watched impatiently for the carrier. There he is, coming out of the next street. He goes down with all haste to open the door himself, and take the precious *Moniteur*.

For it is the *Moniteur de l'Armée*! and he unfolds it with the respect which we owe to holy things, and he reads it all religiously from the first article to the everlasting advertisement of *Rob Boyreau Laffecteur*. He reads it all, not because he is studying tactics or has need of Rob, but because he has set himself the task of reading it all. His servant brings him his morning coffee and brandy, and he believes himself still at father Etienne's or mother Gaspard's, at the garrison café; this makes him quite sprightly.

"Come, mother Gaspard,
It is not late,
Another glass!
Come, mother Gaspard,
It is not late,
To midnight it wants a quarter!"

But it is not the long, tedious military articles which first attract his eye, nor the ministerial decrees, nor the studies on the sabretache, nor the biographies of celebrated skin breeches, nor the improvement of gaiter buttons, nor the changes of police caps; PROMOTIONS AND CHANGES, that is what he wants.

PROMOTIONS AND CHANGES! divine rubrics which have caused so many hearts to beat.

You all recollect it, my old brothers in arms, who have waited long, like me. Years and years have passed. At length the hour is come and the newspaper which is going to transform your life. That folded paper gleams with all the fires of hope, it glitters like a sun, for it contains the magic word which out of nothing is going to make you everything, to draw you out of the obscure ranks to place you in the brilliant phalanx, which, from a passive despised instrument, is going to create you an active and respected head.

How you are dazzled as you open it; with what palpitations and haste you look for the blessed page, skipping the regiments, glancing over the ranks, flying over the names in order to arrive at your own. Ah! you know well where it ought to be; it is among the last; but what does it matter, it is here above all that the last can arrive first.

Here it is! here it is at last! What intoxication! young and old, we all were twenty once.

And meanwhile....

And meanwhile, the best days of your youth are lost in barren, vulgar, common-place, at times repulsive occupations. Your spirit is extinguished, your responsibility as an intelligent man is destroyed at settled hours by the sound of the bugle or of the trumpet, those flourishes of gilded servitude; and beneath the heavy hammer of passive obedience your temples are already growing grey; you have wrinkles on your forehead and on your heart, for you have reached that part of the cup of life, at which one drinks little else than bitterness ... But you forget all that; a new life full of enchantment is beginning. You are an officer! an officer! Ah! those who have never borne the harness, do not know what fairy-land that magic word contains. But you—you know it, and you took at your name, you spell each letter of it and you say: "At last! It is I, it is really I! Sub-lieutenant! I am sub-lieutenant!"

Thus, ten to fifteen years of struggles, tribulation, obstacles, humiliations, devotion, dangers, in order to reach the salary of a grocer's clerk!

But the old Captain, what was he looking for in the columns of the Service newspaper?

He had nothing to expect. No new promotion could swell his aged breast. He had completed his career. Like a rejected charger whose ear has been slit, or whose right flank has been branded, he had been laid aside for ever. Henceforth he had nothing else to do but to plant his cabbages, until his legs were seized by anchylosis, absolutely forgotten.

And so with all those who go away.

Amidst the thousand incidents of military life, so filled in its leisure and so empty in its employments, has anyone the time to give a thought to the absent one who must return no more? His place is taken; a new face is seated there where we used to see him, and his is no longer familiar to us. A few years hence and his name will be known no more. The army is for the young!

But does he forget? Does a man forget his youth, his glory, his dearest memories, his whole life? Retired into some country nook, completely buried in an obscure market-town, or become the modest citizen of some provincial city, the old officer follows afar off with solicitude and envy the different fortunes of his brothers in arms, living ever in thought amidst that forgetful and ungrateful family which he loves as much as his own—the Regiment.

> And that is why you, brave veterans, understand it well,
> that is why Captain Durand used to read the *Moniteur*.

XVII
THE VOLTAIRIAN

"For them religion is the most skillful of juggling, the most favourable veil, the most respectable disguise under which man can conceal himself to lie and deceive."

BARNUM (*Les Blagues de l'Univers*).

But, as I have said, he was a bad parishioner, a bunch of tare in the field of God, a scabby sheep in the flock of the Lord.

Taking no heed of his religious duties, reading the *Siècle*, speaking evil of priests and refusing the blessed bread, he was the scandal of the godly and not one of them in the village augured any good of him.

Never did a publican from Belleville or a novice of freemasonry proclaim with so much boldness his contempt for the things which everybody venerates. He did not uncover himself in presence of funerals, saying he did not want to bow to the dead; he called the church the priests' bank, the altar a parade of mountebanks, the confessional the antechamber to the brothel.

"That man will perish on the scaffold!" the former Curé of the village cried out one day in righteous indignation.

How had he come by this hatred, vigorous as that which Alcestis demands from virtuous souls against hypocrites and evil-doers? What had the *black-coats* done to him? He did not say, and perhaps he would have been embarrassed to say. There are certain natures which will love at any price, there are others on the contrary which need to hate. He was doubtless one of the latter, and he discharged all his excess of gall on the servants of Jesus.

"They are criminals," he cried, "all without exception, from the first to the last. Hypocrisy engenders wickedness. It is a sore which spreads and becomes leprosy. Everything which touches it catches it. Those who associate with hypocrites become hypocrites, and then scoundrels, slowly but surely by infection. That is the logic of the scab. It is not necessary to dress up in a black gown and to swallow God in public to make a perfect priestling, it is enough to rub against the priest's cap. Look at the sacristans, the beadles, the lackeys of the Bishop's palace, the hirers of chairs, the choirmen, the sellers of tapers, the tradesmen by appointment to the religious houses, the beggar who stretches out his hand to you at the door, and the man who hands you the holy-water sprinkler, have they not all the same hypocritical face, the same cunning, devoutly sanctimonious look? Well! scratch the skins of the godly and you will find the hide of the scoundrel."

An honourable man and brutally frank like many old soldiers he had kept in private life the tone and ways of barracks and camps. As he said himself, he did not mince the truth to anybody, and he repeated readily, without understanding it, the saying of Gonsalvo of Cordova, the great captain, "*The cloth of honour should be coarsely woven.*"

When one evening, on returning home, he found the card of the Curé, he nearly fell backwards.

—What, he has had the audacity to come to my house, this holy water merchant. They have not told him then what I am!

—Good heavens, I cried, my dear Captain, what has this poor man done to you?

—To me! nothing at all. I don't know him. He is part of the holy priesthood; that is enough for me. He is a scoundrel like the rest.

—But it is not enough to call a man scoundrel, you must prove that he is.

—Don't trouble me about your proofs. Do you suppose I am going to rummage into this gentleman's private life and see what passes in his alcove? No, indeed, I have no desire to do so, and I leave that care to my cook.

—Come, Captain, you admit that this is to vilify a man on rather slender grounds. There are fagots and fagots, and so there are Curés and Curés. This one, I assure you, is an excellent fellow.

—It may be so, but as I have no desire to make his acquaintance, I laugh at his good qualities.

—Everybody is not of your opinion, and it appears that all the women are distracted about him.

—Another reason why I detest him; women usually place their affections very badly.

—And he turns the heads of all the girls.

—That is good! Oh, the good Curé. He reminds me of the one at Djidjelly when I was a non-commissioned officer, the greatest girl-hunter that I have ever known. The Kabyles used to call him *Bou-Zeb*, which means capable of the thirteenth labour of Hercules, and they held him in high esteem, but when he went near their tents they used to make all the women go inside. Ah! that was a famous Curé! I wish that ours resembled him, and that he would get a child out of all the girls, and that he would make cuckolds of all the husbands.

—Why so?

—To teach these idiots to let their wives and their daughters be idle and dance attendance at the churches, and relate all the details of their household and their little sins to these bullies, as to their grand-dad.

—I grant there is some danger when the confidant is a handsome bachelor.

—There is no need to be handsome, sir. With the women, the cassock gives charms to the ugliest. I have known a sweet and lovely creature become mad after one of these rogues who had a head like a pitchfork. He did with her what he wished. He made her devout, shrewish, and the worst of whores. Yes, yes, they say that the red breeches get over the women, but the black gown bewitches them. Explain that if you can. They want to know what is underneath that wicked cassock. Something strange, mysterious, monstrous attracts them. Women love enormities, and besides it must be said, especially and above all, forbidden fruit.

The Captain had mounted his favourite hobby, I could only let him go on.

—They are vice incarnate, and know how to employ every means to seduce. Religion, the confessional, the bible, the Mass, Vespers, the New Testament, all the holy business is an auxiliary for them. For instance, conceive anything more disgusting than that pardon promised beforehand to guilty women. Play the whore all your life, deceive your husband, have fifty lovers, provided that at the end you lament your faults, God will have only tenderness for you, and will receive you with open arms. I should like to know if by chance their Jesus had taken a wife, what would have been his opinion then of the woman taken in adultery; but he remained single and consequently incompetent to decide upon that delicate matter. All that, you see, is an encouragement to debauchery and a stimulant to lewdness. A devout woman, when she is young and pretty, is on a slope which leads quite straight to Monsieur le Curé's bed.

XVIII
THE VISIT

"Stupefied, the pedant closed his mouth, and opened his eyes."

LÉON CLADEL (Titi Foyssac IV).

If there are any beings as blind as the husbands, they are certainly the fathers; with the latter, as with the former, blindness reaches its utmost limits. Since Molière no one laughs at them any more, and I don't know why, for they always deserve to be laughed at, while all the sarcasms have fallen on the head of the unhappy husbands.

Folly and injustice! Conjugal love is as respectable as paternal affection. Love is as good as affection, and what the heart chooses is quite as good as what the blood gives you.

Why then do they complain if it is papa who is deceived, and laugh if it is a husband. Exactly the contrary ought to occur. Paternal love is egotistic. It is for the most part vanity and self-love. The father looks for his own likeness in his offspring, and if he believes himself to be an eagle, his son naturally must be an eaglet. Most frequently he is only a foolish gosling, but the father insists on finding on him an eagle's plumes. If then he is deceived in his hopes, which are only a deduction from his own infatuation, it is certainly permissible to laugh at it.

While the husband….

This is what I observed to Durand, which put him in a great passion.

—Because my daughter has gone to Mass? And you say: "fathers are blind." Here is a self-contradictory individual. One can see plainly that you are not a father, or you would alter your theories. Hang it! You can't say I am enchanted at it, but you must put yourself in a man's place. She is a child, who leaves school, mark that well, where she was obliged, compelled to perform her religious duties, and one does not break off in a couple of days the habits of ten years like that. Give her time to reach it. I reason with her; hang it, I can't do everything in a day. When she goes from time to time to Mass, on Sunday, it does not follow that she is becoming religious. I am a free-thinker, but I am a father also, and what would you have a father do when two pretty arms take hold of your neck and a sweet little coaxing voice whispers to you, "Let me go there, my darling papa." Hang it, one is not made of wood, after all!

—Neither is the Curé made of wood.

—You make one shiver. Can my daughter have anything in common with your peasants' Curé? I say again that it is purely for diversion that she goes to Mass. And I understand it. Where can she show her new dress? And what place is more favourable for this little display than going into and coming out of church?

—Then the Church is a spectacle like another. There are chants, music, tapers, perfumes, flowers, the half-light which comes through the coloured windows.

—Without speaking of the fellows covered with gold-tinsel who repeat in unknown language the pater-nosters to which no one listens. It is enough to make one burst with laughing, and, if I had not my cabbages to plant, I would go myself now and again and entertain myself at these masquerades which are as good as the theatres at the fair, and to complete the resemblance, it only costs a couple of sous.

—But the principal person of the troop attracts the looks, and the danger is there.

—Your priestling is young then?

—And vigorous. Strong appetites. When I see him rambling in the village, I begin to say: "Good people, the cock is loose, take care of your hens." It is like your Curé of Djidjelly.

—I am easy on that ground. The black cock will not come and rub his wings here. He knows now that he has mistaken the door; they have informed him regarding me, and he will not be so rude as to come again.

But just at that moment the servant came into the room quite scared, and said:

—Here is Monsieur le Curé.

—Who? what? said Durand; and turning towards me, Shall I receive him? Well, we shall have a laugh!

He was still undecided, when Marcel glided into the room.

XIX
HARD WORDS

"I will speak, Madame, with the liberty of a soldier who knows but ill how to varnish the truth."

RACINE (*Britannicus*).

The old soldier, upright, with his hand leaning on the back of his armchair, let the priest come forward with all the agreeableness of a mastiff which is making ready to bite.

The latter bowed gravely, and, although he felt himself to be in hostile quarters, took the seat offered him with an easy air.

Meanwhile his bearing and pleasant look produced their usual effect.

Imbued with the theories of the army, which of all surroundings is that in which one judges most by the appearance, where a good carriage is the first condition of success, where in fact they salute the stripes and not the man, the Captain was, in presence of this handsome young fellow, recalled to less aggressive sentiments.

—Hang it! he said to himself, what a splendid cuirassier this fellow would have made! What devil of an idea has shoved him into a cassock?

War being the most sublime of arts, as Maurice de Saxe remarked, there are few old officers who understand how a man can choose another profession by inclination.

—I come, Monsieur le Capitaine, said Marcel, to pay you my visit as pastor, although perhaps a little late. But you are aware doubtless that I have had the honour of knocking once already at your door.

—You should not have troubled yourself, my dear sir, and you should adhere to that; I belong so little to the holy flock.

—I owe myself to all, said Marcel smiling, to the bad sheep—I mean to the wandering sheep, just as to the good ones; to watch over the one, to bring back and cure the others.

—Oh! Oh! Well, sir shepherd, you are losing your time finely, for I am a worn-out goat.

—There will be more joys in heaven over one sinner that repenteth....

—That is the story of the 99 just persons that you are going to tell us; we know it, and, let me tell you, it is not encouraging for the 99 just persons.

The Curé, seeing himself on dangerous ground, hastened to leap elsewhere.

—This is a charming little house, Captain; it is a sweet retreat after toilsome and glorious years, for you have had numerous campaigns, have you not?

—Fifteen years in Africa, thirty-two campaigns, thirty years' service, two wounds, one of them received at Rome when we fought for that old bully Pius IX.

Marcel had gone astray again; he quickly seized hold of the wounds.

—Ah! two wounds! And are they still painful?

—Sometimes, when the weather is stormy. And yours?

—Mine, Captain! but I have none. I have not had like you the honour of shedding any blood for our Holy Father.

—A pretty cuckoo. It doesn't matter, you may have got a wound somewhere else.

—Where? enquired Marcel simply.

—How do I know? We get them right and left, when we are least thinking of it.

—Like all accidents.

—Well, if you had been the chaplain of my regiment, you would have had a famous accident. He was a right worthy apostle. He wanted to teach the catechism to the daughter of our cantinière, a bud of sixteen, and the little one put so much ardour into the study that the Holy Spirit made her hatch. Her parents beat her unmercifully, and the poor girl died of grief. Our hero, who knew how to get himself out of it with unction as white as snow, did not all the same betake himself to Paradise. A pretty Italian gave him his reckoning. *Quinte, quatorze* and the *point*. Game finished. He died in the hospital pulling an ugly face. That was the best action of his life. Well, old boy, what do you say to that?

—I have not exactly understood, replied Marcel, trying to keep his countenance.

—You are very hard of understanding. I will tell you another story and I will be clearer. I see what you want—the dots on the i's.

Marcel rose up alarmed.

—No, no, cried Durand. Don't get up. Don't go away. Since you are here, we must talk a little. Stay, it will not be long. It is the story of a cousin of mine, or rather a cousin of my wife. Another of your confraternity. He was curate or deacon, or canon, in fact I don't know what rank in your regiment. At any rate, a bitter hypocrite; you will see. Under pretence of relationship, he used to pay us frequent visits. You can think if that suited me, who already adored the cassock! Besides, on principle, I detested cousins. It is the sore of households, gentlemen; you must avoid it like the plague. Monsieur le Curé, if you have a pretty servant, beware of cousins. I only say that. My wife used to say to me: "What has this poor boy done to you that you receive him so badly? Are you jealous of him? Ah! I know very well, it is because he belongs to my family, and you cannot endure my poor relations." So to have peace I tolerated my cousin. He, convinced that little presents maintain friendship, used to make us little presents. There were tickets for sacred concerts, lotteries for the benefit of the little Chinese, rosaries blessed by the pope, pebbles from Jerusalem. Nothing wrong so far. My wife availed herself of the concert tickets; the rosaries were put into a drawer, and I threw the pebbles into the garden. But soon his gifts changed their character. He brought us some hairs of St. Pancratius, a tooth of St. Alacoque, a rag which had wiped something or other off St. Anastasius or St. Cunegunda. My wife clasped her hands, was in ecstasy and transported with joy, and I went and brought up my dinner. I foresaw the time when he would bring us extraordinary things; a louse of St. Labre, a testicle of St. Origen, the coccyx of St. Antony, the parts of St. Gudule or the prepuce of Jesus Christ.

The Curé rose again.

—I see that my presence is *de trop* here, Captain; pardon my having disturbed you.

—Not at all. Good Lord. Not at all. Sit down. It gives me extraordinary pleasure to talk to you. Besides, I have not finished the story of my cousin. Sit down, I pray you; I resume.

He had given a very pretty engraving, a reproduction of a picture by somebody, *Jesus and the woman taken in adultery.* My wife had had it framed very carefully, and had hung it up in our bedroom: a bad sign. That seemed to say to me, "See, my friend, imitate Jesus." One day returning home very quietly, I surprised both of them, squeezed one against the other, holding each others hand, looking at the picture with emotion. I took the little cousin by the shoulders, and I threw him out of doors. I never saw him again. Do you understand the moral?

—Yes, Captain, I understand, said Marcel rising again, and this time fully decided to go away. But the door opened, and Suzanne showed herself on the threshold.

XX
KICKS

"I should have wished, mischievously, to put him in the wrong, and that a thoughtless or insulting word on his part, should serve as a justification for the insult which I meditated."

A. DE VIGNY (*Servitude et Grandeur militaires*).

She had on her school-girl dress of black, which made the whiteness of her complexion more dazzling, and imparted something grave and serious to her beauty.

She was hardly eighteen, and already by the harmonious outlines of her bust, by the undulating movements of her hips and above all by the flash of her great dark eyes, one foresaw in this young girl, still a child to-day, the woman of to-morrow: a daughter of Eve of our modern civilization; forward, precocious, charming.

She was one of those the sight alone of whom is the most radiant and the most dangerous of spectacles, and who, like others, distilling holiness and blessings from heaven, shed around them a perfume of love.

The bright fire of their heart shines out in their look; it reveals itself in the sound of their voice, in their gestures and in their walk. Everything in them is soft, trembling, passionate. Sweet creatures who see only one goal in life, love, and, when the goal is missed, death.

There are women who are but half women. They are quickly recognized; vulgar and awkward, they hide under their ungraceful petticoats the instincts of man, and masculinity is displayed up to their corsage. They form the fantastical cohort of learned women, of the disciples of Stuart Mill and rivals of Miss Taylor, hybrid natures which may possess a heart of gold and a manly soul, but are incapable of being the joy of the hearth.

Others are women to the tips of their rosy nails, to the root of their abundant hair; women above all by their faults, that is to say their weaknesses, and this weakness is one of their attractions. Impressionable and easily led, they become, according to the surroundings which hold them and the destiny which urges them, heroines or saints, courtesans or nuns, but invariably martyrs of that blind despot, their heart.

They are Magdalene or St. Theresa, Madame de Guyon or Heloïse, the nun in love with Jesus or the light girl in love with the passer-by.

In a second the priest had understood this sweet nature, or rather he had felt it, and his quivering nostrils inhaled the keen perfume of pleasure, while his look was lost in ecstasy. It was but a flash, but if beneath the watchful eye of the Captain it appeared impossible, the young girl could read the dumb language which every woman understands.

She came forward, blushing.

—This is my daughter, said the Captain.

—I believe, said the Curé, with a bow, that I have had the pleasure of seeing Mademoiselle several times already in our modest church.

—And you concluded therefore that my daughter was going to increase the blessed flock. Don't be misled, comrade.

Suzanne cast a look of reproach upon her father.

—What! said Marcel, hurt, must not Mademoiselle follow her religion? work out her salvation?

—Her salvation? There is a word which always makes me laugh. It reminds me of my Colonel's wife who, when her husband gave orders for a review and parade for Sunday, said, "My dear, you want then to deprive the poor soldiers of the holy Mass, ought they not to work out their salvation?" A magnificent creature, sir, but too much inclined to the cassock.

Her husband, however, had nothing to complain of, for one fine morning he picked up the stars of his epaulets in some sacristy or other. What have you come for, my child?

—Nothing, papa. I knew Monsieur le Curé was there and I came in.

—I was having a little edifying conversation with Monsieur, and you have interrupted us, but we can talk of something else: You hold the first rank now, gentlemen, continued the Captain, I must do you that justice; and as times go, it is better to be the son of a bishop than of a general. I myself, if I had only had some high influential canon for my father, should have reached the highest offices. Come, you seem to me to be a good fellow, and I want to give you a word of advice. If papa is a bishop, make use of him, and don't stagnate in this village, you will get no good there: I tell you so on my word of honour! I suppose that with you, promotion is as it is with us?

"The cup of humiliation is full," said Marcel to himself. Nevertheless, he answered, I don't understand exactly what you mean by that.

—I mean by that that promotion is a lottery from which they begin by withdrawing all the big numbers to distribute them to Monsieur Cretinard whose papa is a millionaire, to Monsieur Tartuffe whose papa is a Jesuit, or to a Marquis de Carabas whose mamma has the good graces of my Lord the Bishop, and they make the poor devils draw from the rest. It is so in the army—and with you?

—Among the clergy, sir, promotion is generally given to merit.

—I don't believe it; for if it were so, you would be a bishop at least. Don't blush, it is the general report.

—Captain....

—No false modesty. I hear your virtues praised everywhere. There is a chorus of praises from every quarter. My friend here was just declaring to me that all the women are wild about you.

—Sir ... cried the Curé, blushing up to his ears, and not daring to raise his eyes to Suzanne, who sat in a corner, convulsively turning over the leaves of an album.

—Don't protest, we know that true merit is modest; besides, I was by way of asking myself, if I should not beg you to complete my daughter's education.

—You are making pleasant jokes, Captain, and I ask your pardon for not being able to rise to the level of these witticisms. I see that my visit has been unseasonable. It only remains for me to make my excuses and to say to Mademoiselle, how pained I am to have made her acquaintance under such unfavourable auspices, but I hope....

—Stop that, Monsieur le Curé, interrupted Durand in a curt tone.

Marcel made a low bow, but as he withdraw, he caught an appealing look from Suzanne.

XXI
THE PAST

"Look not upon the past with grief, it will not come back; wisely improve the present, it is thine; and go onwards fearlessly and with a strong heart towards the mysterious future."

LONGFELLOW (*Hyperion*).

Marcel returned home exceedingly indignant. Although he had not expected an over-cordial reception from the old Captain, whose irascible character and surly ways were known to all, he did not think that he would have carried so far his disregard of the most elementary propriety.

"It serves me right," he said to himself, "what business had I there? Nevertheless, on reflection, I have lost nothing. My reception by this old dotard has taken away for ever my wish to go back there: and who knows what might have happened, if I had had free admission to that house, if I had met a friendly face and a kindly welcome? Oh, fool! I have found all that in the sweet look of his adorable daughter, that appealing look which seemed to implore my indulgence and pardon for the malevolent words of that ill-bred soldier. Come, think no more of it, drive back to the lowest depths those foolish thoughts which excite the brain. All that he does, God does well. I was on the brink of the abyss; one step more and I should have rolled to the bottom. Let me stop then, there is still time. Let me forget, forget. Forget! better still, I will write and ask to be changed. Could I forget her if I were to meet again that burning look, which pursues me to the steps of the altar, and troubles me to the bottom of my soul?"

He wrote in fact and began his letter ten times afresh. What could he say? What reason could he bring? He had filled this cure for scarcely six months. What pretext could he raise before his superiors? And how would any complaint from him be received at the Palace?

Night came. He felt himself oppressed by a vague and indefinable grief.

Then little by little the present vanished. His infancy rose up before him. He saw it again as in a glass, smiling, simple, pure; and he forgot himself in these sweet memories.

In proportion as we advance in life, we are attached to the things of the past. It clothes itself then with those brilliant colours with which we love to invest what we have lost. Youthful years, bright with poetry and sunlight, come and gild the gloomy and prosaic nooks of ripened age, the twilight of the eternal night.

The young man full of illusions and dreams pursues his road without casting a look backwards. What matters, indeed, the past to him? He expects nothing but from the future. Proud at having escaped from infancy, at arriving at the age of man, at flying on his wings, he pities the years when he was small and weak, ignorant and credulous.

But when he has met with obstacles and ruts on that road which appeared to him so wide and so fair, when he has torn his heart with the first briars of life, when his thought has ripened beneath the sun of passions, and his soul, stripped of its illusions, feels all chilly and bare amidst the ice of reality, then he returns to the joys of infancy, he warms himself again with the memory of his mother, and sits once again in the pleasant corner of the family fire-side, on the little stool of his childhood.

Marcel saw himself again at the little seminary of Pont-à-Mousson, on the benches, all blackened with ink, of the school-room, studying with ardour the *Epitome* or the *De Viris* beneath the paternal eye of Father Martin, a father aged 24, a deacon with curly hair, as timid as a maid. Then he ran in the long corridors, or in the great square court lined with galleries shaded by the chapel. He remembered his joy when he had slipped on some excuse into the Seniors' garden: "Ah! there is little Marcel, come here, you brat!" And everyone wished to give him a caress.

Then, the first time when he was called to the honour of serving the Mass. He had thought of it a week beforehand, full of emotion and fear. At length the day has come. He is dressed in the white surplice, wearing on his head the red cap. He would have wished the whole world to see him; but the pupils alone were present, and that diminished his happiness.

Father Barbelin, the censor, a severe but just man, officiated. He trembled in every limb, as he responded the sacramental verses to this formidable functionary. That was a great business; his little comrades called him in a whisper from behind: Marcel! Marcel! and laughed and nudged each other, while the elder ones, their nose in their book, with sanctimonious face and ecstatic look were wrapt in God.

Then his success, his entrance to the great seminary at Nancy, his first sermon in the chapel. His voice trembled at the commencement, but little by little, growing stronger, taking courage, inspired by the sacred text, he forgot everything, and the Superior, old Father Richard, who watched him with his little bright cunning eyes, and the unmoved professors, and his watchful fellow-students, jeering and scoffing at first, then at last astonished and jealous. "There is the stuff of an orator in him," the Professor of Sacred Eloquence had said, "we must push this lad forward." "He is full of talent and virtue," the Superior had replied, "he will get on. He is our chosen vessel." And the same day he had dined at the master's table, and they had spoken of him to Monseigneur. He had in fact been pushed forward ... and with his talents, his learning, his virtues and his eloquence, he had come to teaching the catechism to the little peasants of Althausen!

Althausen! That was the blow of the hammer which recalled him to reality. He found himself again the poor village Curé, and he began to laugh.

"Poor fool!" he cried, "I shall never be but a common imbecile! Is not my way all traced out? I must continue my career, and let myself go with the current of life. Is it then so hard? Why delude myself with phantoms? I will try to slay the muttering passions, to drive away the fits of ambition which rise to my brain; and perhaps by dint of subduing all that is rebellious in me, I shall come to follow piously the line marked out by my superiors. I will watch patiently amidst my flock, by the corner of my fire, among the Fathers and my weariness.

"Weariness, that cold demon with the gloomy eye, but I will remain chaste ... and after a life filled with little nothingnesses and little works I shall pass away in peace in the bosom of the Lord. And there is my life. Nothing else to choose. No turning aside to the right or to the left. I must remain a martyr, a martyr to my duty, or an apostate, and infamous renegade. The triumph or the shame!"

And, as he just uttered these words with bitterness, a soft voice answered like an echo:

—The shame?

The Curé started and raised his head. His lamp was out, and the dying embers on the hearth cast only a feeble light into the room.

He distinguished, however, a few steps from him the outline of a woman's form.

—Who is there? he cried with a sort of terror.

The shadowy outline stood forth more clearly.

He recognized his servant.

—Why the shame? she said.

XXII
THE SERVANT

"I have already said that dame Jacinthe although little superannuated, had still kept her bloom. It is true that she spared nothing to preserve it: besides taking a clyster every day, she swallowed some excellent jelly during the day and on going to bed."

LE SAGE (*Gil-Blas*).

She looked at him fixedly with burning, feverish eyes.

She was a lusty lass, already arrived at the age of discretion, as Le Sage says, that is to say, she had passed her fortieth year, the canonical period for the servants of Curés, but was fair and fresh still, in spite of some wrinkles and her hair growing gray. She possessed that modest and appetizing plumpness, somewhat rare among mature virgins, the sign of a quiet conscience, a good digestion and feelings satisfied.

What pious souls call holiness exuded from every pore: cast-down eyes, chaste deportment, gentle movements. She did not walk, she glided over the ground as if she already felt the wings of seraphim hanging on her shoulders; she did not speak, she murmured unctuous words with a soft, low, mysterious voice like a prayer. When she said: "Would Monsieur le Curé he pleased to come to breakfast? Perhaps Monsieur le Curé could eat a boiled egg?" or "Ah! the sermon which Monsieur le Curé has been pleased to give has gone to my heart!" it was in the same tone as she would say: "*Lamb of God which takest away the sins of the world....*" and one was tempted to answer: *Kyrie eleison*.

And she wiped her moist eyelid, and cast on her master her veiled, long, silent look.

She said so well: "my duty," "I wish to do my duty," that one felt filled with admiration for this holy maid.

Oh! divine modesty, perfume of woman, sweet enchantment which gently penetrates the heart of man, ready always to unfold.

Besides, what hearts had unfolded for her! what ravages had been caused by her austere deportment and her substantial charms. More than one buxom village lad had made warm proposals with honourable intentions, and the gallant corporal of gendarmes had tried on several occasions to enter upon this delicate subject with her.

But she had willed to remain a maid and virtuous, and vowed herself body and soul to the service of the Church, to the glory of God, and the fortune of her pastor.

She approached the hearth with slow steps, blew on the embers, relighted the lamp, and placing it so as to throw the light on her master's face, she said to him anxiously:

—You are in pain, are you not?

—You were there then? said the Curé dissatisfied.

—Yes, she answered him with the affectionate tone of a mother, I was there, pardon me; I was going to bed, and I heard you talking aloud, there was no light; I feared you were ill, and I ventured to come in.

—And you have heard?

—I have heard that you were not happy, that is all.

—No one is happy in this world, Veronica.

—Yes, we are so only in the other, I know that. And yet happiness is so easy.

The Curé put his head between his hands without replying.

The servant went on:

—Can it be that I, your servant, a poor ignorant village girl, should say that to you, Monsieur le Curé?

—What, Veronica?

—But what matters our condition on earth? We are in a state of transition. Holy Mary, she too, was a poor servant and now she is far above a queen.

—Without doubt, said the Curé.

—We must then despise nobody. Under the most humble appearance, God often conceals his most faithful servants.

—Most certainly. But what are you driving at?

—At this, Monsieur le Curé; that we must be good and indulgent to everybody: that the great sometimes have need of the little, and that when we are able to render a service to our neighbour we must do it without hesitation.

—It is Jesus who commands it, Veronica. But explain yourself, I pray.

—Well! yes, I will speak, she replied, for I am pained to see you thus, and the more so as it is certainly allowed me to tell you so, me who am destined, please God, to live with you. I have only known you since you were our Curé, but you have been so good to me that I love you like ... a sister. I was all alone here, like a poor forsaken creature, after the death of my old master, the Abbé Fortin—may God keep his soul,—and you consented to keep me when taking the parsonage. It is good of you, for you might have brought with you your former servant, or again some niece, as many do.

—I have no niece, Veronica.

—A niece, or a sister, or a relation. After all you have kept me, although you could have found a better than myself. Oh, very easily, I know ... and I thank you from the bottom of my heart, yes, from the bottom of my heart. But could you have found one more devoted, more discreet? I believe not; as much, perhaps; but more, I believe not. Ah! I tell you here, Monsieur le Curé, you can do everything you want, nobody shall ever know anything of it.

The Curé looked at his servant with amazement.

—What do you mean by that, Veronica? he asked in a stern voice.

—Oh! nothing, I mean nothing. I mean that you can have entire confidence in your poor servant.

—I thank you, Veronica, but I don't know what you mean.

—I explain myself badly doubtless, Monsieur le Curé. Ah! pardon me, I was forgetting ... here, there is a letter which I have just found and which has been slipped under the door at night.

He looked at the address. It was an elegant and bold hand, the hand of a woman.

XXIII
THE LETTER

"The beauty then, to end this war,
Offers but a single way which we can hardly guess."

R. IMBERT (*Nouvelles*).

A sweet perfume was exhaled from it.

He opened it with a trembling hand.

That strange intuition of the heart which is named presentiment, told him that it came from Suzanne.

Pale with emotion he read:

"MONSIEUR L'ABBÉ,

"I do not wish the day to pass without coming to ask your pardon for my father's conduct towards you, and assure you that he does not think a single one of his wicked words.

"Do not keep, I pray, an evil memory of me, and believe that I should he grieved if a single doubt were to remain in your mind as to the sympathy and respect which you inspire in

"Suzanne Durand.

"P.S. I have much need of your counsels."

Marcel, full of a delicious trouble, read and re-read this letter. He did not take careful note of his sensations, but he felt an ineffable joy overflow his heart, and at the same time a vague anxiety.

His servant's voice recalled Him to himself.

—Doubtless it is a sick person who asks for religious aid, she said.

Was there a slight irony in that question?

The priest thought he saw it. He called out sharply:

—You are still there, Veronica? Who has called you? I don't want you any longer.

—Pardon me, Monsieuur le Curé, she answered humbly and softly, I was waiting.... I thought that perhaps you were going out *to visit this sick person* and that then I could be useful to you in some way.

—You cannot be useful to me in any way, Veronica, But truly you astonish me. What have you then to say to me? Come, explain yourself at once.

—No, Monsieur le Curé, there is midnight striking. It is time to repose, I wish you good-night, sir.

—Good-night, Veronica.

"What a strange woman," said Marcel to himself, "what can she want with me. One would say that she had a secret to confide to me and that she does not dare.... Could she have any suspicion? No, it is impossible. How could she know what I want to hide from myself. She has caught two or three words perhaps; but what could she understand, and what have I let drop to compromise me? She has evidently heard others, for she was here before me, and these old walls have been witnesses, I am sure, of many groanings of the soul.... Let us be cautious, nevertheless, and repress within ourselves the thoughts which would come forth. A wise precept. It was a precept of my master of rhetoric. Yes, let us be cautious; in spite of this woman's appearance of devotion, who would trust to such marks of affection? The servant's enemy is his master; and I clearly see that independently of my dignity, I must not make the least false step; what torments I should reserve to myself for the future.

"And this letter of Suzanne, the adorable and lovely Suzanne! What an emotion suddenly seized me at the sight of that unknown handwriting, which I had a presentiment was here. Oh! what a strange mystery is man's heart. I, a priest, with a nature said to be energetic and strong. I trembled and was affected like a child, because it has pleased a little school-girl to write me a couple of lines in order to excuse her father's rudeness. What is more natural than such conduct? Is it not the act of a well-bred girl? And yet already my foolish brain is beating the country and travelling into the land of fancies ... of abominable fancies.

"She asks me for counsel; doubtless I will give it her. Is it not my duty and business as priest? but where, but when can I see her?..."

And he went very thoughtfully to bed, with his head full of dreams.

XXIV
THE FIRST MEETING

"Ah! let him, my child,
Ah! let him proceed.
When I was a Curate
I did much the same."

ANONYMOUS (*Le chant du Curé*).

The first person he saw the next day at morning Mass was Suzanne Durand. She had not yet come to these low Masses, which are affected usually by the devout, because the church is then more empty, and they feel themselves more alone with God or with the priest; therefore the Curé was deeply affected by this pious eagerness.

It is doubtful whether, on that day, his prayers reached the throne of the Eternal, for he brought but little fervour to the holy sacrifice.

A good woman who had given twenty sous to buy a place in the firmament for her defunct spouse, was quite scandalized to remark that the Curé was eating in a heedless manner the wafer which, for nearly 2000 years, serves as a lodging for Christ.

His words rose with the incense to the arches of the old church, but his soul remained below, fluttering round that fair young girl, as if to envelop her with embraces.

When he had dismissed the faithful with the sacramental words *Ite missa est*, he felt a momentary confusion and he felt his knees tremble. He was afraid of himself, for he saw the Captain's daughter rise from her seat and slowly make her way to the confessional.

What! It was perfectly true then, she had asked for his counsel, and while he, the priest, was hesitating and seeking where he could converse with her without exposing himself to the brutal invective of the father or the senseless scandals of the village, this simple girl had found, without any aid from him, the safest spot, the sanctuary of which he had inwardly dreamed.

He was then about to listen all alone to the divine accents of that charming mouth; to see her kneeling before him, her face wreathed with a modest blush,—before him who had wished to kiss her foot-prints.

Oh, God supreme! who could depict his transports, his emotion, the thrill which ran through all his frame. She, she so near to him, so near that her sweet breath caresses his face like a breeze come from heaven.

He felt wild with joy. But she also is affected, she also trembles, and beneath her palpitating breast, he seems to hear the beatings of her heart. What passed? What avowal did this maiden of ardent feeling make to this hot-passioned man? There is one of those mysteries which remain for ever buried between priest and woman, between penitent and confessor. What they said to one another no one knows, but from that confessional into which he entered pensive, wavering, it is true, but still contending, he went out with his face radiant, and his heart intoxicated with love.

XXV
LOVE

"All loves around us: all around is heard,
Hard by the warbler's quivering kiss,
That voiceless song of flowers, which the lark,
by love distracted, to his mate translates."

EMILE DARIO (*Sonnets*).

He returned to the parsonage with a light step, hearing the birds singing in the lime-trees the same joyous song which his own heart was singing. He breakfasted with a good appetite, smiled at his servant, and gave pleasant answers to her questions.

It seemed to him that a new world was opening. New ideas sprang up in him, and he discovered sensations till then unknown.

He felt better; life smiled upon him, and all the things of life.

The past had altogether vanished; the present was radiant, the future was laden with rosy dreams.

That same morning he had risen as usual, with no settled wish, aimless and hopeless. Till then, he had acted like a machine, hardly knowing whither he went, following his road by chance, walking onwards in the line which had been traced out for him, with no relish, full of weariness and sadness.

What was he expecting then? Nothing. He was clinging to the fragments of his beliefs, he remained hanging there, not daring to stir, to think, or to turn, for fear of rolling to the bottom of some unknown abyss. But suddenly everything is changed, everything is transformed, everything takes another aspect. The whole world is illumined. Religion, dogma, mysteries, altar, priest, what is all that? God even. He thinks no more of him.

A woman's look has obliterated all.

A woman's voice has murmured in his ear and he perceives that he is young, that he is strong, that he has a heart, and that all cries to him at once: Love! Love!

Oh! what a wonderful thing love is! What frenzy, what delirium, what madness! Sublime madness, ravishing delirium, delicious frenzy.

First and last mystery of nature, first and last voice of the universe.

It is thou, oh God, who givest life to all, who dost animate all, who art the principle of all. Thou art Alpha and Omega; thou art the potent arm which has caused the worlds to rise, which has re-united the scattered forces of matter, which has made order out of chaos.

And there are found men, creatures, works of love like everything which moves, breathes, buds, shoots forth, there are found creatures who have dared to say: Love is evil.

They have sworn to renounce love. They have spat in thy face, fruitful, creative Divinity, they have denied thee on their impure altars.

But it is their God who is evil, as Proudhon said, that senseless and ludicrous God who delights in grotesque saturnalia, in ridiculous prayers, in shameful mummeries, in vows contrary to nature.

Marcel felt himself transformed.

A new feeling was born in him and plunged him into ineffable delight.

Nevertheless, as I have said, he experienced a vague fear; he had had a glimpse of the unknown, and he was one of those delicate and timid souls with their thoughts in some way turned upon themselves, which are terrified at the unknown.

Seized with a restless apprehension and with a mysterious trouble, he felt the hour coming which was about to change his life.

XXVI
OF YOUNG GIRLS IN GENERAL

"You tell me, Madame, that this description is neither in the taste of Ovid nor that of Quinault. I agree, my dear, but I am not in a humour to say soft things."

VOLTAIRE (*Dict. Phil.*).

The great fault, in my opinion, both of the writer and of the poet, is to idealize woman too much, and especially the young girl.

On the stage just as in the novel, the heroines are placed on a sort of pedestal where they receive haughtily the incense and homage of poor mankind.

They are perfect beings, of superior essence, gifted with all the beauties and all the virtues, whose white robes of innocence never receive, amidst all the impurities, of our social state, the slightest splash.

Why then raise thus upon a pedestal of Parian marble these statues of clay? Why place reverentially beneath a tabernacle of gold these pasteboard divinities?

Good Heavens! women are women, that is to say: the females of man, nothing more. They are above all what men make them, and as we are generally vicious and spoilt, since from the most tender age we take care to defile ourselves in the street, in the workshop or on the school-benches; as the atmosphere we breathe is corrupt, we have no claim to believe that our wives, our sisters and our daughters can remain unspotted by our touch, and that this same atmosphere which they breathe, will purify itself in passing through their chaste nostrils.

If then the woman is not worse than we, as some assert, assuredly she is no better.

And how could they be better, who are our pupils, and when the share we have given them in society is so slight and so strangely ordered that, if they cannot by means of supreme efforts expand and grow in it morally and intellectually, every latitude is allowed them on the other hand to corrupt themselves in it beyond measure, and to fall lower than the man into the lowest depths.

"Fools!" said Machiavelli, "you sow hemlock and pretend you see ears of corn growing ripe."

Why then idealize and make a divinity of this creature, when we know that the education she ordinarily receives, takes away from her, little by little, all which remains attractive, divine and ideal!

Certainly a chaste and simple young girl, fair and fresh as a spring morning, sweet as the perfume of the violet, and whose mind and body alike are as pure as the petals of a half-opened lily, is the most heavenly and the most adorable thing in the world.

But, outside the pages of your novel, how many of them have you met in the world?

I have often heard the modest virtues of the middle classes extolled, and it is from such surroundings that the novelist of to-day most frequently draws his feminine ideal. It is among the middle classes indeed that all the qualifications seem to unite at first. It is the intermediate condition, the most happy of all, as the excellent Monsieur Daru said in 1820, since it is only disinherited of the highest favours of fortune, and the social and intellectual advantages of it are accessible to a reasonable ambition.

But they evidently benefit very little by their advantages, for I, and you also, have always found them coquettish, ignorant, frivolous and vain, bringing up their children very badly, but in revenge, generally deceiving their husbands very well.

"In middle-class households, bickering; among fashionable people, adultery. In fashionable middle-class households, either one or the other and sometimes both."[1]

And how could it be otherwise?

The daughters of devout and consequently narrow-minded and ignorant mothers, of sceptical and libertine fathers, they spend five or six years at school, where they consummate the loss of what may have escaped the baneful example of their family.

They have taken from their mother foolish vanity, ridiculous prejudices, the art of lying; from their father scepticism and an elastic conscience; perhaps they will preserve their virtue and modesty? The pernicious contacts of the school soon carry them away.

They still have a blush on their face, a down-cast eye, a timid bearing. But their affected timidity is the token of their knowledge of *good and evil*; like Eve, if they have not yet tasted of the forbidden fruit, they burn to taste it, for their thought is sullied, their imagination is vagrant and at the bottom of their soul there is a germ of corruption.

They leave the boarding-school *virgins,* but chaste, never.

Let us then represent the world as it la, women such as they are, and not such as they ought to be; let us call things by their names, and when there is moral deformity somewhere, let us show that deformity.

When we make wonders of the heroines of a novel, possessing the charms of the *three Graces* and the virtues of the seven sages of Greece, who when they fall, fall in spite of themselves, impelled by a fatal concurrence of circumstances, but with so much candour and innocence, that we cannot do otherwise than pardon their fall and even fail to comprehend that they have fallen, we are completely amazed when we descend from this imaginary world to enter the world of reality.

The idealization of woman has therefore, besides other faults, that of causing as to take a dislike to our ordinary companions. How, indeed, after being present at the devotion of Sophonisba, at the suicide of the chaste Lucretia, at the display of the virtues of Mademoiselle Agnes, and at that of the form of Venus at the bath, can we contemplate with ravished eye the wife no less plain than lawful, who is sitting with sullen air at our fire-side, who has no other care than that of her person, no other moral capital than a round enough sum of prejudices and follies, and whose charms, finally, resemble more those of a Hottentot Venus than those of Venus Aphrodite.

The picture of virtues is an excellent thing, but still it is necessary that these virtues should exist. We must not enunciate an idea simply because it is moral, but because it is true. *Amicus Plato, sed magis amica veritas.*

That is why I shall not depict the little person, whom I am going to make better known to you, as a model of virtue. She is an inquisitive girl, she is vehement, she has been brought up in an atmosphere where depravity is more generally inhaled than holiness. I should then be badly advised in presenting you with an angel of candour and wisdom.

An angel! She is at that age indeed, at which foolish men call women angels.

"Before they are wed, they are angels so gentle,
But quickly they change to vulgarian scolds,
She-demons who truly make hell of their homes."

[Footnote 1: H. Taine (Notes sur Paris).]

XXVII
OF SUZANNE IN PARTICULAR

"An exalted, romantic imagination of vivid dreams, peopled with sumptuous hotels, with smart equipages, fêtes, balls, rubies, gold and azure. This is what I have most surely gathered at this school and is called: a brilliant education."

V. SARDOU (*Maison Neuve*).

But she was a ravishing demon, this child, and more than one saint might have damned himself for her black eyes, those deep limpid eyes which let one read to her soul. And there one paused perfectly fascinated, for this fresh resplendent soul displayed in large characters the radiant word, Love.

Have you never read this word in a maiden's two eyes? Seek in your memory and seek the fairest, and you will have the delightful portrait of Suzanne.

I am unable to say, however, that she was a perfect girl. What girl is perfect here below? She had left school, and it would have been a miracle if she were, and we know that away from Lourdes, God works no more miracles.

She had even many faults: those of her age doubled by those which education gives to girls. Many a time, when opening the holy Bible, the only book capable of cheering me in the hours of sadness, I have come across these words of Ezekiel,

"They are proud, full of appetites, abounding in idleness."

It is of the daughters of Sodom that the holy prophet is complaining! What would he say to-day to *the young ladies* of our modern Sodoms?

But if the little Suzanne had all the darling faults of forward flowers forced in the warm soil of our enervating education, and our decayed civilization, she was better than many plainer ones, and I do not think that the sum total of her errors could weigh heavy on her conscience. Perhaps she was culpable in thought; but if the imagination was sick, the heart was good and sound. She had not sinned, but she said to herself, that sinning would be sweet!

Well! there is no great crime there. Does not every woman love instinctive pleasure? Among them there are few stoics. They who are so, are so by compulsion, and so they cannot make a virtue of it. Suzanne loved pleasure then, and she loved it the more because she only knew it by hearsay.

The education of Saint-Denis had contributed no little to develop her natural disposition.

Everything has been said about the *House of the Legion of Honour*, about its curious system of education with regard to young girls, nearly all of them poor, and brought up as if, when they left school, they would find an income of £2,000 a year.

It is known that in this establishment intended for the daughters of officers *with no fortune*, everything is taught except that which is most necessary for a woman to know. They leave having a barren, superficial education, principally composed of words, and in which consequently, to the exclusion of the intelligence and the heart, the memory plays the principal part; none of the childish rules of ceremonial are spared them, none of the frivolous accomplishments indispensable for access to a world which, for the greater part, they will never be invited to see; and they return to their father's humble roof, dreaming of balls, fêtes, equipages, hotels, drawing-rooms, the only surroundings in which they could profitably display the useless accomplishments with which they have been endowed, but also perfectly incapable of darning their stockings or of boiling an egg.

And so they soon blush at their father's obscure condition and evince a mortal disgust of the modest joys of the poor fire-side.

"Heavens! how little it all is!" Such was the first word which escaped her when she returned to her father's house.

She had grown, and everything she saw on her return had shrank; her father like the rest, perhaps more than the rest. She loved him all the same, but she could not help finding him common.

She, the dainty young lady, brought up with the daughters of country-gentlemen and generals, she said to herself that she was only the daughter of an obscure captain, and it humiliated her. Ah! if her haughty friends with whom she had exchanged confidences and dreams, had seen her coming down the sumptuous stairs of her castles in Spain to go and live in a poor village, while her father perspired over his cabbage-planting.

Her dreams! You know them well, and have also told them in quiet at the age when you know how to form them:

At the age when you cease to be called a little girl, when the dressmaker has just lengthened your dress, when your father's friends are no longer familiar, but say with a smile: *Mademoiselle.*

At the age, when you feel the attraction of the unknown redouble its power, when for the first time you feel a conscious blush at the look of a man.

At the age when the likeness of the young cousin you saw yesterday, appears all at once on the page of your history or grammar, and strange to say, pursues you at your games; when the noisy games of your companions weary you, and you betake yourself to solitude in order to screen your thoughts.

And solitude, a bad adviser, takes possession of your thoughts, isolates them from the rest of the real world, in order to immerse them in imaginary worlds, and then agitates, reflects, whirls, polishes all that marvellous enchanted universe in which the daughters of Eve wander with each wild license, whom the base-born sons of Adam approach only a single step.

But when that step is taken, the enchanted world vanishes. The scaffolding cracks and falls down. Palaces, geail, heroes and bounteous fairies disappear pell-mell into the lowest depth. The old farce of humanity, the comedy of love is played out.

Ah! how ugly it all is then! Under the smoky lamp of reality you vaguely distinguish the battered grotesque shapes, rising in the ruins.

Suzanne therefore, like all her young friends, like you, Mademoiselle, and also like you formerly, Madame, had commenced her little romance, had sketched her little plot. She had loved, oh truly loved, with a love necessarily confined to the platonic state, the handsome young men with tasty cravats, whom she had seen on days when she walked out. What delightful chapters were sketched upon their brown or fair heads! Oh! when would she be free? When would she cease to have the ever-open eye of an inquisitive under-mistress upon her slightest gesture?

And then the day of liberty had come, and under the breath of that liberty, so eagerly and impatiently expected, the chapters she had begun were blotted out, and so was the handsome head of a cherub or an Amadis in a sublieutenant's cap or in a chimney-pot.

Fallen from these enervating heights of fictitious passions and hair-dressers' scents into the prosaic but generous and brave arms of paternal lore, on the breast of true and mighty nature, she had forgotten for a moment her dreams.

She lavished on her father all the treasures of affection which her heart contained, and treated him with all manner of solicitude and caresses; and the old soldier before this youthful future which shone before him, himself forgot his dreams of the past.

XXVIII
THE SHADOW

"Troubled by a vague emotion, I said to myself, I wanted to be loved, and I looked around me; I saw no one who inspired me with love, no one who appeared to me capable of feeling it."

BENJAMIN CONSTANT (*Adolphe*).

But what is the liberty that a well-behaved girl can enjoy? She had run like a wild thing in the meadows, letting her hair fly in the wind, and elated by the kisses of the breeze. She had relished the long mornings of idleness in bed, recollecting, in order to double her enjoyment, that at that very moment the friends she had left at school, were turning pale beneath the smoky lamps of the school-room; and in the evening she read the delightful novels of Droz by her lamp, and thought with pleasure that her same friends had been in bed for a long while. Then she closed her book, and reflected again and said with a yawn: "They are asleep, poor little things, and I am awake, I am free to be awake."

And she wrote long letters to them in which she told them, how happy she was, assuming a charming air of superiority, treating them as children who knew nothing yet of life. But she thought that she knew nothing more of it herself, and yearned to be instructed.

She felt that there was something wanting, and that her father's affection was not enough to fill her heart.

She had looked well about her, but she had found only what was commonplace. No more young clerks with curled hair, who darted inflammatory looks at the women from behind the shop-windows, no Saint-Cyrion with delicate moustache, no doctors of twenty-five or poets of eighteen. Besides her father and the notabilities of the village, middle-aged dignitaries, nothing but peasants only.

She held the belief which all girls hold; a nice little belief very convenient and very simple: the sweet Jesus, the Paschal Lamb, and the Immaculate

Conception. Around this trio gravitated all the rest, but graceful and light as the mists which float at sun-rise.

Therefore the Captain had not thought it his duty to disappoint his daughter, when she said to him one Sunday morning, "My darling papa, I am going to Mass." He let her go, grumbling; and she noticed Marcel.

The fine figure of the priest struck her; she was touched by the sound of his voice, and while she fixed her gaze upon him, she encountered his, and their eyes fell.

In the days when she took her walks at Saint-Denis, and saw for the first time that she was admired by some handsome young men, she had not experienced a more delicious emotion.

She was astonished and almost ashamed at it, and nevertheless she returned for Vespers on purpose to see the Curé. She soon gained the certainty that she had attracted his attention, and she was flattered at it. What! she, a little school-girl, was she distracting from his prayers, at the very foot of the altar, a minister of the altar? She felt herself rise in importance. But her natural modesty made her reflect directly: "Has he looked at me because I am a stranger, or because I am pretty?"

She was almost afraid that it was not this latter reason; Marcel's eyes reassured her.

Nevertheless, the first impulse of self-love satisfied, what did it concern her? How did this priest's admiration affect her? Is a priest a man? It must be no more thought of. But she could not prevent herself from thinking of him, being pleased at his finding her pretty. Others, doubtless, had found her pretty before he did; perhaps had told her so in a whisper, but was that the same thing?

The silent admiration of this grave personage, clothed in a sacred character, raised her all at once in her own eyes more than a thousand warm glances or timid declarations from insignificant and common-place youths. Besides, he was young, he was handsome, and his position, his studies placed him far above the ignorant and common people, whom she elbowed since her return.

At night, the pale fine countenance of the Curé of Althausen crossed her dreams several times; she was not disturbed at it, but she said to herself that she would like to have a closer acquaintance with this shepherd of men, who had made so deep an impression on her.

She was affected by his grave voice, soft and sad, more than by his look, and, with a school-girl's simplicity, she asked herself, if a heart could not beat beneath that black robe.

The visit of Marcel filled her with a strange trouble, and she hesitated a long time before showing herself to him. Then the bitter raillery of her father tortured her heart and wounded her in her delicate maidenly sentiments. She suffered more than he from the insults which he received, and she vowed to herself to have them forgiven.

XXIX
OTHER MEETINGS

"There was no seduction on her part or on mine: love simply came, and I was her lover before I had even thought that I could become so."

MAXIME DU CAMP (*Mémoires d'un suicidé*).

They saw one another again very soon: sometimes on the road which leads to the little chapel of Saint Anne, sometimes behind the village gardens, other times on the high-road lined with poplars. From the furthest point at which he caught sight of her dress or her large straw-hat, trimmed with red ribbon, he trembled and became pale.

The first time he quickened his pace as he passed her, as though he were afraid of being retained by a force stronger than his own will, or perhaps from fear of ridicule, and he bowed to her as one bows to a queen.

She returned his bow graciously, and that was all. He had his sum of happiness for the rest of the day.

The second time they met, they had both thought so much of one another that they accosted one another like old acquaintances. The heart of each had broken the ice and made all the advances before they had taken the first steps. The young girl had read in the priest's eyes the wish to accost her, and he saw that he would be welcome.

Was anything more necessary? Therefore, mutually content, when they separated, they each had the desire to see the other again.

It was very often then that they saw one another; but especially at the morning Masses; then, when he turned towards the nave, and raising his look towards the gallery encountered hers, he asked no other joy from heaven.

XXX
SERAPHIC LOVE

"How many times does it not occur to me to blush at my tastes? to hide them from myself? to feign with myself that I have them not? to find some covering for them beneath which I conceal them, in order to play a part a little less foolish in my own conscience?"

JULES SIMON (*Le Devoir*).

But one day the Curé awoke full of dismay. The first intoxication had slightly dissipated, he had taken time to look closely within himself, and when he sought to analyze in cool blood this new and ravishing sensation, he saw the abyss beneath his feet.

"What! he said to himself, whither am I going? What am I doing? I, a priest, a minister of the altar, I should be at that point a slave of sin; I shall continue to cast myself from darkness to darkness until the definite and final fall. Oh! Lord, stop me, come to my aid; suffer not this shame and this crime."

But he altered his mind. When the devil has succeeded in bringing a soul to sin, there is no artifice he does not use to blind him beforehand, and to turn away his thought from everything capable of making him see the unhappy state in which he is. That is what the Church teaches.

Soon he viewed this passion under a new aspect, and he asked himself why he had not the right to love. Had not all the saints loved? Had not St. Jerome loved St. Paula? Had not Francis de Sales loved Madame de Chantal? Had not Fénélon loved Madame Guyon? St. Theresa, her spiritual director, and Venillot, his cook?

Were there not two kinds of love? The ethereal, ideal, chaste, seraphic love, the love of the creature grateful for the perfect work of the creator; platonic love, free from all impurity, allowed to the virtuous confessor for his virtuous penitent, the love of the wise man in fact; or—the other. Then with that art of the rhetorician which sacred scholasticism teaches to every Levite, he said to himself, "Yes, I can love, for it is the spotless love of the angels."

But his conscience protested and cried to him: "It is the other!"

XXXI
THE VIRGIN

"In whatever place I was, whatever occupation I imposed on myself, I could not think of women, the sight of a woman made me tremble. How many times have I risen at night, bathed in sweat, to fasten my mouth on our ramparts, feeling myself ready to suffocate."

A. DE MUSSET (*Confession d'un enfant du Siècle*).

It was the other. He was soon obliged to confess this to himself; for slumber abandoned his couch.

In vain in the day-time he wearied his body under the labour which kills thought. He sought to fly from the seductive image. He did not go out, for fear of seeing her. He rushed upon every hard and unfruitful labour that he could find. He rooted up his trees in order to re-plant them elsewhere; dug useless banks in his garden; changed his library from its place, and carried one after another his enormous folios to the upper story. He would have liked to go upon the road, sit at the bottom of some ditch, and take the stone-breaker's hammer.

But the thought which he silenced by day, took its revenge by night. How many times, during the long silent hours, his servant heard him get up all at once and march with long steps in his room, as if he had to accomplish some terrible vow.

It was the devil, whispering low mysterious words in his ear, while his impetuous desires constrained him with all the power of his vitality. He walked like a madman from his bed to his window, which he dared not open. He had often formerly, leant his elbows there during the hours of sleeplessness, and breathed with delight the keen freshness of the valley. But now he dared no longer; warm vapours rose up to him and completed the conflagration of his senses. Nature was re-awakening from the long slumber of winter, and already setting to work, was accomplishing from every quarter the mysterious work of love. And within and without he felt its formidable power growing and enveloping him.

Nameless thoughts tumultuously invaded his sick brain and ruled there as despots. They attached themselves to him like an implacable furious old woman, who attaches herself the more closely to her young lover, the more she feels he is going to escape her.

He saw again in continual hallucinations, sometimes the lascivious player as she had appeared to him near her little white bed, sometimes the fresh face of the religious school-girl who smiled to him from the height of the gallery. At other times he saw them both together, and each of them called him and said to him: Come, come.

Oh! why all these obstacles, these doors, these walls, these prejudices and that formidable barrier which he dared not pass, duty.

It seemed to him that a burning lava was escaping from his heart, running into his veins and devouring him. His limbs were heavy and bruised; his head was on fire like his heart, and his thoughts were enveloped in mire. Often with his eye fixed on space, he contemplated some phantom visible to himself alone; then big tears rolled slowly on his cheeks and fell one by one on his bare chest, and he felt that they relieved him.

He had placed a statue of the Virgin at the foot of his bed: the one which has a heart in flames and open arms. He looked on it as he went to sleep and prayed the Mother, eternally chaste, to watch over his dreams.

But many times in his delirium he saw the Virgin come to life and take the well-known face of her from whom he sought to flee, and come and find him in his couch. And he woke with a start full of terror of himself at the moment when, in his impious sacrilege, he felt the chaste bosom of the Mother of God quiver beneath his kisses.

Then he opened his scared eyes and perceived before him the sweet form which stretched its plaster arms to him in the shadow, and full of agony he cried:

"*Mater inviolata, ora pro nobis!*"

But once he thought he heard a voice which answered:

"*Christe, audi nos.*"

XXXII
THE DEATH'S-HEAD

"God is my witness that I did then everything in the world
to divert myself and to heal myself."

A. DE MUSSET (Confession d'un enfant du Siècle).

One night he went out by stealth, crossed the market-place, and descended the hill. He had the look of a man who was hiding himself, and he went back several times, as if he was afraid of being followed. He reached the cemetery, took a key from his pocket, cautiously opened the gate and closed it behind him. At the bottom of the principal path there was a little chapel which served for an ossuary. In it was a hideous accumulation of the remains of several generations. The cemetery was becoming too full and it had been necessary to make room. Here as elsewhere the cry was: "Room for the young." And it is only justice. What would become of as if all the old remained? There is overcrowding under ground as there is above. "Keep off! Keep off!" Therefore their ancestors' bones were in the way, and they had cast them into this retreat to wait for the common grave. But the common grave is again a place which must be taken, and the recent gluttonous dead want everything. "Keep off! Keep off!" Let us not say anything ourselves, perhaps they will dispute with us the corner of ground which should shelter our bones!

Marcel went into the gloomy chapel; he lighted a dark lantern and began to search among the pile.

Then he returned to the parsonage like a thief, afraid of being caught, and shut himself up in his room.

He had a parcel under his arm; he opened it and, carefully placing its contents on the table, he sat down in front of it and contemplated it for a long time.

XXXIII
FRENZY

"Abstinence has its deadly exhaustions."

BALZAC (*Le Lys dans la Vallée*).

A few days before, the gravedigger, while digging up the whitened bones of the ancient dead, had broken up with his pick-axe a mouldering coffin, and a head rolled to his feet It was of later date, for the lower jaw was still fastened to it and it had not the calcareous colour of bones buried long ago. It was the more horrible.

The gravedigger threw it into his wheel-barrow with its neighbour's shin-bones, and carried it to the common heap. It was this *thing* that the Curé of Althausen had coveted and stolen.

He had then placed it on his table and contemplated it in silence. The top of the skull was polished and blunt, the front narrow, the bones small and apparently not having attained their full development. It was therefore a youthful head, the head of an adolescent cut down at the moment, when life completely unfolds itself to hope; while the elliptical shape of the lower maxillary, the small and similarly-shaped teeth, the slight separation of the nasal bones, a few long hairs still adhering to the occiput, clearly indicated its feminine origin.

"A young girl!" murmured Marcel, "a young girl! beautiful perhaps; loved without doubt ... and there is what remains. Ah! if he who was pleased to kiss your lips, could see your dreadful laugh."

And, after he had meditated a long while, he went to his bed, took the plaster virgin from its pedestal, and taking in his two hands the skull, he put it in its place between the serge curtains.

And when the fever seized him, when he was burning with all the flames which the fiery *simoom* of passion breathed on him, and he felt the frenzy taking possession of his pillow, he turned towards the wall and looked at this new companion. Sometimes a moon-beam came and lighted up the hideous skull and played in the gloomy cavities of its sightless eyes. The head then seemed to become animate and its bare teeth gave an infernal grin.

This was his remedy for love.

But we grow used to everything. Custom destroys sensations. Death and its mysteries, the horrible, and all its threatening shapes soon present nothing to our eyes but worn-out pictures. He accustomed himself to contemplate without emotion this lugubrious ruin. As before, the frenzy seized him and shook him before the skull. It did more. It clothed it again with flesh. It planted long hairs upon that shining, yellow forehead. It placed in the hollow orbits large eyes full of love; it hid the wasted cartilages under quivering nostrils, and upon that horrible jaw it laid rosy lips and a sweet mouth, like a maiden's first kiss. And it is thus that it appeared to him in the shadow, wrapped in the curtains of his bed, like a modest girl who hides herself from sight.

"Oh! sweet phantom, return to life," he said. "Take again thy body adorned with its graces and with its charms; come, clothed in thy sixteen years."

And he stretched his arms towards the enchanting vision, while the death's-head, with its bare jaw, gave its eternal grin.

He woke and found himself kneeling near his bed, facing the wreck of humanity.

Horror soiled him. His empty room was filled with spectres. He saw hell-hags with death's-heads sporting and swarming on his bed. At the same time, little sharp, hasty, shrill knocks shook his window.

Fall of terror he ran to open it. A gust of wind, mingled with rain and hail, heat against his face. He was ashamed of his fears and leant his head out to catch the beneficent shower. His brain cooled and his blood grew calm.

He was there for a few minutes, when all at once, under the trees in the market-place, he thought he distinguished two motionless shadows. He thought for an instant that his hallucination lasted still, but soon the shadows drew near. They seemed to walk carefully under the young foliage of the limes in order to avoid the rain, and in one of them he recognized distinctly Suzanne.

XXXIV
THE PROHIBITION

"Do you know any means of making a woman do that which she has decided that she will not do?"

ERNEST FEYDEAU (*La Comtesse de Chalis*).

That same day, after supper, the Captain had entered the drawing-room where
Suzanne was playing the *Requiem* of Mozart.

—So you are playing Church airs now? he said to her.

—Don't you like this piece, father?

—Not at all.

—Perhaps, said Suzanne smiling, because it is a Mass.

—My dear child, do you want me to tell you what you are with all your Masses?

—What?

—Where did you go this morning?

—At what time?

—At the time when you went out.

—I only went out to go to Mass.

—And the day before yesterday?

—Why this questioning, dearest papa?

—Ah! dearest papa, dearest papa. There is no dearest papa here, I want to know the truth.

—But what truth? I have nothing wrong to hide from you. I went to Mass. Is that forbidden?

—To Mass! Good Heavens! To Mass! That is most decidedly making up your mind to disobey me!

—But papa, you have not forbidden it to me.

—Not in so many words, it is true; because I counted on your reason and good sense. Have I not spoken loudly enough my way of thinking on this subject?

—But, papa, your way of thinking is completely contrary to that which I have been taught. You ought to have said when you sent me to Saint-Denis: "You are not to teach my daughter any religion." They have taught me religion, what is more natural than for me to follow it.

—And what has your religion in common with your Mass? If you want to pray to God, can you not pray to him at home?

—Am I not a Catholic before all?

It was the first time that Suzanne had spoken to her father in this firm and decided tone. Nothing more was wanted to irritate the irascible soldier:

—Ah! I know the hidden and villainous insinuation! he cried, Catholic before all! It is that indeed. Before being daughter! before being wife! before being mother! the Church, the priest first; the rest only comes after. The Mass, the Church! the Church, the Mass! With that they cover every vileness. Well, do you want me to tell you what I think of women who frequent churches? They are either lazy, or hypocrites, or idiots, or finally hussies in love with the Curé. There are no others. In which category do you want to be placed, my daughter?

—And all that because I discharge my religious duties!

—You have spoken to that Curé? I see it. Where have you spoken to him?

—I have nothing to hide from you, father; but Monsieur Marcel had not given me any bad advice, I ask you to believe.

—So it is true then; you have spoken to this man: unknown to me, in secret.

—I had no secret to make of it. I went to confession, that is all, as I was accustomed to do at school.

—Confession! what, good Heavens! You went and knelt before that rascal, after what I have told you concerning all his like!

—All priests are not alike.

—Ah! you are under his influence already. Doubtless, he is the pearl, the model, the saint. Thunder of Heaven! my daughter too, but you do not know that your mother died of remorse of soul because she found a saint, a model of virtue in that black crew of scoundrels. Stay, be silent, you make me say too much.

—I don't understand you.

—I will be obeyed and not questioned. Have I the right to expect that from my daughter?

—You have every right, father.

—Well, I forbid you for the future to put your foot inside the church.

—In truth, father, would not one say that you were talking of some ill-reputed place?

—Worse than that. Those who enter a place of ill-repute, know beforehand where they go and to what they expose themselves, which the little fools who frequent churches never know.

Suzanne made no reply and went down into the garden.

The old governess who bad brought her up and who loved her tenderly, came to meet her.

—Your father is after the Curés again. What can these poor people of God have done to the man?

They walked a long time round the kitchen-garden, then they sat down under an arbour of honeysuckle.

—What time is it, Marianne? the young girl said all at once, fixing her eyes on the window of her father's room.

—It is late, my child, it is ten o'clock at least; everybody in the village has gone to bed. Come, your father has finished his newspaper, there is no longer any light in his room; he has just blown out his lamp. Let us go in.

They were near the little back-gate which led out to the meadows. Suzanne opened it cautiously: "No, let us go out," she said.

XXXV
THE SHELTER

"Is it a chance? No. And besides; chance, what is it after all
but the effect of a cause which escapes us?"

ERCHMAN-CHATRIAN (*Contes fantastiques*).

As soon as Marcel had recognized Suzanne, he did not take time to
reflect, and say to himself:

"What is it you are going to do, idiot?" He ran downstairs, stumbling
like a drunken man, and gently opened the door. What did he intend? He
did not know. Was he going to call these women? He did not know. He
opened his door, that was all, and his thought went no further.

The same morning at church, he had seen Suzanne, and said to himself,
"I will not look at her." He did not look at her. He kept his eyes lowered
when he turned towards the nave, but he could have said how many times
Suzanne lifted hers, if she were joyous or sad, and if she had a red ribbon or
a blue ribbon at her neck.

Oh! the eternal contradiction of mankind. He had not wanted to look
at her by day, and here he is throwing himself in her path in the middle of
the night.

The steps approached and his heart beat with violence; he was so
agitated that, at the moment when the two women passed before his door to
reach the lane which led to the bottom of the hill, he could hardly articulate
in a hesitating voice:

"Mademoiselle Durand."

They uttered a cry.

—It is I, he said coming forward. Is it possible? You here at such an hour
and in the rain?

—I had gone out with my maid, said Suzanne, and the rain has surprised
us.

—Do not go farther. Shelter yourselves under my door. It is an April shower; it will soon have passed.

At the same time he went down the steps before the house and took Suzanne's hand. Never had he felt such boldness.

—I pray, Mademoiselle, do not refuse me the pleasure of offering you a refuge for a few moments beneath my humble roof.

Suzanne accepted without making him plead any more. She went up the stairs and entered the corridor. The servant followed her. At the end, on the first steps of the stair-case, a lamp swung to and fro in the wind.

The Curé shut the door again and, passing near the two women, drawn up against the wall, he brushed against the young girl's damp dress with his hand.

—But you are wet, Mademoiselle, he said to her. Perhaps it would not be wise to remain in this cold passage. Should I dare to ask you to go upstairs an instant, and warm yourself at my fire?

His voice trembled with emotion, and he found that his hand was so near hers that he had only to close his fingers to take Suzanne's. He seized it therefore and inflicting on her a gentle violence: "Go up, I pray, go up," he said.

She allowed him to conduct her. He showed them into his library, which was his favourite apartment, the sanctuary of his labours, his griefs and his dreams. He took some vine-twigs which he threw in the fireplace, and soon a cheerful flame lighted up the hearth.

XXXVI
THE HOT WINE

"I looked at her; she tried to show nothing of what she felt in her heart. She held herself straight, like an oarsman who feels that the current is carrying him away, and her nostrils quivered."

CAMILLE LEMONNIER (*Contes flamands et wallons*).

Suzanne was sitting in the old arm-chair of straw, the seat of honour of the parsonage, her huge dark eyes followed the curling flames, while Marianne, standing up against one of the sides of the chimney-piece, cast around her an inquisitive and timorous look. The priest with one knee on the ground, was drawing up the fire.

—Here is quite a Christmas fire, he said as he got up. Come close, Mademoiselle, your feet are doubtless damp. It is cold; don't you find it so?

He was trembling in all his limbs as if indeed he were frozen near this blazing fire.

Suzanne put forward a little delicate arched foot which she rested on one of the fire-dogs. The priest's eyes stayed with ecstasy on the white line, the breadth of two fingers, displayed between her boot and the bottom of her dress.

—I am truly ashamed, she murmured, yes, truly ashamed to disturb you at such an hour.

—Ought not the priest's house, said Marcel, to be open to all at any hour? It is open to the poor man who passes by; it is open sometimes to the vagabond; why should it not be to an angelic young lady who seeks a shelter against the storm?

—It is true, it is the house of God, said Marianne. The young girl looked at the priest, smiled and then became thoughtful. She appeared soon no longer to be conscious where she was, nor of the priest who remained standing before her. She knitted her eyebrows and a feverish shudder ran through her frame.

Marcel stooped down towards her with anxiety.

—Are you in pain? he said.

She shook her head as if to drive away a world of thought which possessed her and answered with a kind of hesitation:

—No, Monsieur, thank you; I am not in pain. But I tremble to find myself here. What will my father say? And you, Monsieur, what will you think of me?

—But what are you frightened at, Mademoiselle? said Marianne. We are here because Monsieur le Curé has had the goodness to bring us in. Don't you hear the rain outside? As to your father, he is not obliged to know that we are at Monsieur le Curé's.

—Reassure yourself, Mademoiselle; your father cannot be offended because you have accepted a shelter against the bad weather. You are here, as the good Marianne has just said, in the house of God, and I will say in my turn, beneath the eye of God. These are very great words about so small a matter, he added with a smile. But you are in pain? Ah! you see, you have a cold already.

He proposed making her take a little warm wine, which Marianne declared to be a sovereign remedy, and spoke of going to wake up his servant.

Marianne opposed this with all her power.

—Since you have the kindness to offer something to our dear young lady, she said, let me make it. Good Heavens! to wake up Mademoiselle Veronica! what would she say? that I am good for nothing, and she would be right.

—Well, said Marcel, I am going to show you where you will find what is necessary.

They both went down to the kitchen, as quietly as possible, so as not to disturb Veronica's slumber, and Marianne declared that with an armful of dry wood, she would have finished in a few minutes.

—Then I leave you, said the priest; I must not leave Mademoiselle Suzanne alone.

He remained several seconds longer, hesitating, following the movements of the old governess without seeing them, then all at once he quickly remounted the stair-case.

XXXVI
TÊTE-À-TÊTE

"'Tis yours to use aright the hour
Which destiny may leave you,
To drain the cup of oldest wine,
And pluck the morning's roses."

A. BUSQUET (*La poésie des heures*).

He halted at the threshold, pale and trembling as if he were about to commit a crime.

He passed his hand over his brow, it was damp with a cold sweat. What! Suzanne was there, in his house, alone, in the middle of the night, in his own room, beside his fire, seated in his arm-chair. Oh, blessed vision! Was it possible? Was he dreaming? Would the charming picture disappear? And he remained there, motionless, anxious, not daring to move a step, for fear of seeing her disappear. But yes, it is she indeed; she has hidden her charming face in her hands, and it seems to him that tears are stealing through her fingers.

He sprang towards her.

—Oh! Mademoiselle, what is the matter? What is the matter? Why these tears, which break my heart? Confide your troubles to me, and, I swear to you, if it be in my power, I will alleviate them.

—You cannot, answered Suzanne sadly, lifting to him her great moist eyes.

—I cannot! do not believe that, my child: the priest can do many things; he knows how to comfort souls, it is the most precious of his gifts. Do not hesitate to confide your griefs to the priest, to the friend.

He sat down, facing her, waiting for her to speak. But she remained silent; he only heard the rapid breathing of the young girl, and the storm which raged in his own heart.

At length he broke the silence.

—Mademoiselle, dear young lady, he said with his most insinuating voice, do you lack confidence then in me? Ah! I see but too well, your father's prejudices have left their marks.

—Do not believe it, she cried eagerly, do not believe it.

—Thank you, dear young lady. I should so much wish to have your confidence. And in whom could you better repose it? What others could receive more discreetly than ourselves the trust of secret sufferings? Ah, that is one of the benefits of our holy religion; it is on that account that she is the consolation of those who are sad, the relief of those who suffer, the refuge of the humble and the weak, the joy of all the afflicted. Her strong arms are open to all human kind; but how small is the number of the chosen who wish to profit by this maternal tenderness. Be one of that number, dear child, come to us, to us who stretch out our arms to you, to me, who now say to you: "Open your heart to me, confide to me your troubles. However sick your soul may be, mine will understand it."

The priest's voice was troubled, and it went to the bottom of Suzanne's heart. She cast on him a look full of compassion: You are unhappy, she asked.

—Do not say that, do not say that! Unhappy! yes, I may have been so, but now I am so no longer. Are you not there? Has not your presence caused all the dark clouds to fly away? No, I am no longer unhappy; it would be a blasphemy to say so, when God has permitted you, by some way or other of his mysterious and infinite wisdom, to come and bring happiness to my hearth!

—Happiness! I bring happiness to you! But who am I? a little girl just out of school, who knows nothing of life.

—And that is what makes you more charming. You are a rose which the breath of morning, pure as it is, has not yet touched. Life! dear child, do not seek to know it too soon. It is a vale of tears, and those who know it best are those who have suffered most deception and weeping.

—But a priest is safe from deception and sorrows....

—Ah, Mademoiselle, you with that clear and honest look, you do not know all that passes at the bottom of a man's heart.

Alas, we priests, we are but men, more miserable than others, that is the difference ... yes, more miserable because we are more alone. Ah, you cannot understand how painful it is never to have anybody to whom you can open your heart; no one to partake your joys and mitigate your griefs; no loved soul to respond to your soul; no intellect to understand your intellect. Alone, eternally alone, that is our lot. We are men of all families; friends of all, and we have no friends; counsellors to all, and no one gives us salutary advice; directors of all consciences, and we have no one to direct ours, but the evil thoughts which spring from our weariness and our isolation. But why do I speak to you of all that, am I mad? Let us talk about yourself. Come, dear child, I have made my little disclosures to you, make yours to me, open your heart to me … speak … speak.

—Well, yes, I wanted to see you, to speak with you, to ask your advice. I used to meet you before from time to time in your walks, now you never go out. I have gone to Mass, notwithstanding the displeasure it causes my father, I thought your looks avoided mine. What have I done to you? I don't believe I have done anything wrong. This evening I had a dispute with my father. I went out not knowing where I went; the rain overtook us and I met you.

Marcel trembled. He had taken the young girl's hand, but he quickly dropped it, fearing she might observe his agitation.

—Ah! Suzanne continued, there are hours when I miss the school, my companions, the long cold corridors, our silent school-room, even the under-mistresses. I am ashamed of it, and angry with myself, but I must confess it. Is this then that liberty I so desired? I was a prisoner then, but I was peaceful, I was happy: I see it now. Weariness consumes me here. I see no aim for my life. I had one consolation; my religious duties. That is taken away from me. For my father has formally forbidden me this evening to go to church. If I go there again, I disobey my father and I grieve him. If I obey his orders, I take away the only happiness of my life.

She had spoken with volubility, and the priest listened to her in silence. Hanging on her look, he drank in her words. He heard them without comprehending exactly their meaning. It was sweet music which charmed him, but he only thought of one thing. She had said: "Your looks avoided mine."

When she had finished speaking, he was surprised to hear her no longer and listened afresh.

—I have spoken with open heart to my confessor, said Suzanne timidly, astonished at this silence.

—To the confessor! no, no, dear child; to the friend, to the friend, is it not? Do you want him? Will you trust yourself to me? Will you let yourself be guided by me? I will bring you by a way from which I will remove all the thorns.

—But my father?

This was like the blow from a club to Marcel.

—Your father! Ah, yes! your father! Well, but what are we going to do?

—I have just asked you.

—It is written in the Gospel: "No one can serve two masters at the same time." You have a master who is God. Your father places himself between God and your duty. You must choose.

Suzanne did not reply.

—Consult your conscience, my child. What says your conscience?

—My conscience says nothing to me.

Marcel thought perhaps he had gone a little too far, he added:

—You must decide nevertheless. It is also written, "Render unto Caesar the things that are Caesar's, and to God the things that are God's."

—How am I to unite the respect and submission which I owe to my father with my duties as a Christian? That, repeated Suzanne, is what I wanted to ask you.

—And we will solve the problem, dear child. Yes, we will come forth from this evil pass, to our advantage and to our glory. Nothing happens but by the will of God, and it is He, doubt it not, who has guided you into my path in order that I may take care of your young and beautiful soul. The ancients were in the habit of marking their happy days; I count already two days in my life which I shall never obliterate from my memory, two days marked in the golden book of my remembrances. The one is that on which I saw you for the first time. You were in the gallery of our church. The light was streaming behind you through the painted windows and surrounded you with a halo. I said to myself: "Is it not one of the virgins detached from the window?" The other is to-day.—Do you believe in presentiments, Mademoiselle?

—Sometimes.

—Well! I had a presentiment as it were of this visit. Yes, shall I dare to tell you so? The whole day I have been wild with joy! I had an intuition of an approaching happiness, a very rare event with me, Mademoiselle.

—Of what happiness?

—Why of this, of this which I enjoy at this moment; this of seeing you sitting at my hearth, in front of me, near to me, this of hearing your sweet voice, and reading your pure eyes. But what am I saying? Pardon me, Mademoiselle. See how happiness make us egotistic! I talk to you about myself, while it is about you that we ought to occupy ourselves, of you, and of your future.

And he looked at her with such glowing eyes, that she was a little frightened.

XXXVIII
THE KISS

"That strange kiss makes me shudder still."

A. DE MUSSET (*Premières poesies*).

—Are you not cold? said Marcel; and he stooped down to draw up the fire.

But on sitting down again it happened that his seat was quite close to that of Suzanne, so close that their knees were touching, and that he had only to make a slight movement to take one of her hands.

—Dear, dear child.

And he began to talk to her of God in his unctuous voice. He talked to her also of her duties as a Christian, and of the probable struggles she would have to undergo. He talked to her again of the purity of her heart and compared her to the angels.

And while he talked, he began to fondle this little soft white hand, lifting delicately the slender fingers with their rosy nails, drawing over the soft and satiny tips his brown and muscular fingers.

Soon his warm hand became burning. Magnetic influences were evolved. Invisible sparks broke forth suddenly at the contact of these two epidermises, ran through his veins, inflamed his heart and set his brain a-blaze.

[PLATE II: THE KISS. She tried to release her imprisoned hand, but he bent over it, and pressed it to his lips.]

He lost his presence of mind, his will wavered and sank in the molten lava of his desires; he lost perception of his surroundings, of all those formidable things which until then had bound him with the strong bands of moral authority; he thought no longer of anything, he paused no longer at anything, he saw nothing but this fair young girl whom he coveted, who was alone with him, her hand in his, sitting by his fire-side, in the silence and the mystery of the night. His clasp became convulsive. Under the fire of his burning gaze Suzanne raised her head, and a second time fell back in dismay. She tried to release her imprisoned hand, but he bent over it, and pressed it to his lips.

The door opened wide.

—Don't get impatient, said Marianne, there is the hot wine. I have been a long time, but the wood was green. Are you better?

But Suzanne, trembling all over, remained silent.

XXXIX
THE DEVIL IN PETTICOATS

"I know an infallible means of drawing you back from the precipice on which you stand."

CHARLES (*Des Illustres Françaises*).

—Wretch that I am. I have defiled a pure confiding child, who came in all loyalty to sit at my fire-side. Vile and cowardly nature, like some base Lovelace, I have grossly abused the confidence which was placed in me. My priestly robe, far from being a safeguard, is but a cloke for my iniquities. I have reached that pitch of cowardice that I am no longer master of myself.

Incapable of commanding my feelings; become the slave and the plaything of my shameful desires and of my lustful passions!... It must have happened. Yes, it must have happened. Sooner or later I was obliged to fall: it is the chastisement of my presumption and pride. Ah! wretch, you wish to subdue the flesh, you wish to reform nature, you wish to be wiser than God. They tried at the seminary by means of *nenuphar* and *infusions of nitre* to quench in you the desires of youth and its rebellious passion. Vain efforts, senseless attempts, which served only to retard your fall. In vain you try, in vain you struggle, in vain you invoke the angels and call God to your aid; there comes a time, a moment, a minute, a second, in which all your life of struggles and efforts is lost. The angry flesh subdues you in its turn, baffled nature revolts, and the Creator, whose laws you have not recognized, abandons the worthless creature and lets him roll over, falling into an abyss of iniquity.

Oh! my God! where is all this going to bring me? What will become of me? How can I show my brow all covered with shame? Is not my infamy written there?... She, she, what will she think of me?... To kiss her hand, her soft perfumed hand. Oh God, God all-powerful, where am I? where am I going? I said it; martyrdom or shame! It is shame which awaits me.

So spoke the Curé, when Marianne had taken away her young mistress, and his conscience exaggerated the gravity and the consequences of his imprudent rapture.

—Yes, it is shame, it is shame.

—Do not despair in this way, said a jeering voice.

Marcel turned round, terror-struck.

His servant was behind him.

She had approached, noiselessly, and was looking at him with her strange, green eyes.

—Shame lies in scandal, she added sententiously. Reassure yourself; that pretty young lady will hold her tongue.

She spoke low, slowly, with perfect calm, and each word penetrated the priest's heart like a steel blade.

Like all persons ashamed of having been caught, he put himself in a passion.

—You! he cried. You here? Who called you? You were not gone to bed then? What do you want? What have you just been doing? You are always listening then at the doors?

—That is useful sometimes, the woman said sententiously.

—What, you dare to admit that wretched fault without blushing at it?

—There are many others who ought to blush and yet don't blush.

—What do you mean? Come, speak? what do you want?

—Only to talk with you. You have had a long talk with Mademoiselle Suzanne
Durand! you can well listen to me a little in my turn.

—What do you say? wicked creature! what do you say?

—Oh, Monsieur le Curé, you are wrong to call me wicked, I am not so.

—You are, at the very least, most indiscreet.

—Oh, sir, it is not my fault; it is quite involuntarily that I have been a witness of what passed.

—Eh! what has passed then?

—Sir, don't question me, she said in a pitying tone, *I have heard and seen.*

—You have seen! cried the priest in a stifled voice. What have you seen then, wretched woman?

And mad with anger, with blazing eyes and clenched fists, he sprang upon the servant, who was afraid and retreated to the door.

—Please, Monsieur le Curé, she implored, don't hurt me.

These words recalled the priest to himself.

—No, he said as he sat down again, no, Veronica, I shall not hurt you. I flew into a passion, I was wrong; pardon me. Reassure yourself; see, I am calm; come closer and let us talk. Come closer. Sit here, in front of me.

—I will do so. Ah! you frighten me....

—It is your fault, Veronica; why do you put me into such passion?

—It was not my intention; far from it. I wanted to talk with you very peaceably, like the *other*, it is so nice.

—Please, enough of that subject.

—Oh, Monsieur le Curé, it is just about that I want to speak to you.

—Do not jest, Veronica. You have been, thanks to your culpable indiscretion, witness of a momentary error, which will not be repeated any more.

—A momentary error, which would have led you to some pretty things, Monsieur le Curé. Good God! if Marianne had not arrived in time, who knows what might have happened.

—It is not for you to blame me, Veronica. There is only God who is without sin.

—I know that well. Therefore, I have not said that to you in order to blame you. Quite the contrary, I was astonished that with a temperament ... as strong as yours, you have remained free from fault till to-day.

—And, please God, I will always remain so.

—Oh! God does not ask for impossibilities, as my old master, Monsieur le Curé Fortin, used to say: he was a good-natured man. He often repeated to me: "You see, Veronica, provided appearances are saved, everything is saved. God is content, he asks for no more."

—What, the Abbé Fortin said that?

—Yes, and many other things too. He was so honest, so delicate a man—not more than you, however, Monsieur le Curé—but he understood his case better than any other. He said again: "Beware of bad example, keep yourself from scandal. Dirty linen should be washed at home." Good rules, are they not, Monsieur Marcel?

—Certainly.

—He knew so well how to compassionate human infirmities. Ah! when nature speaks, she speaks very loudly.

—Do you know anything about it, Veronica?

—Who does not know it? I can certainly acknowledge that to you, since you are my Curé and my confessor.

—That is true, Veronica.

—And to whom should a poor servant acknowledge her secret thoughts, if not to her Curé and her confessor? He is her only friend in this world, is he not?

The Curé did not reply. He considered the strange shape the conversation was taking, and cast a look of defiance at the woman.

—You do not answer, sir, she said. You do not look upon me as your friend, that is wrong. Is it because I have surprised your secrets?

—I have no secrets.

—Yes?…. Suzanne?

—Enough on that subject. Do not revive my shame, since you call yourself my friend.

—Oh! sir, it is precisely for that, it is because I do not want you to distress yourself about so little. Listen to me, sir, I am older than you, and although I am not so learned, I have the experience which, as they say, is not picked up in books: well, this experience has taught me many things which perhaps you do not suspect.

—Explain yourself.

—I would have explained already, if you had wished it. The other evening you were quite sad, sitting by that fireless grate; you were thinking of I don't know what, but certainly it was not of anything very lively, so much so that it went to my heart. I suspected what was vexing you; I wanted to speak to you, but you repulsed me almost brutally. Nevertheless, if you had listened to me that day, what has just happened might not have occurred.

—I don't understand you.

—I will make myself understood … if you allow me.

XL
LITTLE CONFESSIONS

"To relate one's misfortunes often alleviates them."

CORNEILLE (*Polyeucte*).

The Curé laid his forehead between his hands, and rested his elbows on his knees, a common attitude among confessors.

—I am listening to you, he said.

—I said to you, Monsieur le Curé, do not despair. You will excuse a poor servant's boldness, but it is the friendship I have for you which has urged me; nothing else, believe me; I am an honest girl, entirely devoted to my masters. You are the fourth, Monsieur le Curé, yes, the fourth master. Well! the three others have never had to complain about me a single moment for indiscretion, or for idleness, or for want of attention, or for anything, in fact, for anything. Never a harsh word. "You have done well, Veronica; that's quite right, Veronica; do as you think proper, Veronica; your advice is excellent, Veronica." Those are all the rough words which have been said to me, Monsieur Marcel. Therefore, I repeat, really it went to my heart to hear you speaking harshly sometimes to me, and to see that you did not appear satisfied with me. I had not been accustomed to that.

And the servant, picking up the corner of her apron, burst into tears.

—Why! Veronica, are you mad? Why do you cry so? Who has made you suppose that I was not satisfied with you? I may have spoken harshly to you, it is possible; but it was in a moment of excitement or of impatience, which I regret. You well know that I am not ill-natured.

—Oh, no, sir, that is just what grieves me. You are so kind to everybody. You are only severe to me.

—You are wrong again, Veronica. I may have felt hurt at your indiscretion, but that is all. Put yourself in my place, and you will allow that it is humiliating for a priest....

—Do not speak of that again, Monsieur le Curé. You are very wrong to disturb yourself about it, and if you had had confidence in me before, I should have told you that all have acted like you, all have gone through that, all, all.

—What do you mean?

—I mean that young and old have fallen into the same fault.... If we can call it a fault, as Monsieur Fortin used to say. And the old still more than the young. After that, perhaps you will say to me that it is the place which is wicked.

—Be silent, Veronica. What you say is very wrong, for if I perfectly understand you, you are bringing an infamous accusation against my predecessors. Perhaps you think to palliate my fault thus in my own eyes. I thank you for the intention, but it is an improper course, and the reproach which you try to cast upon the worthy priests who have succeeded one another in this parish, takes away none of my remorse.

—Monsieur Fortin had not so many scruples. He was, however, a most respectable man, and one who never dared to look a young girl in her face, he was so bashful. "Well," he often used to say, "God has well done all that he has done, and He is too wise to be angry when we make use of His benefits!"

—That is rather an elastic morality.

—It was Monsieur Fortin who taught me that. After all, that is perhaps morality in word, you are ... morality in deed.

—Veronica, you are strangely misusing the rights which I have allowed you to take.

—Do not put yourself in a rage, Monsieur le Curé, if I talk to you so. I wanted to persuade you thoroughly that you can rely upon me in everything, that I can keep a secret, though you sometimes call me a tattler, and that I am not, after all, such a worthless girl as you believe. We like, when the moment has come to get ourselves appreciated, to profit by it to our utmost.

—Veronica, said Marcel, I hardly know what you want to arrive at; but I wish to speak frankly to you, since you have behaved frankly towards me. I recognize all the wisdom of your proceeding, although you will agree it has something offensive and humiliating for me, but after all, it is preferable that you should come and tell me this to my face, than that you should go and chatter in the village and tattle without my knowledge.

—Oh, Monsieur le Curé, Veronica is not capable of that.

—Therefore, since you have discovered ... discovered a secret which would ruin me, what do you calculate on making from this secret, and what do you demand?

—I, Monsieur le Curé, cried the servant, I demand nothing ... oh! nothing.

—You are hesitating. Yes, you want something. Come, it is you now who hang your head and blush, while it is I who am the culprit.... Come, place yourself there, close to me.

—Oh! Monsieur le Curé, I shall never presume.

—Presume then to-day. Have you not told me that you were my friend?... Yes. Well then, place yourself there. Tell me, Veronica, what is your age?

—Mine, Monsieur le Curé. What a question! I am not too old; come, not so old as you think. I am forty.

—Forty! why you are still of an age to get married.

—I quite think so.

—And you have never intended to do so?

—To get married? Oh, upon my word, if I had wanted to do so, I should not have waited until now.

—I believe you, Veronica. You could have done very well before now. But you may have changed your ideas. Our characters, our tastes change with time, and a thing displeases us to-day, which will please us to-morrow. There are often, it is true, certain considerations which stop us and make us reflect. Perhaps you have not a round enough sum. With a little money, at your age, you could still make an excellent match.

—And even without money, Monsieur le Curé. If I were willing, somebody has been pestering me for a long time for that.

—And you are not willing. The person doubtless does not suit you?

—Oh, I have my choice.

—Well and good. We cannot use too much reflection upon a matter of this importance. I am not rich, Veronica, but I should like to help you and to increase, if it be possible, your little savings, your dowry in fact.

—You are very good, sir, but I do not wish to get married.

—Why so?

—It depends on tastes, you know.... You are in a great hurry then to get rid of me, Monsieur le Curé.

—Not at all: do not believe it.

—Come, come, Monsieur le Curé. I see your intentions. You say to yourself: "she holds a secret which may prove troublesome to me; with a little money I will put a padlock on her tongue, I will get her married, and by this means she will trouble me no more." Is it a bad guess?

—You have not guessed it the least in world, Veronica.

—Oh, it is! But it is a bad calculation, and for two reasons. In the first place, if I marry, your secret is more in danger than if I remain single. You know that a woman ought not to hide anything from her husband.

—There are certain things....

—No, nothing at all: no secret, or mystery. The husband ought to see all, to know all, to be acquainted with all that concerns his wife. Ah! I know how to live, though I am an old maid.

—You are a pearl, Veronica.

—You want to make fun of me; but others have said that to me before you, and they were talking seriously. On the other hand, she continued, if you keep me, you need not fear my slandering you, since I am in your hands and the day you hear any rumour, you can turn me away.

—Your argument is just, and believe me that my words had but a single object, not that of separating myself from you, but of being useful to you. Since you are desirous of remaining with me, at which I am happy, let us therefore try to live on good terms, and do you for your part forget my weaknesses; I for mine will forget your inquisitiveness; and let us talk no more about them.

—Oh yes, we will talk again.

—I consent to it. Let us therefore make peace, and give me your hand.

—Here it is, Monsieur le Curé.

—Ah, Veronica. *Errare humanum est.*

—Yes, I know, Monsieur Fortin often repeated it. That means to say that the devil is sly, and the flesh is weak.

—It is something like that. So then I trust to your honesty.

—You can do so without fear.

—To your discretion.

—You can do so with all confidence.

—To your friendship for me. Have you really a little, Veronica?

—I have, sir, said the servant, affected. You ask me that: what must I then do to convince you?

—Be discreet, that is all.

—Oh! you might require more than that. But could I also, in my turn, ask something of you?

—Ask on.

—It will be perhaps very hard for you.

—Speak freely. What do you want? Are you not mistress here? Is not everything at your disposal?

—Oh, no.

—No! You surprise me. Have I hurt you without knowing it? I do not remember it, I assure you. Tell me then, that I may atone for my fault.

—I hardly know how to tell you.

—Is it then very serious?

—Not precisely, but....

—You are putting me on thorns. What is it then?

—Oh, nothing.

—What nothing? Do you wish to vex me, Veronica.

—I don't intend it; it is far from that.

—Speak then.

—Well no, I will say no more. You will guess it perhaps. But meanwhile....

—Meanwhile....

—It is quite understood between us that you will never see that little hussy again.

—What hussy?

—That little hussy, who was here just now.

—Oh, Veronica! Veronica!

—It is for your interests, Monsieur le Curé, in short ... the proprieties.

—My dignity is as dear to me as it is to you, my daughter, be answered sharply.

—Good-night, Monsieur le Curé; take counsel with your pillow.

XLI
MORAL REFLECTIONS

"Ah, poor grandmamma, what grand-dam's tales
You used to sing to me in praise of virtue;
Everywhere have I asked: 'What is this stranger?'
They laughed at me and said, 'Whence hast thou come?'"

G. MELOTTE (*Les Temps nouveaux*).

The Curé of Althausen had no need of reflection to understand the kind of shameful bargain which his servant had allowed him to catch a glimpse of.

The lustful look of the woman had spoken too clearly, and when he had taken her hand, he had felt it burn and tremble in his.

Then certain circumstances, certain facts to which he had not attended at first, came back to his memory.

Two or three times, Veronica, on frivolous pretexts had entered his bedroom at night; and each time, he remembered well, she was in somewhat indecent undress, which contrasted strangely with her ordinarily severe appearance.

He recalled to himself all the stories of Curés' servants who shared their masters' bed. Stories told in a whisper at certain *general repasts*, when the priests of the district met together at the senior's house to observe the feast of some saint or other—the great Saint Priapus perhaps—and where lively talk and sprightly stories ran merrily round the table.

And what he had taken for jokes in bad taste, and refused to believe till now, he began to understand.

For he could no longer doubt that he had set his servant's passions aflame, and he must either expose himself to her venomous tongue and incur the shame and scandal, or else appease the erotic rage of this kitchen Messalina.

He tried to drive away this horrible thought, to believe that he had been mistaken, to persuade himself that he was the dope of erroneous appearances; he wished to convince himself that he had been the victim of errors engendered by his own depravity, that he judged according to his secret sentiments; his efforts were vain; the woman's feverish eyes, her restless solicitude, her jealous rage, her incessant watching, the evidence in short was there which contradicted all his hopes to the contrary.

And then, the latest confessions regarding his predecessors: "All have acted like you, all," possessed his mind. Like him! What had they done? They also had attempted then to seduce young girls, and perhaps had consummated their infernal design. What? respectable priests, ministers of the Gospel, pastors of God's flock! Was it possible? But was not he a respectable priest and respected by all, a minister of God, a leader of the holy flock, a pastor of men, and yet....

How then? where is virtue?

"Virtue," answered that voice which we have within ourselves, that voice odious to hypocrites and deceivers, which the Church calls the Devil's voice, and which is the voice of reason. Virtue? Of which do you speak, fool? Without counting the *three theological*, there are fifty thousand kinds of virtues. It is like happiness, institutions, reputations, religions, morals, principles: Truth on this side the mount, error on that.

There are as many kinds of virtues as there are different peoples. History swarms with virtuous people who have been so in their own way. Socrates was virtuous, and yet what strange familiarities he allowed himself with the young Alcibiades. The virtuous Brutus virtuously assassinated his father. The virtuous Elizabeth of Hungary had herself whipped by her confessor, the virtuous Conrad, and the virtuous Janicot doted on virtuous little boys; and finally Monseigneur is virtuous, but his old lady friends look down and smile when he talks of virtue.

See this priest of austere countenance and whitened hair. He too, during long years, has believed in that virtue which forms his torment. Candid and trustful, he felt the fervency of religion fill his heart from his youth. He had faith, he was filled with the spirit of charity and love. He said like the apostle: *Ubi charitas et amor, Deus ibi est.* And he believed that God was with him, and that alone with God he was peacefully pursuing his road. But he had counted without that troublesome guest who comes and places himself as a third between the creature and the Creator, and who, more powerful than the God of legend, quickly banishes him, for he is the principle of life and the other is the principle of death; it is the fruitful love and the other is the wasting barren love; it is present and active, while the other is inert, dumb and in the clouds of your sickly brain.

"It is in vain that in his successive halts from parish to parish, he has resisted the thousand seductions which surround the priest, from the timid gaze of the simple school-girl, smitten with a holy love for the young curate, to the veiled smile of the languishing woman. In vain will he attempt, like Fénélon formerly, to put the warmth of his heart and the incitements of the flesh upon the wrong scent by carrying on a platonic love with some chosen souls; what is the result in the end of his efforts and his struggles? Now he is old; ought he not to be appeased? No, weighty and imperious matter has regained the upper hand. He loves no longer, he is not able to love any longer, but the fury urges him on. He seduces his cook, or dishonours his niece."

And yet those most courageous natures exist, for they have resisted to the end. We blame them, we are wrong. Who would have been capable of such efforts and sacrifices? Who would sustain during ten, fifteen, twenty years, similar straggles between the imperious requirements of nature and the miserable duties of convention? They, therefore, who see their hair fall before their virtue are very rare.

The crowd of priests strike themselves against the obstacles of the road from the first steps, they tear their catechumen's robe with the white thorns of May, and when they have arrived at the end of their career, they have stopped many a time under some mysterious thicket, unknown by the vulgar, relishing the forbidden fruit.

Let us leave them in peace. It is not I who will disturb their sweet tête-à-tête.

XLII
MEMORY LOOKING BACK

"Man can do nothing against Destiny. We go, time flies, and that which must arrive, arrives."

LÉON CLADEL (*L'Homme de la Croix-aux-Baufs*).

Marcel was one of those energetic natures who believe that struggle is one of the conditions of life. He had valiantly accepted the task which was incumbent upon him.

But there are hours of discouragement and exhaustion, in which the boldest and the strongest succumb, and he had reached one of those hours.

And then, it is so difficult to struggle without ceasing, especially when we catch no glimpse of calmer days. Weariness quickly comes and we sink down on the road.

Then a friendly hand should be stretched towards us, should lift us up and say to us "Courage." But Marcel could not lean on any friendly hand.

He had no one to whom he could confide his struggles, his vexations, and the apprehension of his coming weaknesses.

Although his life as priest had been spotless up to then, his brethren held aloof from him, for there was a bad mark against him at the Bishop's Palace. It had been attached at the commencement of his career. He was one of those catechumens on whom from the very first the most brilliant hopes are founded. Knowledge, intelligence, respectful obedience, appearance of piety, sympathetic face, everything was present in him.

The Bishop, a frivolous old man, a great lover of little girls, who combined the sinecure of his bishopric with that of almoner to a second-hand empress, whose name will remain celebrated in the annals of devout gallantry or of gallant devotion, the Bishop, a worthy pastor for such a sheep, passed the greater portion of his time in the intrigues of petticoats and sacristies, and left to the young secretary the care of matters spiritual.

It was he who, like Gil-Blas, composed the mandates and sometimes the sermons of Monseigneur.

This confidence did not fail to arouse secret storms in the episcopal guest-chamber.

A Grand-Vicar, jealous of the influence which the young Abbé was assuming over his master's mind, had resolved upon his dismissal and fall.

With a church-man's tortuous diplomacy, he pried into the young man's heart, as yet fresh and inexperienced.

He insinuated himself into the most hidden recesses of his conscience, seized, so to say, in their flight the timid fleeting transports of his thought, of his vigorous imagination, and soon discovered with secret satisfaction that he was straying from the ancient path of orthodoxy.

Marcel, indeed, belonged to that younger generation of the clergy which believes that everything which alienates the Church from new ideas, brings it nearer to its ruin. And the day when the foolish Pius IX presumed to proclaim and define, to the great joy of free-thinkers and the enemies of Catholicism, the ridiculous dogma of the Immaculate Conception in the presence of two hundred dumb complaisant prelates, on that day he experienced profound grief. According to his ideas this was the severest blow which had been inflicted on the foundations of the Church for centuries.

He had studied theology deeply, but he had not confined himself to the letter; he believed he saw something beyond.

—The letter killeth, he said, the spirit giveth life.

—The spirit giveth life when it is wholesome and pure, the Grand-Vicar answered him with a smile, but is it healthy in a young man who believes himself to be wiser than his elders?

Marcel then without mistrust and urged by questions, developed his theories. He believed in the absolute equality of men before God, in the transmutation of souls: and the resurrection of the flesh seemed to him the utmost absurdity. He quite thought that there were future rewards and penalties, but he had too much faith in the goodness of God to suppose that the expiation could be eternal. He allied himself in that to the Universalists, who were, he said, the most reasonable sect of American Protestantism.

—Reasonable! reasonable! repeated the Grand-Vicar scoffingly; in truth, my poor friend, you make me doubt your reason. Can there be anything reasonable in the turpitude of heresy?

Then he hurried to find the Bishop:

—I have emptied our young man's bag, he said to him. Do you know, Monseigneur, what there was at the bottom?

—Oh, oh. Has he been inclined to debauchery? He is so young.

—Would to heaven it were only that, Monseigneur. But it is a hundred times worse.

—What do you tell me? Must I fear then for all my little sheep? We must look after him then.

—I repeat, Monseigneur, that that would be nothing.... It is the abomination of abomination, a whole world of turpitude, heresies in embryo.

—Heresies! Oh, oh! That is serious.

—Heresies which would make the cursed shades of John Huss, Wickliffe, Luther and Calvin himself tremble, if they appeared again.

—What do you say?

—I tell you, Monseigneur, that you have warmed a viper in your bosom.

—Ah, well, I will drive out this wicked viper.

The Bishop, who kept two nieces in the episcopal seraglio, would willingly have pardoned his secretary if he had been accused of immorality, but he could not carry his condescension so far as heresy. He wanted, however, to assure himself personally, and as Marcel was incapable of lying, he quickly recognized the sad reality.

The young Abbé was severely punished. He was compelled to make an apology, to retract his horrible ideas, to stifle the germ of these infant monstrosities; then he was condemned to spend six months in one of those ecclesiastical prisons called *houses of retreat*, where the guilty priest is exposed to every torment and every vexation.

He was definitely marked and classed as a dangerous individual.

His enemy, the Grand-Vicar, pursued him with his indefatigable hatred, so far that from disgrace to disgrace he had reached the cure of Althausen.

XLIII
ESPIONAGE

"A sunbeam had traversed his heart; it had just disappeared."

ERNEST DAUDET (*Les Duperies de l'Amour*).

Since the fatal evening when the secret of his new-born love had been discovered by his servant, Marcel had observed the woman on his steps, watching his slightest proceedings, scrutinizing his most innocent gestures.

He encountered everywhere her keen inquisitive look.

He wished at first to meet it with the greatest circumspection and the most absolute reserve. He avoided all conversation which he thought might lead him into the way of fresh confidences, and he affected an icy coldness.

But he was soon obliged to renounce this means.

The woman, irritated, suddenly became sullen and angry, and made the Curé pay dear for the reserve which he imposed on himself. The dinner was burnt, the soup tasted only of warm water, his bed was hard, his socks were full of holes, his shoes badly cleaned, finally, he was several times awakened with a start by terrible noises during the night.

He attempted a few remonstrances. Veronica replied with sharpness and threatened to leave him.

—You can look for another maid, she said to him; as for me, I have had enough of it.

—Oh! you old hussy, he thought; I would soon pack you off to the devil, if I were not afraid of your cursed tongue.

Then, for the sake of peace he changed his tactics. He was affable and smiling and spoke to her gently; and the servant's manners changed directly.

She also became like she had been before, attentive and submissive.

Several days passed thus in a continual constraint and hidden anger; at the same time, a restlessness consumed him, which he used all his power to conceal.

He had not seen Suzanne again, either at the morning Masses, or in her usual walks. He looked forward to Sunday; but at High Mass her place remained empty; he reckoned on Vespers: Vespers, and then Compline passed without her. In vain he searched the nave and the galleries, his sorrowing gaze did not find Suzanne, and he chanted the *Laudate pueri dominum* with the voice of the *De profundis*.

Where was she? He had no other thought. Her father had prevented her from coming to church, without any doubt; but why had he not seen her as before upon the roads, which they both liked? He made a thousand conjectures, and with his thoughts completely absorbed in Suzanne, he forgot aught else. He saw no longer those attractive members of his congregation, who admired him in secret as they accompanied him with their fresh voices, and were astonished at the mysterious trouble which agitated their sweet pastor; he forgot even the odious spy who watched him in some corner of the church, and whom he would meet again at his house.

Ashamed of himself, he recalled with a blush the hand he had kissed in a moment of frenzy, which must have let Suzanne suspect what was the plague which consumed his heart, and he would have sacrificed ten years of his life to become again what he was in the eyes of this young girl, hardly a month ago; only a stranger.

Unaccustomed to the world, he did not yet know women well enough to be aware that they are full of indulgence for follies committed for their sake, and more ready to excuse an insult than to pardon indifference. Under these circumstances vanity takes the place of courage, and gives to the commonest girl the instincts of a patrician. There is no ill-made woman but wishes to see the world at her feet.

And the espionage which laid so heavy on him, became every day more irritating and more insupportable.

In vain he fled from the house, and walked on straight before him; far, very far, as far as possible, he felt his servant's gaze following him, and weighing upon him with all the burden of her furious and clear-sighted jealousy.

He felt that lynx eye pierce the walls and watch him everywhere, even when he had put between himself and the parsonage, the streets, the gardens, the width of the village and the depth of the woods.

She received him on his return with a smile on her lips, but her eager eye searched him from head to foot, studied his looks, his gestures, the folds of his cassock and even the dust on his shoes; as though she wished to strip him and bare his heart in order to feast upon his secret conflicts.

XLIV
THE GARRET WINDOW

"Do I direct my love? It directs me.
And I could abide it if I would!...
And I would, after all, that I could not."

V. SARDOU (*Nos Intimes*).

Other days passed, and then others.

From a garret-window in the loft of the parsonage, the eye commanded a view of the whole village. Over the roofs could be seen the house of Captain Durand, quite at the bottom of the hill. Marcel went up there several times, and with his gaze fixed on that white wall which concealed the sweet object which had torn from him his tranquillity and his peaceful toil, he forgot himself and was lost in his thoughts.

Then his eyes wandered over the verdant plain, and the length of the stream edged with willows which wound along as far as the wood, side by side with the little path, where often he had met with Suzanne.

Sometimes the keen April wind blew violently through the ill-closed timber and the cracks of the roofing. It shook the joists and filled the loft with that shrill sinister sound, which is like an echo of the lamentable complaint of the dead, and it appeared to him that these groanings of the tempest mingled with the groanings of his soul.

But he soon discovered that the garret-window was also a post of observation for Veronica, for to their mutual embarrassment, they caught one another climbing cautiously up the wooden stair-case, or slipping under the dusty joists. Again he was caught in fault. What business had he in that loft?

He resumed his walks and prolonged them as much as possible; he resumed his pastoral visits with a zeal which charmed the feminine portion of his flock; but nowhere did he see or hear anything of Suzanne. That name filled his heart, and he dreaded the least suspicion, the slightest comment.

He was seen always abroad. He fled from his house, his books, his flowers, that little home which he loved so well when it was quiet, and where now he heard the muttering storms; he suspected some infernal plot.

And the remembrance of that hand which was surrendered to him, and on which he had placed his lips, that remembrance consumed his heart. He saw again Suzanne's emotion, her large dark eyes full of amazement, yet without anger, and he would have wished to see them again, were it only for a second, in order to read in them the impression which his presence left there.

XLV
TREACHEROUS MANOEUVRE

"He stepped more lightly than a bird; love traced out his progress."

CHAMPFLEURY (*La Comédie Académique*).

"I must know," he said to himself, "where I stand."

And one morning, after saying Mass, he went out of the village.

He took the opposite direction to the part where Captain Durand dwelt. But after following the high road for some time, sure that he was not being watched, he retraced his steps, quickly entered the little path, hedged with quicksets, which runs by the side of the gardens, and rapidly made the circuit of Althausen.

Hitherto in his walks, he had avoided, from shame as much as from fear, the Captain's house, now he directed his steps thither, with head erect, resolute and assuming a careless air, as if the peasants whom he met could suspect his secret agitation.

He hurried his steps, desirous of settling the question one way or the other.

To discover Suzanne! that was his only desire, and his heart beat as though it would break.

In spite of the reproaches and invectives which he addressed and the fine argument which he formed for himself, he had fallen again more than ever under the yoke, precisely because he saw obstacles accumulating.

Love had taken absolute possession of his heart, it had hollowed out its nest therein, like the viper in the old Norway ballads, and while ever increasing, consumed it.

To see Suzanne, simply the hem of her gown, or her pretty spring hat crowned with bluebirds, to pass near the spot where she breathed and to inhale there some emanation from her, was his promised treat.

And he walked along joyously, his step was light, and he no longer felt the load of his grief; his apprehensions and anxiety disappeared, and he was filled with a wild hope.

A few steps more and he would see behind the clump of old chestnuts the little house, always so smart and white.

Ah! he knew it well. Many a time he had passed in front of it and behind it, pensive and indifferent, without dreaming that the sanctuary of a goddess was there, the only one henceforth whom his heart could adore.

There was a little garden, surrounded with palings, with two paths which crossed, and placed in the middle, a statue of the Little Corporal in a bed of China-asters. In one corner an arbour of honeysuckle, where more than once he had caught sight of a crabbed face.

Perhaps the maid with the sweet eyes will be sitting beneath that arbour embroidering thoughtfully some chosen pattern.

What shall he do if Suzanne is there? Will he dare to look at her?

Yes, he must! He must read the expression in her look. And if that look is sweet and free from anger, shall he stop? Certainly. Why should he hesitate? What is there surprising in a priest, stopping to talk to a young girl? Is he not her Curé? More than that, her Confessor. Her confessor! Has he still the right to call himself so? And the weather-beaten soldier, the disciple of Voltaire, the malevolent, unmannerly father? Come, another blunder! he sees clearly that he cannot dream of stopping. And then, after what he has done, what would he dare to say? He will pass by therefore rapidly, without even turning his head; she will see him, and that is enough.

He quickens his step, then he slackens it. Where will she be. Here are the old chestnut-trees, and behind is the white house, the corner of paradise.

What is that open window, garnished with flowers, that room hung with rose, and at the back those white curtains which the morning sun is gilding? Oh, that he might melt into those subtle rays, and penetrate, like a ray of love, into that chaste virgin conch.

Now he is near the garden. His heart is beating. He looks. A sound of footsteps on the path, and the rustling of a dress make him start. Is it she?

He turns round.

Veronica is behind him.

XLVI
THE LETTER

"Let them take but one step within your door. They will soon have taken four."

LA FONTAINE (Fables).

She was red and out of breath, and her large breasts rose and fell like the bellows of a forge, while her air of triumph said clearly to Marcel: "Ah, ah, I have caught you here."

—Come, Monsieur le Curé, it is quite a quarter-of-an-hour that I have been looking for you. I ought to have thought before where to find you. Somebody is waiting for you.

—Who!

But the servant avoided making any reply, as she took the lead towards home. The Curé followed her hanging his head.

He reached the parsonage directly after her.

—Who is waiting for me then? he said again.

—It's the postman, she replied with an air of frankness; he could not wait till to-morrow. He had a letter for you ... for *you* only, she added, lingering over these words with a scornful smile.

Marcel blushed.

—Another mystery, Veronica went on. Ah, Jesus! My God! What a lot of mysteries there are here. Really it's worse than the Catechism. Your letters for you only! Isn't that enough to humiliate me? You have reason then to complain of my discretion that you tell the postman to hand your letters to *yourself only*. Holy Virgin! it's a pretty thing. What can they think of me then at the Post-office? They will surely say that I read your letters before you do. Upon my word. Your letters don't matter to me. Would they not say...? Ah, Lord Jesus. To make a poor servant suffer martyrdom in this way?

—There you are with your recrimination again!

-Oh, Monsieur le Curé, I make no recriminations, I complain that is all: I certainly have the right to complain; my other masters never acted in that way with me.

—Your masters acted as they thought proper, and I also do as I wish.

—I see very well, that you don't ask advice from anyone.... And with the insolence of a servant who has got on a footing with her master, she added: You have gone again to the part where Durand lives? After what has happened, are you not afraid of compromising yourself?

—Mind your own business, you silly woman, and leave me alone for once. I consider you are very impudent in trying to scrutinize my actions.

—My business! Well, Monsieur le Curé, yours is mine just a bit, since I am your confidante. As to being impudent, I shall never be so much as others I know.

—Insolent woman.

—Ah, you can insult me, Monsieur le Curé. I let you do as you like with me.

—Veronica, said Marcel, this life is unendurable. I hate to be surrounded with incessant spying; what do you want to arrive at? tell me, what do you want to arrive at?

And the Curé approached her, his fists clenched, and with glaring eyes.

—Take care of yourself, woman, for I am beginning to get tired.

—I am so too: I am tired, cried Veronica.

Marcel's wrath passed all bounds.

—Yes. I understand, you ought indeed to be so. Tired of odious spying; tired of your unwholesome curiosity; tired of your useless narrow-mindedness. Do not drive me too far for your own sake, I warn you. Twice already you have made me beside myself, beware, you miserable woman, beware of doing it a third time.

—Be quiet, Monsieur le Curé, said Veronica softly, be quiet.

—Oh, you are driving me mad, cried Marcel, throwing himself into an arm-chair, and covering his face with his hands.

The servant came near him:

—It is you who are making me ill with your fits of anger, she said with solicitude: shall I make you a little tea?

—I don't want anything.

—Come, Monsieur Marcel, be yourself. I am not what you think, no, I am not.

—It is my wish that you leave me, Veronica.

—Everything I do is for your interest, Monsieur le Curé, you will understand it one day.

—Leave me, I say.

The servant withdrew.

—It cannot last thus, he thought. What a scandalous scene! And what a horrible fatality thrusts me into this ridiculous and miserable situation! Ah, the apostle is right: "As soon as we leave the straight path, we fall into the abyss." And I am in the abyss, for I am the laughing-stock of this servant. What will become of me with this creature? How can I get rid of her? Can I turn her out? She would proclaim everywhere what she has discovered.... Ah, if it were only a question of myself alone! What a dilemma I am involved in! But that letter, that letter! Suzanne!... dear Suzanne ... no doubt it is she who has written to me, my heart tells me so loudly.

He waited with feverish impatience for the postman's return.

Expecting news from Suzanne, and fearing with good reason his servant's inquisitiveness, he had indeed asked him for the future to deliver his letters to himself only.

He sought for various pretexts to send Veronica away, but the woman too discovered excellent reasons for not going out.

She was present therefore, in spite of her master, at the delivery of the mysterious letter.

Marcel's countenance at first displayed deep disappointment, but as he read on, it was lighted up by a ray of joy.

XLVII
GOOD NEWS

"Alleluia, alleluia, alleluia
O filii et filiae...
Et Maria Magdalena
Et Jacobi, et Salome!
Alleluia."

(Easter-Mass Hymn).

"Rejoice, my son, and sing with me *Hosannah! Hosannah!* The ways of the Lord are infinite.

"Your personal enemy, Saint Anastasius Gobin, Grand-Vicar, Arch-Priest, Notary Apostolic and, like the ancient slave, as vile as anyone, *non tum vilis quam nullus*, has just left Nancy secretly, and in disgrace, like a guilty wretch as he is.

"Ah, my poor friend, let us veil our faces like the daughters of Sion. It is written: 'If ye live after the flesh, ye shall die.' Anastasius Gobin has lived too much after the flesh. Alas! we know it, and you know it. *Nemo melius judicare potest quam tu*, as Brutus said to Cicero; so you will not share in the astonishment of the Cathedral worshippers. I will relate the matter to you in private.

"*Ergo.* You are henceforth safe from his persecution for ever; it is now only a question of regaining Monseigneur's favour. The serpent is no longer there to whisper perfidious insinuations into his too complaisant ear. When the beast is dead, the venom is dead.

"I hope that adversity has been of use to you. You have experienced what it costs not to be sufficiently yielding. Now the future is yours; nothing has been lost except a few years, and those few years have brought, I hope, experience and knowledge of life. Courage then. *Filii Sion exultate et laetimini in Domino Deo nostro.*

"I have faith more than ever in your lucky star, and I hope that you will form the consolation and the pride of my declining years. Yes, my friend, you will do honour to your old master. *Tu quoque Marcellus eris!*

"As for myself, I am going to move heaven and earth for you, or, what is worth more, I am going to stir up the arrière-ban of the sacristies.

"I know some worthy sheep of influence, who, for my sake, will do anything in their power. I have shown your photograph to the old Comtesse de Montluisant; she finds it charming, yes charming! and she has promised that before six months, Monseigneur shall swear by the Abbé Marcel alone.

"That is rather too much to presume, for the old man is as obstinate as an Auvergne mule; but what I can promise you is a change of cure—that at length you shall leave your Thebaid.

"Once again then, my dear fellow, courage. As soon as I have a few days to dispose of after Easter, I will hurry to you. And while we are tasting your wine, provided it is good (which I doubt, you dreadful stoic), we will discuss what is best to do.

"Have patience then till then. *Vos enim ad libertatem vocati estis, fratres,* said St. Paul to the Galatians. I say so to you.

"I embrace you tenderly,

"Your spiritual Father

"MARCEL RIDOUX

"*Curé of St. Nicholas.*"

XLVIII
RECONCILIATION

"The fair Eglé chooses her part on a sudden
In the twinkling of an eye, she becomes charming."

CHAMPFORT (*Contes*).

"Here is salvation," said Marcel to himself, "the solution of the problem, the end of my misery and shame, the blow which severs this infernal knot which enfolds me and was about to hurry me on to my ruin. God be blessed!" And he turned joyfully to his servant who was watching him:

—Good news! Veronica.

—I congratulate you, sir, she said, perplexed and disturbed. Are you nominated to a better cure? Does Monseigneur give notice of his visit?

—Better than that, Veronica. My excellent and worthy uncle, the Abbé Ridoux, gives notice of his.

—Monsieur le Curé of Saint Nicholas?

—Himself. Do you know him?

—Certainly. He came one day to see Monsieur Fortin (may God keep his soul) regarding a collection for his church. Ah, he has a fine church, it appears, and a famous saint is buried there. My poor defunct master was in the habit of saying that there was not a more agreeable man anywhere in the world, and I easily credited it, for he was always in a good temper. It's he then who has written to you. Well, if he comes here, it will make a little diversion, for we don't often laugh.

—That is wrong, Veronica. A gentle gaiety ought to prevail in the priest's house. Gaiety is the mark of a pure heart and a quiet conscience. Where there is hatred and division there is more room for the spirit of darkness. Our Saviour has said: "Every house divided against itself shall perish."

—He has said so, yes, Monsieur le Curé.

—We must not perish, Veronica.

—I have no wish to do so; therefore I do not cause the war.

—Listen, Veronica. It would be lamentable and scandalous that my uncle might possibly be troubled on his arrival here by our little domestic differences, and particularly that he might suspect the nature of them. We are both of us a little in the wrong; by our each ascribing it to oneself, it will be easy for us to come to an understanding; will it not, Veronica?

—Oh, Monsieur le Curé, we can come to an understanding directly, if you wish it. God says that we must forgive, and I have no malice.

—Then it is agreed, we will talk of our little mutual complaints after supper.

—I ask for nothing better; I am quite at your service.

—And we will celebrate the good news.

—I will take my share in the celebration. Ah, Monsieur le Curé, you do not know me yet; I hope that you will know me better, and you will see that I am not an ill-natured girl. My heart is as young as another's, and when we must laugh, provided that it is decent and without offence, I know how to laugh, and do not give up my share.

—Good, said Marcel to himself, let me flatter this woman. That is the only way of preventing any rumour. I must leave Althausen, I will pass her on to my successor, but I do not want to have an enemy behind me. If you have my secret, you old hypocrite, I will have yours, and I will know what there is at the bottom of your bag of iniquity.

XLIX
CONFIDENCES

"To thee I wish to confide this secret,
Speak of it to no-one, we must be discreet
They love too much to laugh in this unbelieving age."

BABILLOT (*La Mascarade humaine*).

That evening, contrary to his usual custom, the Curé of Althausen had coffee served after dinner, and told his servant to lay two cups.

—You have asked somebody then? she enquired.

—Yes, replied Marcel, I ask you, Veronica.

The woman smiled.

She went and assured herself that the door below was shut and that the shutters were quite closed, put together a bundle of wood which she placed partly on the hearth, and without further invitation, sat down facing her master.

—We are at home, and inquisitive people will not trouble us.

Marcel was offended at thus being placed on a footing of equality with his servant. Nevertheless he did not allow it to be seen. "It is my fault," he thought, and he answered quietly:

—We have no reason to dread inquisitive persons, we are not going to do anything wrong.

—Ah, Jesus, no. But, you know, if they saw your servant sitting at your table, they would not wait to look for the why and wherefore, they would begin to chatter.

—It is true.

—And one likes to be at home when one has anything to say, is it not so, Monsieur le Curé?

Marcel bent his head:

—You are a girl of sense, and that is why I can behave to you as one cannot usually with a ... common housekeeper. I am sure that you understand me. Then, after a moment's hesitation:

—Twice already I have flown into a passion with you, Veronica; it is a serious fault, and I hope you will consent to forgive it.

—Do not speak of that, Monsieur le Curé, I deserved everything that you have said to me. It is for me to ask your pardon for not behaving properly towards you.

—I acknowledge all that you do in my interest: I know how to appreciate all your good qualities, so I pardon you freely.

—Monsieur le Curé is too good.

—No, I am not too good. For if I were so, I should have behaved differently towards you. But you know, there is always a little germ of ingratitude at the bottom of a man's heart. After all, I have considered, and I believe that with a little good will on one side and on the other, we can come to an understanding.

—Yes, I am easy to accommodate.

—Let us save appearances, that is essential.

—You are talking to me like Monsieur Fortin. That suits me. No one could ever reproach me for setting a bad example.

—I know it, Veronica; your behaviour is full of decency and dignity: it is well for the outside world, and as Monsieur Fortin used to say to you, we must wash our dirty linen at home.

—Poor Monsieur Fortin.

—That is what we will do henceforth. Come, Veronica. I have made all my disclosures to you, or very nearly. I have confessed to you my errors, and you know some of my faults as well as I do. Will you not make your little confession to me in your turn? You have finished your coffee? Take a little brandy? There! now sit close to me.

—Monsieur le Curé, one only confesses on one's knees.

—At the confessional before the priest, yes; but it is not thus that I mean, it is not by right of this that I wish to know your little secrets, but by right of a friend.

—I am quite confused, Monsieur le Curé.

—There is no Curé here, there is a friend, a brother, anything you wish, but not a priest. Are you willing?

—I am quite willing.

—You were talking to me lately about my predecessors, and, according to you, their conduct was not irreproachable. What is there then to say regarding them? Oh, don't blush. Answer me.

—What do you want me to tell you?

—They committed faults then?...

—I have told you so, sir,—sometimes—like you.

—Ah, Veronica, the greatest saint is he who sins only seven times a day.

—Seven times!

—Seven times, quite as much. You find, no doubt, that I sin much more, but I am far from being a saint. As to my predecessors, were they no greater saints?

—Saints! Ah, Jesus! Do you wish me to tell you, sir? Well, between ourselves, I believe that there are none but in the calendar.

—Oh, Veronica, Veronica.

—Yes, sir, I believe it in my soul and conscience, and I can add another thing still. If, before they canonized all these saints, they had consulted their servant, perhaps they would not have found a single one of them.

—What! you, the pious Veronica, you say such things?

—One is pious and staid and everything you wish, but one sees what one sees. Monsieur Fortin was accustomed to say that no one is a great man to his *valet de chambre*; and I add, that no one is a saint to his cook. I tell you so.

—But that is blasphemy, Veronica.

—Blasphemy possibly, but it is the truth, Monsieur Marcel.

—Have you then surprised my predecessors in some act of culpable weakness?

—Oh, holy Virgin! I did not surprise them, it was they on the contrary who surprised me.

—You!... And how then?

—Monsieur le Curé, you don't understand me. You were speaking of their weakness, I meant to say that they had taken advantage of mine.

—Ah, here we are, thought Marcel. Is it possible? What! of your weakness? these ecclesiastics?

—Sir. You are an ecclesiastic too and yet … if Mademoiselle Suzanne Durand….

—Don't go on, Veronica. I have asked you not to recall that remembrance to me. It is wrong of you to forget that.

—Sweet Jesus! I don't want to offend you. I wanted to make you understand that since you, you have erred, the others….

—And what have they done?

—Ah, it is very simple, Lord Jesus!

—Let us see.

—I hardly know if I ought to tell you that, I am quite ashamed of it.

—Come, let us see, speak … you have nothing to be afraid of before me … speak, Veronica, speak.

—Where must I begin?

—Where you like; at the beginning, I suppose.

—There are several of them.

—Several beginnings?

—Yes; I have had three masters, you know.

—Well, with the last one, with Monsieur Fortin, that worthy man whom I knew slightly.

—He was no better than the rest, Jesus! no.

—The Abbé Fortin?

—Lord God, yes, the Abbé Fortin!

—What has he done then?

—My God … you know well, that which one does when one … is a man … and has a warm temperament.

—To you, Veronica, to you?

—Alas, sweet Jesus. Ah, Monsieur le Curé, I am so good-natured, I don't know how to resist. And then, you know, it is so hard for a poor servant to resist her master, particularly when he is a priest, who holds all your confidence, and possesses all your secrets, and with whom you live in a certain kind of intimacy; and besides a priest is cautious, and one may be quite sure that nothing of what goes on inside the parsonage, will get out through the parsonage door.

—Assuredly; he will not go and noise his faults abroad.

—And so with us, the priests' servants, who could be more cautious than we are? We have as much in it as our masters, have we not? and a sin concealed is a sin half pardoned.

—Yes, Veronica, it was said long ago: "The scandal of the world is what causes the offence. And 'tis not sinning to sin in silence."

—Those are words of wisdom; who is it who said so?

—A very clever man, called Monsieur Tartuffe.

—I see that. Be must have been a priest, at least?

—He was not an ecclesiastic, but he was somewhat of a churchman.

—That is just as I thought. Certainly we must hide our faults. Who would believe in us without that? I say *us*, for I am also somewhat a church-*woman*.

—Undoubtedly.

—I have spent my life among ecclesiastics. My father was beadle at St. Eprive's and my mother the Curé's housekeeper.

—That is your title.

—Is it not? Then I have the honour to be your maid-servant, and I am the head of the association of the Holy Virgin.

—No one could contest your claims, Veronica; add to that you are a worthy and cautious person, and let us return to Monsieur Fortin. Ah, I cannot contain my astonishment. Monsieur Fortin!... And how did he go to work to ... seduce you? He must have used much deceit.

—All the angels of heavens are witnesses to it, sir, and you shall judge.

L
MAMMOSA VIRGO!

"The monk could not refrain from admiring the freshness and plumpness of this woman. For a long time he made his eyes speak, and he managed it so well that in the end he inspired the lady with the same desire with which he was burning."

BOCCACIO (*La Décaméron*).

Veronica took several sips of the brandy which remained at the bottom of the cup, collected her thoughts for a moment, and casting her eyes down with a modest air, she proceeded:

—The good Monsieur Fortin, as perhaps you know, used to drink a little of an evening.

—Oh, he used to drink!

—Yes, not every day, but every now and then; two or three times a week: but you know ... quite nicely, properly, without making any noise; he was gayer than usual, that was all. But when he reached that point, though he was ordinarily as timid as a lay-brother, he became as bold as a gendarme, and he was very ... how shall I say?... very enterprising. I may say that between ourselves, Monsieur le Curé, you understand that strangers never knew anything about it. If by chance anyone came and asked for him at these times, I used to say that he had gone out, or that he was ill. One day, I was finely put out. Christopher Gilquin's daughter came to call him to her mother who was at the point of death. He took it into his head to try and kiss her. The little one, who was hardly fifteen, did not know what it meant. I made her understand that it was to console her, and through pure affection for her and for her mamma. It passed muster. But when she had gone I gave it to him finely, and I made him go to bed ... and sharply too.

—And he obeyed you?

—I should think so, and without a word. He saw very well he was wrong. One evening then ... I had been in his service hardly six months—I must tell you first that he had looked at me very queerly for some time; I let him do so and said to myself: "Here is another of them who will do like the rest." And I waited for it to happen. I was better-looking then than I am now: I was ten years younger, Monsieur le Curé.

—Ten years younger! but you were thirty then. How could you be a Curé's servant at that age? Our rules are opposed to it.

—I passed as his relation. And that was tolerated. Besides, when Monseigneur made his visitation, I did not show myself ... for form's sake, for Monseigneur knew very well that I was there. I met him once on the stairs; he took hold of my chin, looked at me very hard, and said in a sly way: "Here is this little *spiritual sister* then; faith, she is a pretty little rogue." I was so bashful. I asked Monsieur Fortin what a *spiritual sister* was, and he told me that they used formerly to call women so who lived with priests. They say that all had two or three *spiritual sisters*. What indecency! I should not have allowed that.

—Spiritual sister is not exactly the expression, said Marcel, it is *adoptive sister*, because they were adopted.[1] Alas, Veronica, the clergy were slightly dissolute in former times: it is no longer so in our days, in which so many holy ecclesiastics give an example of the rarest virtues.

—Oh, three wives, Monsieur le Curé! three wives! sweet Jesus! they must have torn out each other's eyes.

—No, Veronica. They agreed very well among themselves. They had different ideas at that time to what we have now.

—One evening then Monsieur Fortin had drunk at table a little more than usual. I was going to bring the dessert and I leaned over to take up a dish which was before him. As the dish was heavy and rather far from my hand, I supported myself on the back of his chair, and involuntarily I rubbed against his body with my stomach. "Oh, oh," he said, "if that happens again I shall pinch that big breast."

—What! Monsieur Fortin used that expression?

—Yes, sir, and many others besides. I blush when I think of it.... Then I looked at him quite astounded. He began to laugh. I went to look for the cheese, and I passed again beside him on purpose, and supported myself on his chair again to place it on the table. "Ah," he cried, "she is beginning again. O, *mammosa virgo!*"—he repeated it so many times to me that I remember it—"so much the worse, I keep my promises." And he pinched me.

—Where?

—Where he had said. He made no error. I blushed for shame and drew back as quickly as possible: "How can he," I said to myself, "use Latin words to deceive poor women?" Then he cried: "Are you ticklish?"—Yes, sir. "Ah, you are ticklish. The big Veronica is ticklish! Who would have believed it?" And he laughed, but I saw clearly that his laugh was put on, and that something else preoccupied him. And from that moment, each time that I passed near him and stooped down to clear away, he tried to pinch me where he could: "And there," he said, "are you ticklish? are you ticklish there?" I was so stupefied that I could not get over it. "It is a little too much, Holy Mother of God," I said to myself, "a man like him! to pinch me in this way! who would believe it! One would not credit it, if one saw it! Ah, I will see how far he will go, and to-morrow I will give him an account." At last, when I saw that he would not stop it, and that he was going too far, I said to him severely: Monsieur le Curé, if you continue to tease me in this way, you shall see something.

—What shall I see? he said getting up suddenly, I want to see it directly. Ah, *mammosa virgo*! you threaten your master! Wait, wait, I will teach you respect.

And, pretending to punish me, he caught hold of as much as he could grasp with both hands; yes, sir, as much as he could. Ah, I was very angry, God can tell you so.

—And did he stop?

—Not at all, sir; quite the contrary. I escaped from his hands, and I turned round the table saying: "Ah, sweet Jesus, what is going to happen? Divine Saviour! How far will he dare to go?" To complete the misfortune, I let the lamp fall, and it went out. Then he put himself into a great passion, and soon caught me. "You have upset the oil," he cried. "I will teach you to spill the oil." He held me with all his might. Then I got angry in earnest, in earnest, you know.

—Well?

—Well, that was useless. I was taken like a poor fly. It was too late. It was all over.

—All over!

—All over. Monsieur Fortin let me go then. Ah! sir, if you knew how ashamed I was.

[Footnote 1: They are still called *sisters agapetae* or *subintroduced* women. Perhaps it is not unnecessary to recall the fact that Gregory VII was the first of the popes to impose celibacy on the clergy. He nullified acts performed by married priests and compelled them to choose between their wives and the priesthood. In spite of this, and in spite of excommunication with which he threatened them, many kept their wives secretly, the rest contented themselves with concubines. Besides, the majority of the bishops, who lived after the same manner, tolerated for bribes infractions of the rule by the lower and higher clergy. The Council of Paris, in 1212, forbade them to receive money, proceeding from this source. At the present time, however, the Catholic priests of the Greeks-United, those of Libar and different Oriental communions, all under papal authority, not only may, but must take wives.

St. Paul said: "Choose for priest him who shall have but one wife." Would he find many of them at the present time?]

LI
CHAMBER MORALITY

"Practise moderation and prudence with regard to certain virtues which may ruin the health of the body."

THE REV. FATHER LAURENT SCUPOLI (*Le Combat Spirituel*).

—What a strange story, said Marcel. Oh, Veronica. But did you not make more resistance?

—Resistance! I was lame from it for more than a fortnight. I walked like a duck. People said to me: "What is the matter with you, Mademoiselle Veronica? They say you have broken something!" Ah, if they had suspected what it was.

—What a scandal! Monsieur Fortin!

—He was stronger than I; but I don't give him all the blame. We must be just. It was my fault too. That is what comes of playing with fire.

—But it seems to me, Veronica, that you displayed a little willingness.

—Ah, Monsieur le Curé, you are scolding me for telling you all this so plainly. Was it not better for me to act thus, than to let Monsieur Fortin run right and left and expose himself to all sorts of affronts, as some do? That man had a temperament of fire. And that temperament must have expended itself on someone. The business about little Gilquin made me reflect. I sacrificed myself, and I acted as much in his interests as in the interests of religion.

—And does not temperament speak in you also, Veronica?

—Ah, that is only told in confession.

—Nevertheless it is fine to rule your passions, to be chaste.

—Ah, yes, as you were saying once when I came in: "Chaste without hope." All that is rubbish. God has well done all that he has done; I can't get away from that.

—How can you bring the holy name of God into these abominable things?

—Abominable! that is rubbish again. Monsieur Fortin and I often asked ourselves what evil that could do to God, when neither of us did any to other people. Monsieur Fortin used to say to me: "Are we doing evil to our neighbours, Veronica?" "Not that I know of, Monsieur le Curé." "Are we causing a scandal?" "Ah, Jesus, no, Monsieur le Curé." "Are we setting a bad example?" "No, Monsieur le Curé, no." "Are we populating the land with orphans?" "Oh, as to that, no." "Well then, in what way can we be offending God?" That was very well said all the same, the more so as his health depended on it.

—But, replied Marcel, wishing to change the conversation which was verging upon dangerous ground, have you not told me that you have been in the service of ecclesiastics for nearly five-and-twenty years. That appears to me to be very extraordinary for, after all, you are hardly forty.

—Thirty-nine, corrected Veronica, who was past forty-five.

—Reason the more.

—That is true, Monsieur le Curé, but I began early. At fifteen I went to the Abbé Braqueminet's.

—I was acquainted with a Braqueminet, who was Bishop *in partibus*. A very worthy prelate.

—That he is, sir; he went to America.

—Come! this is too much, Veronica; you want to make a fool of me. At fifteen, do you say, that is too much! At thirty you were with the Abbé Fortin. I have no objection to that, since you passed as his relation, although with regard to this, our rules are precise, and we cannot take a housekeeper, till she is over a certain age. Sometimes, it is true, they smuggle in a few years: but fifteen years!

—It is the exact truth, however, sir. I was fifteen years old, and no more at the Abbé Braqueminet's, and you will believe me, when I tell you that I was his niece.

-Monseigneur Braqueminet's niece! you, Veronica?

-Yes, sir, his niece; the Holy Virgin who hears me, will tell you that I was his niece, and I will explain to you how.

LII
THE POSSET

"This little maid, so fair, with teasing ways,
Was made to be a lovely man's support.
For many a foolish thing in former days
He did to gain a face less fair than thine."

BÉRANGER (*la Célibataire*).

My father, as I have told you, was beadle at Saint Eprive's, and my mother was servant to Monsieur le Curé. These were two good situations, but they had a number of children, and not much time to attend to them. Therefore when I was thirteen, they entrusted me to an old aunt who was willing to take charge of me. She was servant to Monsieur Braqueminet, who was then at Mirecourt. She placed me at first with a lady who made me look after her little children. At the end of a year Monsieur l'Abbé had a change, and went away to a village near Saint-Dié. He said to my aunt: "You cannot leave Veronica alone at Mirecourt; she will soon be fifteen; she is tall and nice-looking; she will run too much risk, and we must take her with us; but as it would make these foolish peasants chatter if their Curé had a strange young girl in the house, she shall pass as my niece. What do you say to this proposal?" My aunt was delighted and agreed to it directly, and all the more because I would have to assist her in the household work, and that her labour would thus be lightened. They took me away from my situation, they taught me my lesson, and I went away with them, very pleased to be Monsieur le Curé's niece. Ah! that was the best time of my life. My aunt spoilt me, Monsieur le Curé was excessively fond of me, I had all my wishes. All the ladies in the neighbourhood spoke to me civilly, the Collector's wife, the lawyer's wife, the Mayoress, the wife of the exciseman, they all, in short, made much of me. Mademoiselle Veronica here! Mademoiselle Veronica there! I had my place in the gallery. They invited me to dinner and they were rivals as to who should make me little presents, as if I were really his true niece; everybody believed it, and my aunt herself, by dint of hearing it said, ended by believing it herself, for she never called me anything else than Mademoiselle Veronica.

Unfortunately after some time my aunt died. When we had both of us wept copiously for her, Monsieur le Curé said to me: "Now your aunt is dead, Veronica, what are you going to do?" I made no answer and burst again into tears. "You must not cry like that, little one, you will spoil your pretty eyes; will you remain with me? will you continue to be my niece?" That was my dream; I asked for nothing more. I thanked Monsieur Braqueminet with all my soul, and told him that as he wanted me to be his niece, I would remain his niece all my life.—"That is agreed," he said to me, "you shall keep my little house for me, and I will take another maid-servant for the heavy work only." For he was so nice to me that he would not allow me to fatigue myself in anything. Ah, the men, Monsieur le Curé, who can trust the men! See what he has made of me after all his fine promises: a poor servant, nothing more.

—Had he then any reason to complain of you?

—To complain of me! ah, sweet Paschal Lamb! Never has he said a word of reproach. But since I am in the mood to tell you everything, I may as well do so at once. It was he who had my innocence.

—What! it was not the Abbé Fortin then?

-No, Monsieur le Curé, it was the Abbé Braqueminet.

—And how did he go to work to have your innocence?

—Ah, he was a very clever man. First he knew how to inspire affection, he was so kind to me. It was I who managed everything. I was mistress of all, although so young, and, pray believe me, everything proceeded well. But … one fine day a real niece turned up, no one knows whence … and, faith, I was obliged to retire. I might have made an exposure, but I preferred to sacrifice myself.

—Was she younger than you then?

—The same age, sir, but she was fresh fruit. She appeared so innocent that one would have given her the sacrament without confession. Monsieur Braqueminet, he undertook to give her the Sacrament…. Yes, he undertook it, that man!…

—But was she really his niece?

—Yes, sir, his own sister's daughter. I have had proofs of it; do you think I should have gone away, without that? This sister hated me, and I thoroughly returned it; but when I saw her daughter arrive, I said to myself: I am well revenged.

—But your innocence…. how did he have it?

—Ah, you are anxious to know that. I must tell you everything then! everything! this is how it happened. He suffered a little from his chest, and every evening my aunt used to carry him up a posset. When my aunt was dead, I was obliged to take her place, for the servant we had taken was married, and went home at the end of the day. He knew very well what he was doing, and I, poor little lamb of God, believed everything. I was like a new-born child. It is not right to be so silly as that. God has punished me for it: it is quite right. I don't complain at it. So I used to take him up his posset every evening. Then he used to kiss me and squeeze me to his heart, calling me his dear niece, and charging me to be good:

—You will always be good? he used to say to me.

—Yes, uncle.

—Always! you promise me.

—Yes, uncle.

—Ah, let me kiss you for that kind promise. I found that he kissed me for rather a long time and although it was very pleasant to me, still it used to give me reason for reflection: "How can he love me so much, I thought, when he is not my uncle?"

You can judge by that if I was not silly. But it is perfectly conceivable, for I had never been to school, so who was there then to teach me naughtiness. A young girl's brain is active, and I formed a thousand fancies of every kind. "Perhaps he has some interest concealed underneath," I said artlessly to myself, "and perhaps he does not love me as he wishes me to believe." I was hardly fifteen, and you see I was quite candid and simple. I thought I would pretend to be ill, in order to make a trial of him, and see if he would be grieved and if he would come and nurse me. So one evening, when he had finished supper, I told him that I was not well, and that I was going to bed. He was reading his newspaper and did not appear to hear me. At least he made no reply. I went away very sadly and sorrowfully, thinking that his affection for me was not very great, as he did not give the least attention to my complaints. In short, I went to bed.

"He will go to bed too very soon," I said to myself, "he will call for his posset and he will be obliged to get up to see why I do not bring it to him."

Indeed, about an hour after, I heard his bell. I wrapped myself up in the sheets and pretended to be asleep. He rang a second time. "Veronica, Veronica," he cried, "my posset; what are you doing then? Have you forgotten it? Veronica!"

I turned a deaf ear.

LIII
THE LEG

"One is compelled sometimes to say to oneself, 'On what does ruin or safety depend?'"

J. TOURGUENEFF (*Les eaux printanières*).

Then I heard him come upstairs cautiously and stop at the door of my room. All at once he opened it. He remained standing still for a moment, then he came near my bed on tip-toe.

I half-opened my eyes quickly, and the first thing I saw was his naked legs — my word, he had a very well-made leg! I looked again and saw that he was covered with an old black cloak which served him as a dressing-gown.

I closed my eyes again quickly, and, without giving an account of my feelings, I was overcome by a strong emotion.

My uncle passed his hand over my forehead. He found it burning, for he cried out directly: "But she is really ill, she is really ill, poor child." Then leaning over me: "Little one, little one, where are you in pain?"

I pretended to wake up with a start, and I stared wildly at him, as if I was much surprised to see him there. We women have the instinct of deceit from birth; believe me, what I tell you is true, Monsieur le Curé.

— It is possible, Veronica.

— Well, then be said to me, "Where are you in pain, little one?" I put my finger on the pit of my stomach, and replied in a feeble voice "Here."

He put his hand there, and I saw that he moved it about with complacency on that part.

This touch seemed to make him beside himself, "Oh, the pretty little girl, the pretty little girl!" he said, "she is ill, poor dear child." And his hand continued to caress me.

You may think how I was trembling. Although he did it very decently, I said to myself that it was not altogether proper, but I took good care not to utter a word. A girl is inquisitive, you know, and I was not displeased to see what he would come to.

"Will you have a fomentation?" he said to me after a moment. "No, uncle," I answered, "I feel I am getting better, it is not worth while; I am even going to get up to make you your posset." "To get up, do you dream of it?... All the same, perhaps you are right, there is still some fire in my room: will you come there? you will warm yourself better than in your bed." "I will, if it does not disturb you." "Disturb me! no, no, don't be afraid of disturbing me; come, put on a dress and come."

I sat up in bed, thinking that he would go out of the room to let me dress, but he remained standing in front of me, and his looks frightened me.

I remained sitting on the bed, without stirring. "Well, well, little girl, you are not getting up?"

"I dare not get up before you, uncle." "Are you silly? What are you afraid of? Are you not my niece? Come, come, out of bed, little stupid." He said that in a gentle insinuating voice, and I dared not hesitate any more. I put one leg out of bed. He followed my movements with the greatest attention; "Well, well, and that other leg?"

I put out the other leg, blushing all over with shame, and I wanted to take my petticoat.

But he came near directly and said: "Oh, the lovely little lass, how pretty she is like this…. You will always be good, will you not?"

"Yes, uncle."

"How pretty you are when you are good. You will always be so? You promise?"

"Yes, uncle."

"Oh, I want to kiss you for that kind promise."

—I held out my cheek to him without resistance, but it was my mouth which received the kiss. It was followed by a thousand others. One is not of iron, Monsieur le Curé, and that was how … I … lost my innocence.

—What, Veronica, you fell so easily! They say that it is only the first step which is painful, but it seems hardly to have been painful to you.

—Oh, Monsieur le Curé, we women are full of faults, and we deserve only eternal damnation.

—I do not say that, Veronica. Certainly in this circumstance all the fault lies on your seducer, but I should have preferred more struggle on your part.

—You men are very good with your struggle. To hear you, we never make enough resistance. Would one not say that the poor women are made of another paste than you, and that they ought to be harder?

—No, but it is necessary to know how to govern one's passions. That is the noble, the lofty, the meritorious thing. Resist temptation, everything lies in that.

[PLATE III: THE LEG. "Oh, the lovely little lass, how pretty she is like this..."]

—Everything lies in that, I know it well; but what would you? I had lost my head entirely like Monsieur Braqueminet. And I did not know what he wanted, or what he was going to do. I only understood when it was too late.

—Ah, Veronica, you singular woman, you have made me quite beside myself with your stories.

—It was you who wished it.

—The Abbé Fortin! the Abbé Braqueminet! God of heaven! and who besides?

—The Abbé Marcel!

—Yes, it is true, I also ... I have been on the point of transgressing. Ah! temptation is sometimes very strong, Veronica, my good Veronica; the noble thing is to resist.

The greatest saints have succumbed. St. Origen was obliged to employ a grand means, you know what, my daughter?

—Monsieur Fortin has told me. But you must not act like that saint; that would be a pity, it would be better to succumb, dear Monsieur Marcel. How I like your name, Marcel, Marcel, it is so soft to the mouth.

—To resist temptation like Jesus on the mountain....

—There was but one Jesus.

—Like St. Antony in the desert....

—That is rubbish; in the desert no one could tempt him.

—Leave the room, Veronica; since you have talked to me, I understand the fault of your former masters; leave the room.

—Are you afraid of me then? Angels of heaven, a woman like me. Is it possible? Ah, I should have been very proud of it.

—Proud to make me sin?

—Sin! Sin! Monsieur le Curé: why do we call that a sin?

She came nearer to him. He wished to rise from his chair, but his hand went astray, he never knew how, on his servant's waist.

Oh vow of chastity, sentiments of modesty, manly dignity and priestly virtue, where were you, where were you?

LIV
MATER SAEVA CUPIDINUM

"Well, you have found it, this ephemeral happiness."

BABILLOT (*La Mascarade humaine*).

Sadness succeeds to joy, deception to illusion, the awakening to the dream, the head-ache to the debauch.

When the crime is perpetrated, remorse, the avenging lash of virtue, comes and scourges the conscience. "Come, up, vile thing! thou hast slept over long."

And it exposes to the wretch the emptiness of pleasures, purchased at the price of honour.

The dawn found the Curé of Althausen groaning secretly to himself on his couch.

He had made himself guilty of an abominable wickedness, he had just committed an inexcusable crime, he had succumbed cowardly, ignominiously; he had betrayed his faith, abjured his priestly oaths, forgotten his duties, prostituted his dignity on the withered breast of an old corrupted maid-servant.

Suzanne, the adorable young girl, who in the first place had insensibly and involuntarily drawn him on the road of perjury, for whom he would have sacrificed honour, reputation, the universe and his God, he had abjured her also in the arms of this drab.

And that was the wound which consumed his heart the most.

For as soon as we have yielded to the infernal temptation, the lying prism vanishes, the halo disappears, and there only remains vice in all its hideousness and repulsive nudity. It is then that we hear a threatening voice mutter secretly in the depths of our being.

Happy is he who, already slipping on the fatal descent, listens to that voice: "Stop, stop; there is still time, raise thyself up."

But most frequently we remain deaf to that importunate cry. And, weary of crying in vain, conscience is silent. It no more casts its solemn serious note into the intoxicating music of facile love.

And the wretch, devoured by insatiable desire, pursues his coarse and looks not back. He goes on, he ever goes on, leaving right and left, like the trees on the way-side, his vigour and his youth which he scatters behind him. He set forth young, robust and strong, and he arrives at the halting-place, worn-out, soiled and blemished. There is the ditch, and he tumbles headlong into it. He falls into the common grave of cowardice and infamy. The lowest depths receive him and restore him not again.

Seek no more, for there is no more; the worms which consume him to his gums have already consumed his brain, and his heart is but gangrened. Disturb not this corpse, it is only putrefaction.

The poet has said:

> "Evil to him who has permitted lewdness
> Beneath his breast its foremost nail to delve!
> The pure man's heart is like a goblet deep:
> Whe the first water poured therin is foul,
> The sea itself could not wash out the spot,
> So deep the chasm where the stain doth lie."

Marcel had not reached that point, but he felt that he was on a rapid descent, and made these tardy reflections to himself:

"Shall I ever be able to see the light of day? Shall I ever dare to raise my eyes after this filthy crime? Oh Heaven, Heaven, overwhelm me. Avenging thunderbolt of omnipotent God, reduce me to ashes, restore me again to the nothingness, from which I ought never to have come forth."

But Heaven did not overwhelm him that day, nor was there the slightest rumbling of thunder. Nature continued her work peacefully, just as if no minister of God had sinned. The sun, a glorious sun of Spring, came and danced on his window, and he heard as usual the happy cries of the pillaging sparrows as they fluttered in his garden.

There was a movement by his side, and he felt, close to his flesh, the burning flesh of Veronica; she was awake and looking at him with a smile. She felt no remorse; she was proud and happy, and her eyes burning with pleasure and want of sleep were fixed on her new lover with restless curiosity.

[PLATE IV: MATER SAEVA CUPIDINUM. ...he sprang out of bed, surfeited with disgust.... And she rose also, and ran off to her room, laughing like a madcap, and carrying her dress and petticoats under her arm.]

Doubtless she was saying to herself: "Is it really possible? Am I then in bed with this handsome priest? Is my dream then realised?"

And to assure herself that she was not dreaming, that she was really in the Curé of Althausen's bed, she spoke to him in mincing tones:

—You say nothing, my handsome master. You seem to be dejected. What! you are not tired out already?

And she put out her hand to give him a caress. But he sprang out of bed, surfeited with disgust.

—Ah, true, she said, happiness makes us forgetful. I was forgetting your Mass.

And she rose also, and ran off to her room, laughing like a madcap, and carrying her dress and petticoats under her arm.

LV
IN THE FOOT-PATH

"'Tis the comer blest where God's creatures dwell,
The wild birds' haunt and the dragon-fly's home,
Where the queen-bee flies when she leaves her cell,
Where Spring in the verdant glades doth roam."

CAMILLE DELTHIL (*Les Rustiques*).

"Abomination of abomination!" murmured Marcel, and he went out in haste; he would not remain another minute in that cursed house. It seemed to him that the walls of his room reeked of debauchery, and that everything there was impregnated with the odour of foul orgies.

He went out of the village, unconscious of his road, like a hunted criminal; he tried to escape from himself, for that harsh officer, remorse, had laid vigorous hold of his conscience. Be followed at random the foot-paths, lined by gardens by which he had passed so many times with placid brow and a clean heart; he walked on, he walked on, with bare head, and blank and haggard eyes, thinking of nothing but his crime, seeing nothing, hearing nothing, not oven the bell which summoned him to his morning Mass, as it cheerfully filled the air with its silver notes.

The morning was as bright as the face of a bride. May was shedding its perfumes and flowers on the paths, and displaying everywhere its marvellous adornments of universal life,—labour and love. The children were already tumbling about in the foot-paths, the birds were warbling in the hawthorn hedges, and in the moist grass the grasshopper was saluting the rising sun.

And he, in the midst of all this joy and all this life, was walking on with his head filled with vague ideas of suicide. A few peasants passed near him and sainted him: he saw them not; he saw not the children who stopped still and gazed in bewilderment at his strange appearance: he saw not Suzanne who was approaching at the end of the path.

She was only a few paces away when he raised his head, and all his blood rushed to his heart. Vision blessed and cursed at the same time. She,

she there, at the vary moment of the consummation of his shame. She before him when he had just dug an abyss between them. What should he say? Would she not read on his troubled face the shameful secret of the drama within? Was not his crime written on his sullied brow in indelible soars? He would have wished the earth to open under his feet.

Meanwhile she advanced blushing, perhaps as greatly agitated as himself.

And from the smile on her rosy lips, from the brightness of her dark eyes, from the gram of her carriage, from the chaste swelling of her bosom, from the folds of her dress which, blown by the morning breeze, revealed the harmonious outlines of her fairy leg, from all those inexpressible maiden charms, there breathed forth that *something*, for which there is no name in the language of men, but which accelerates the beating of the heart, which pours into the veins an unknown fluid, and bids us murmur low to the stranger who passes by, and whom perhaps we may never see again: "My life is thine, is thine!"

Mysterious sensation, which, in the golden days of youth, we have all experienced once at least with ravishing delight.

And everything seemed to say to Marcel: "Fool! If thou hadst wished it, we were thine. The delights of paradise were thine, and thou hast preferred the impurities of hell!"

Oh, if he had been able, if he had dared, he would have cast himself at this maiden's feet, he would have kissed her knees, he would have grovelled on the ground and cried with tears: "Pardon! pardon! Fate has caused it all. Almighty God will never pardon me, but it is thou whom I implore, and what matters it, if thou, thou dost pardon me."

The feeling of the reality recalled him to himself. Who was aware of his fault, and what was there, besides, in common between this young girl and himself? One evening when alone with her, he had acted imprudently, that was all, and it was now long ago. Then, through desperation and also to show that he attached no importance to that act of imprudence which he had almost forgotten, he assumed an icy demeanour.

She advanced with a smile, but she felt it congeal on her lips before this insolent coldness, while he, gravely bowing to her as before, a stranger, passed on.

LVI
DOUBLE REMORSE

"Ah, how much better are the love-tales which we spelt in our eyes with our hearts."

CAMILLE LEMONNIER (*Croquis d'automne*).

His Mass said, Marcel did not want to return to the parsonage. He made his way slowly to the wood, absorbed by a world of thoughts. All was quite changed since the day before, and what a revolution had been wrought in his soul in one day.

The day before there was still time to stop, there was time to cast far away temptations and impure desires, to avoid the infernal snares and ambushes, to take refuge, according to the Apostle's advice, in the bosom of God; now it was too late, it was no longer in his power; he found himself hemmed in within the circle of abominations, and he did not see how he could get forth.

A double remorse tormented him, and wrung his conscience with fierce fingers.

On the one hand, there was his servant, become his accomplice and his mistress, an odious thing; his servant defiling his couch, hitherto immaculate; his couch of a virtuous priest.

Then, on the other, there was the fair pale face of Suzanne, full of reproaches, surprised and sad. Why had he not stopped? What fury had urged him forward, cold and scornful, when he burned to hear once again the sound of that voice which stirred his heart!

And the memory of that meeting, at the very moment of the consummation of his infamy, was the blow of the lash which laid bare the open wound of his remorse. He did not curse his crime more than the inopportuneness and the awkwardness of that crime.

What! be had given himself up to a despicable old woman, he had slaked the thirst of that ghoul with his generous blood, he had abandoned to that hell-hag the promises of his young body and his virgin soul, while a young girl whose like he had never seen but in fairy tales and dreams, came to him and seemed to say to him: "You may love me."

And he had repulsed her in order to give himself up to the former: that horrible creature, that hypocrite, that sorceress.

And now that his judgment was calm, he could not understand how he had allowed himself to be carried away by such clumsy manoeuvres, that he had fallen in so cowardly a way, and for such an object.

If, at least, it had been in the arms of the lovely school-girl! If his virtue had melted under the kisses of her charming lips! But no, none of all that: none of those unparalleled joys, of those ineffable delights, of those divine and sweet pleasures.

Unclean touches, a withered body, an impure mouth. Lewdness instead of love.

And his servant's caresses recurred to him and froze him like the infernal spectres of a hideous nightmare.

He saw again her face, lighted up by amorous fever, her fiery lecherous look, fastening on him with all the wild fury of her forty-five years, with the cynicism of the sham saint who has thrown away her mask, and who, after long fasting, continence and privation, finds at length the means of glutting herself, and wallows more than any other in the sewer of obscenities and Saturnalia.

He saw her again like the old courtesan of Horace,

....*Mulier nigris dignissima barris*

soliciting horribly her too avaricious caresses, and employing all the arsenal of her filthy seduction to excite him.

Meanwhile the hours were passing away. The spirit travels in vain into the land of phantoms; nature performs her modest functions without caring for the wanderings of the spirit.

He felt by the pangs of his stomach that he had as yet only breakfasted on the body of Christ, a meagre repast after a night consecrated to Venus. In short, he was hungry, and he decided to return to the parsonage.

LVII
THE EXPLOSION

"What dost thou want with me, old vixen, worthy to have black elephants for thy lovers.... With what passion dost thou reproach me for my disgust."

HORACE (*Epodes*).

Veronica was waiting for him with a puckered smile. At another time she would have made a great uproar, for the hour for the meal had struck long ago; but she did not wish to abuse her freshly conquered rights, and she contended herself with asking in accents of soft reproach.

—How late you are. Where have you come from? I was beginning to be anxious.

Marcel made no reply.

—You don't answer me. Why this silence? Are you vexed already? Where have you come from?

—I have just been reading my breviary, replied Marcel sharply.

The servant smiled, and pointed out to him his breviary, lying on the table.

—Why tell a lie? she said, I don't bear you any ill-will, because you went towards the wood, although I should have preferred to see you return here quickly. Ah, you are not like me, you have not my impatience. But men are all like that; they do all they can to have a woman, and afterwards they scorn her.

This sentence struck the Curé to the heart like a pin prick. It opened his wounds, already bleeding overmuch, it recalled the shameful memory which he wished to drive away, and which rose up obstinately before him.

—You are changing our parts in a strange manner, he cried indignantly.

—There you are vexed. Why are you vexed? What have I done to you? Have I said anything wrong to you? Do you then regret? Ah, doubtless I am not young enough or pretty enough for you.

—I pray; enough upon that shameful subject. You are revolting.

—What do you say? replied the woman, wounded to the quick.

—I have no need to repeat it, you heard me, I think.

—I heard you, it is true, but I thought I was mistaken. Ah! I am revolting! revolting! Well, I am content to learn it from your mouth. But it is not to-day that you ought to tell me that, sir, it was yesterday, yesterday, she cried insolently.

—Yesterday! yesterday! Oh! let us forget yesterday, I implore you. I would that there were between yesterday and to-day, the night and the oblivion of the tomb.

—Yes? is that your thought? Well, for my part, I will forget nothing. Oh! you are pleased to wish to forget, are you? Therefore, you give yourself up to all your passions, you make use of a poor girl in order to satiate them, and the next day, when you are tired and weary from your debauchery, with no pity for the unhappy one who has trusted you, you say: "Let us forget." Ah! I know you all well, you virtuous gentlemen, you fine priests who preach continency and morality, you are all just the same, all of you, do you hear?

—Veronica, be silent, in the name of Heaven.

—I will not be silent, I will not. So much the worse if they hear me. What does that matter to me, poor unhappy creature that I am? It is not I who am guilty, it is you. It is not I who am charged to teach morality, it is you. It is not I who preach fine sermons on Sunday about chastity and purity and morals, and who hide myself behind the shutters to watch half-naked tumblers dancing in the market-place, who entice little girls at night under some pretest or other, and who kiss them when the servant has turned her back. Yes, yes, you have done that. I blush for you. And you are Monsieur le Curé! Monsieur le Curé. If that wouldn't make the hens laugh. Ah, what does it matter to me that they hear me telling you the truth, it is not I who will be despised by everybody, it will be you. Have I gone and sought for you, have I? You have made me tell you a lot of stories which ought not to be told except in confession, you have made me sit down beside you, drink brandy,… and then afterwards you have taken advantage of me. Yes, you have taken advantage of your maid-servant, a poor girl who has been all her life the victim of priests like you. No, I will not be silent, I will cry it upon the house-tops, if I must. Ah! you have taken me like a thing which one makes use of when convenient, and which one throws away, when one has no more need of it: I understand you; but I have more self-respect than that, although I am only a poor servant.

You want to forget. Very good. But I do not want to forget, and I shall not forget. Oh, I well know what it is your want, Messieurs les Curés; you want young girls, quite young girls, green fruit, which you pick like that at the Confessional, or in some corner, without appearing to touch it, and all the while praying to God. I am aware of that, you know. You cannot teach any tricks to me. You did not get up early enough, my good master. Your Suzanne! there is what would please you. You would not tell her that she is revolting. Affected thing! But they will give you them, wait a little. *Go and see if they are coming, Jean.* The little girls come like that and throw themselves at your neck! You would allow it perhaps. That is what would be revolting. But the mammas are watching, and the papas are opening their eyes. You hear, Monsieur le Curé? The papas; that is what annoys you. Papa Durand.

—Here! cried a voice of thunder from the bottom of the stair-case, and it resounded in Marcel's ears like the trumpet of the last judgment.

Pale and terrified, he questioned Veronica with his eyes.

—It is he, she said, hurrying to the landing-place.

LVIII
PROVOCATION

"For her, for her I will drink the cup to the dregs."

A. DE VIGNY (Chatterton).

—A thousand pardons, said the Captain, but the door was open and I have knocked twice. Monsieur le Curé, I have the honour to salute you. I am not disturbing you?

—Not at all, Monsieur le Capitaine, quite the contrary, I am happy to see you; please come in, stammered Marcel, trying to conceal his confusion, and to look pleasantly at the old soldier. He eagerly brought forward an arm-chair for him, the one on which Suzanne had sat.

"Ah," he thought, "if he knew that his daughter was there, at this same place!"

The Captain sat down, and, tapping his cane on the floor, seemed to be seeking for a way of entering on his subject; he appeared anxious, and Marcel noticed that he no longer had his decisive scoffing manner.

—Monsieur le Curé, he said after a moment's silence, you must be a little surprised to see me ... although, after what I believe I heard, I may not be altogether a stranger here.

—My parishioners are no strangers, Captain.

—Parishioner! oh, I am hardly that. I was not making allusion to that title, but to my name, which was uttered at the very moment when I was at your door.

—Your name, Captain, said Marcel growing red; but there are several persons of your name.

—That is what I said to myself. There is more than one donkey which is called Neddy, and more than one *Papa* Durand in the world. *Papa*! that recalls to me my position as father, sir, and the purpose of my presence here.

Marcel trembled.

—For you may guess that independently of the pleasure of paying you a call, I have moreover another object in view.

—Proceed, Captain.

—Yes, sir. I wish to talk to you about my daughter.

—About your daughter! cried Marcel.

—About my daughter, if you allow me.

—Do so, I beg of you.

—Monsieur le Curé, you have been in this neighbourhood some six or eight months. People have certainly spoken to you about me; they have told you who I am; a miscreant, a man without religion, who regards neither law or Gospel: that is to say, only worth hanging. In spite of that, you came to see me. Very good. You know that I do not pick and choose my words, that I do not seek a lot of little twisting ways to express my meaning. You have had a proof of it. I am blunt, and even brutal, that is well known; but I am open and true.

—I do not doubt it, Captain.

—After our little conversation the other day, you must have decided on my sentiments with regard to those of your profession. Are those sentiments right or wrong? That is my business. I am not come to begin a controversy, I am come to ask for an explanation.

—Please go on, said Marcel alarmed.

—Not liking the priests, I should have wished to bring up my daughter in these principles. You see I am straightforward. Unfortunately, like many other things, her education has slipped out of my hands. We soldiers do not accumulate property, and those who have the best share, if they have no private fortune, remain as poor as Job. We are not able therefore to bring up our children as we intend. The State, in its solicitude, is willing to undertake this care: we are glad of it, and we are thankful to the State; but our children slip out of our hands; they become what the State wishes them to be, that is to say, its humble servants, and, if they are daughters, anything but what their father has ever dreamed.

Marcel breathed again:

—The vocation of children, he said softly, is often in contradiction to the wishes of parents, and that is precisely the sign of the real vocation ... to shatter obstacles. Where is the great artist, the great man, the hero, the saint, the martyr, who has not had to struggle with his own family?

—I am not speaking of a vocation, sir, but of prejudices, of fatal habits, of disheartening nonsense, which children, and especially young girls, imbibe in certain surroundings. The education which my daughter has received, has inoculated her with ideas which I am far from blaming in a woman—I have my religion myself too—but the abuse of which I resent. I am not then at war with my daughter because she has her own, and her own is more receptive, but what I blame with all my power, and what I am determined to oppose with all my power is the excessive attendance at church and on the priest ... on the priest, above all. You are a man, sir, and you understand me, do you not?

—I understand, Captain, that you do not wish your daughter to go to church.

—As little as possible, sir.

—Nevertheless, as a Christian and as a Catholic, she has duties to perform.

—What do you mean by duties?

—Why, the first elements which the Catechism prescribes.

—I do not remember exactly what your catechism prescribes, but if you mean by that the little box where they tell their sins, that is exactly what I absolutely forbid.

—Nevertheless a young person has need of counsel.

—Undoubtedly; but that counsel I intend to give myself.

—There is also the priest's part, Captain.

—Allow me to have another opinion. Besides, the adviser is too young; that is why, Monsieur le Curé, I ask you to abstain in the future from all advice, and undertake to abandon any intention you may have with regard to the direction of this young soul. Such is the purport of my visit.

—Monsieur le Capitaine, answered Marcel, relieved from a great weight, I am an honourable man. Another perhaps might be offended at this proceeding. I will take no offence at it. Another perhaps might answer: "It is a soul to contend for with Satan; it is the struggle between the Church and the family; an old struggle, sir, an eternal struggle. You are master to impose your will among your own, just as among us, we are masters to act according to our conscience. As a father of a family, your rights are sacred, but they stop at the entrance to the holy place. You desire the struggle. It lies between us." For myself I simply reply: "Let it be done according to your wish, and may the will of God equally be done!"

—And what does that mean?

—That your daughter is and shall be in my eyes like all the souls which Heaven has willed to entrust to my care. If she does not come to church, I will not go to seek her; but if she comes there, I cannot ask her to depart.

—You are really too good. And if she comes and kneels in the little box?

—Then the will of God will be stronger than the paternal will.

—That is no answer.

—Well! what can I do? humbly replied Marcel.

—Allow me, sir; I ask you what you would do in such a case.

—I make you the judge of it; can I treat your daughter differently to the other ladies of the parish?

—That is to say that you will receive her confession?

—That will be my duty, Captain. I am frank also, you see.

—But, Monsieur le Curé, the first of your duties is not to encourage the disobedience of children, and not to place yourself between a father and his daughter.

—I place myself on no side, Captain. I confine myself, as far as I can, to the very obscure and modest character of a poor priest. I am charged with an office; is it possible, I ask you yourself, for me to repel those who address themselves to that office?

—Very good, sir, said the Captain rising; I know henceforth what to rely on.

—Pardon me, Captain, but allow me to say that your proceedings and apprehensions appear to me a trifle superfluous; for indeed, if you have a reproach to make your daughter, it is not that of excessive devotion, for it is a long time since she has come to church.

—I have forbidden it to her, sir. But my daughter is grieved, and that pains me. I came to address myself to you, man to man, and as you see, I am disappointed.

—Believe me, Captain, let the thing alone. Do nothing in a hurry. Young people are irritated by obstacles. They need freedom and diversion. Think of this young lady's position, dropped from her school into the midst of this solitude, having neither friends or companions any longer; at that age, the family is not everything; books, walks, music are not sufficient, What harm is there in her coming sometimes on Sunday, to hear Divine Service? We do not conceal it from ourselves, sir, that many women whom we see at service, come there for relaxation.

—And it is precisely that relaxation which ruins them.

—Not in the church, sir.

—Not there, no. But behind, in the sacristy, or at the back of some well-closed room. Adieu, sir.

—I do not want to criticize your language, Captain But one word more, I ask. Is your daughter acquainted with your proceeding?

—Why that question?

—Because then my task will be all traced out.

—What task?

—To avoid every sort....

—Of intercourse. Do what honour counsels you, and trust to me for the rest. I will act with my daughter as it will be suitable for me to act. As for you, you have asserted that any other priest *less honourable* would have said to me: "We are going to engage in the struggle, it lies between us." I see now that in your mouth the word *honourable* signifies *polite*, for you have been polite, but the other alone would have been frank and honourable. "Between us" is better, "between us" pleases me. It is plainer and shorter. Again, I have the honour to salute you.

LIX
ACTS AND WORDS

"Intrigues of heavy dreams! We go to the right; darkness: we go to the left; darkness: in front; darkness ... the thread which you think you hold, escapes out of your hand, and, triumphant for a moment, you set yourself again to grope your way to the catastrophe, which is a denseness of shadows."

CAMILLE LEMONNIERE (Croquis d'automne).

When the Captain had gone away, Marcel perceived the triumphant face of his servant. Mad with shame and rage he shut himself up in his room, and asked himself what was going to become of him. "What am I to do?" he said to himself; "here is the punishment already."

Nevertheless, on serious reflection, he saw a way all traced out before him; it was the ancient, the good, the old way which he had followed until then, and into which the Captain had just brutally driven him back:

The way of his duty.

To forget Suzanne! He had that very morning, without wishing it, almost unknowingly, commenced the rapture; the father's visit had just completed the work.

To forget Suzanne! Yes, he would forget her, he must; not only his honour, his reputation, but his very existence were involved in it. Material impossibilities rose up before him in every direction where he tried to deviate from the straight path. His servant! The father! He was compelled to be an honourable man anyhow, not lost sight of, watched and spied upon by these two enemies.

To forget Suzanne! How, after what had passed the previous day, would he dream for a moment of remembering her? He was almost thankful to his servant for having stopped him in time on a descent, at the end of which was scandal and dishonour.

In any other circumstances his pride would have revolted at the menaces of the foolish father, he would have been stung in his self-esteem, and he would have disputed with him for his treasure. But where was his pride? Where was his dignity? He had left all that on the lap of a cook.

Reputation was safe; that was henceforth the only good which he must keep at any price.

"Come," said he, "keep it, have courage. Stand up, son of saints and martyrs. Yield not, hesitate not, march forward, without being anxious for what is on the right or left. Do thy duty in one direction, since in the other thou hast failed. Is a man then lost because he has for one moment deviated from his way? Is he dead for one false step? Peter denied his master three times, thou hast done so but once!"[1]

The postman's ring drew him from his reverie. He ran to receive the letter, recognized the writing, hastily put it into his pocket, took up his hat and his breviary, and went out without saying a word.

When he was in the little hollow road which is at the bottom of the hill, he turned round, and, certain that he was not being followed, only then did he open the letter which follows:

"MONSIEUR LE CURÉ,

"Why are you vexed with me? If you have not seen me any more at Mass, it is that I have had to contend with my father, and that I have been obliged to yield. Nevertheless, I am unhappy, and more than ever have I need of your counsel. You have said: 'We cannot serve two masters,' and 'it is very difficult to render to Caesar that which is Caesar's, and to God that which is God's.' One word, if you please, through the medium of Marianne to

"Your very devoted

"S.D."

He tore up the letter into the smallest fragments and returned home in all haste.

A few hours after, Marianne received the following notice:

"*To-morrow evening at 7 o'clock, in honour of the Holy Virgin, there will be Salutation and Benediction at the Chapel of St. Anne. The faithful are besought to attend.*"

[Footnote 1: Thou art man and not God, says the holy book of Consolation, thou art flesh and not an angel. How canst thou always continue in very virtue?]

LX
TALKS

"When from the hills fell balmy night,
'Neith the dark foliage of the lofty trees,
Starred by the moon-beams' placid light,
Often we wandered by the water's side."

CAMILLE DELTHIL (*Poésie inédite*).

As he expected, she did not fail to be at the meeting-place. She was unaware of her father's proceedings; it was Marcel who informed her of them. She was quite terrified; but he reassured her, and knew how to soothe her young conscience; and meeting followed meeting. Dear and innocent meetings. The most prudish old woman would have found nothing to find fault with. The mystery, and their being forbidden, formed all their charm.

The Chapel of St. Anne, half-a-league distant from the village, was a charming object for a walk. You cross the meadow as far as the little river, bordered with willows, then the chapel is reached by a hollow lane hedged with quicksets. The sweet month of May had begun. Three evenings a week the little nave was in festal dress, and filled with light, and perfumes and flowers.

Suzanne went no more to Mass, but she had said to her father:

—Will you not let me go instead and take a walk sometimes beside Saint Anne's, to hear the music and the singing of the congregation?

—Marianne shall accompany you, replied Durand.

They were always the last to leave the chapel, and Marcel soon rejoined them. It was at some winding of the path that he used to meet them *by chance*, and every time he showed great surprise. They walked slowly along, talking of one thing and another. The Spring, the latest books, the *good* Captain's rheumatism, were themes of inexhaustible variety. The future sometimes attracted their thoughts, her own future; and the priest tried to cause a few fresh rays to shine into the young unquiet soul.

They talked also of the school and of friends who had gone out into the world. One of them, a fair child with blue eyes, was her best-beloved and the fairest of the fair, and Marcel sometimes felt jealous of these warm, young-girl friendships.

He did not disdain to talk of fashions; it is one way of pleasing, and he admired aloud the elegant cut of the waist, the twig of lilac fastened to the body of her dress, and the graceful art which had twined her long jetty plaits. She smiled and said: "What, you too; you too; you pay attention to these woman's trifles!"

But what matters the topic of their conversations, all they could say was not worth the joyous note which sang at the bottom of their hearts.

When they drew near the village he bowed to her respectfully, and each one returned by a different way.

Marianne was then profuse in her praises:

-What a fine Curé! she said, so kind and civil. If your father only knew him better!

And Suzanne, who returned very thoughtful, said once: "The Curé! can it be? It is the Curé then."

LXI
LE PÈRE HYACINTHE

"She still preserved for herself that little scene; thus, little by little, we accumulate within ourselves all the elements of the inner life."

EMILE LECLERCQ (*Une fille du peuple*).

She had shown Marcel the portrait of her beloved Rose. "Yes, she is very pretty," he had replied, "but I prefer dark girls ..." Suzanne blushed. He opened his breviary and drew out a card.

—Are you going to show me a dark girl? she said.

He handed it to her without answering.

It was the photograph of a man of about forty, with strongly-marked and characteristic features. The eyes, prominent and slightly veiled, were surrounded with a dark ring, a token of struggle, fatigue and deception. A profile out of a picture of Holbein in every-day dress.

—It is a priest, she cried.

—It is a priest, indeed, answered Marcel. We are recognized in any costume. We cannot conceal our identity. Do you know who that is?

—Is it not that monk who has made such a noise? That Dominican who has married, and broken with the Church?

—Yes, Mademoiselle.

The young girl regarded it with curiosity.

—It must have been a violent passion to come to that, she said.

—No, it was an idea well resolved upon and matured. No transport of youth carried him away. See, he is no longer young, and the companion he has chosen is very nearly his own age, and he had for her only a tender and holy feeling.

—Why then this uproar and scandal?

—In order to protest aloud against a rule which he did not approve. In our days there are so many cowardly and degenerate characters, that we cannot too greatly admire those who have the courage to proclaim their opinion in the presence of the mob, especially when those opinions shock the brutalized mob; for my part I admire this man; but what I admire still more is the woman who has dared to put her hand in his, and brave the derision of the vulgar, and the calumnies of hypocrites.

—But his vows?

—What is a vow when it is a question of the duty which your conscience dictates? I heard him say one day: "If, after reaching middle age, I have decided after long reflection to choose a companion, it is not in response to the cry of the senses, but in order to sanctify my life." He has taken back the word which he had given, as we all do, at an age when we are ignorant of the import, and the consequence of that word. Be assured that his conscience does not reproach him, for you can see on this fine countenance that his conscience is at rest. Besides, is it the case that God enjoins celibacy? The celibacy of priests dates only from the year 1010: Christ never speaks about it.

—And so he has broken with all his past, his relations, his world; he has ruined what you men call his future. He must begin his life again.

—And he begins it again in accordance with his inclinations, his needs and his heart: It is never too late to change the road when we discover that we have taken the wrong way. It takes longer time, there is more hardship, but what matters it, provided we attain happiness, the end which we all have in view. Ah, Mademoiselle, how many, like he, would wish to begin their life again, if they found a courageous soul who was willing to accompany them? The future, do you say? But the future, the present, the past, the whole life lies in the sweet union of hearts. To devote oneself, to renounce everything, to give up everything, even one's illusions, one's beliefs, one's dreams for the loved object, is not a sacrifice: it is the sweetest of joys and the noblest of duties.

He stopped, fearing that he had gone too far, and did not dare to look at Suzanne.

She answered coldly. "Ah, Monsieur le Curé, you approve of that! I did not think you would have approved of Père Hyacinth; truly, I am astonished."

Monsieur le Curé! It was the first time Suzanne had called him *Monsieur le Curé*. That name wounded him like an affront. He remembered what he was, and what he must not cease to be in the eyes of the young girl: the Curé! nothing but the Curé.

And he was sick at heart for several days.

But one fine morning, on coming out from Mass, his countenance lit up, he uttered a cry of joy and fell into the arms of Abbé Ridoux.

LXII
THE HAPPY CURÉ

"Such was Socrates said to have been, because the outside beholders, and those estimating him by his external appearance, would not have given the slice of an onion, so plain was he in his person, and ridiculous in his bearing ... simple in habits, poor in fortune, unfortunate with women, unfit for all the offices of the republic, always laughing, always drinking with one or another, always sporting, always concealing his divine wisdom."

RABELAIS (*Gargantua*).

Monsieur Ridoux was a very good fellow, but he was not handsome. A big nose, a big belly, blinking eyes, an enormous mouth, hair on end, the arm of a chimpanzee, and the legs of a Greenlander. At first sight, he gave me the impression of a monkey with young.

But what is a man's outward form? The vessel, more or less regular, filled with a baneful or beneficent liquid, and you all know that the shape of the flagon has no influence on the quality of the wine.

The outward form is the wrapper of the goods: very often that wrapper is brilliant and gilded, of satin or watered silk, and the goods are adulterated and spoiled. At other times the wrapper is rough and coarse, but it enfolds precious commodities.

The stamp of genius is usually found only on countenances with fantastic features. Have you ever seen on the fair insipid faces of our *young swells* the imprint of a powerful and fertile intelligence?

The body nearly always is adorned at the expense of the mind.

Of all the deformities of nature, the hunchbacks are intellectual in proportion as the handsome men are not.

Enquire of the army its opinion on its pre-eminently *fine man*, the drum-major.

Vincent Voiture, who had, as he confessed himself, the silly face of a dreaming sheep, used to say that nature usually likes to place the most precious souls in ill-favoured, puny bodies, as jewellers set the richest diamonds in a small quantity of gold.

Accordingly, the pitiful wrapper of the Abbé Ridoux covered an excellent soul. With his ugly face and his old stained cassock, he reminded me of those dirty bottles, coated with spider-webs and dust, which we place daintily on the table on days of rejoicing, and which lord it majestically among the glittering decanters, soon to be despised, when their dusty sides appear.

Thus Monsieur Ridoux lorded it amongst his curates, younger, handsomer, fresher, more tasty than himself, and eclipsed them by all the brilliancy of his good-sense, his tact, and his experience.

He had certainly his little failings!... Who can say that he is exempt from them? But his mind was sound. A good companion, besides, and of a cheerful disposition. "We have reached a period," he used to say, "when the priest must lay aside the stern front and the anathema. There is already much to obtain pardon for in the colour of his robe. Let us be cheerful, let us be insinuating, let us be compassionate to human weaknesses. Let us sin, if need be, with discretion and propriety; but, in heaven's name, let us not terrify. Let us promise paradise to all. There are always plenty enough whose life is a hell."

In that he was not of Veuillot's opinion, that rigid saint, who wished to see all the world damned for the love of God.

Therefore, on seeing this cheerful countenance, this openness of manner, this freedom of speech, this unrestrained good-nature, even those who had been warned, could not help saying: "Well indeed! this Curé has a pleasant phiz!"

Slanderous tongues, Voltairians—who is sheltered from the stings of that race of vipers?—slanderous tongues affirmed that beneath this Rabelaisian exterior, he was profoundly vicious, artful, and hypocritical. Marcel, who had been brought up by him, and was acquainted with the most secret details of his inmost life, has always assured me that he was nothing of the kind, and that his uncle Ridoux, endowed with the ugliness of Socrates, had also his wisdom.

Nevertheless, I would not dare to assert that he did not like to pinch the young girls' chins, especially of those who had made their first communion and were near to the marriageable age; a familiarity which, thanks to his gray hairs, and the development of his abdomen, he thought was permitted him, but which, however, is not always without danger.

Cazotte, a wise man, used to say to his daughters: "When you are alone with young people, distrust yourselves; but if you find yourselves with old men, distrust them, and avoid allowing them to take hold of your chin."

Cazotte was right, for old men begin with that. I would not dare either to assert that the charms of his cook were safe from his indiscreet curiosity, for it is there too that old men finish; and we must swear not at all. Everybody knows the wise man's precept: "When in doubt, abstain."

At the period of which I am speaking to you, he reigned in a good parish, well frequented by devout ladies, both young and middle-aged, where from the height of his pulpit he laid down his laws to his kneeling people, without hindrance or control.

He was happy, as all wise men ought to be. Happy to be in the world, satisfied to be a Curé. "It is the first of professions," he often used to say, and there is not one of them which can be compared to it.

> "I am a village Curé,
> Where I live most modestly;
> I'm no important person,
> But I'm happy and content
> No, I do not envy aught,
> For my wants they are but small.
> How I love to pass my days
> Within the house of God!"

But if he had complained, it would have been very hard, and everybody in the diocese, from Monseigneur the Bishop to his sexton, would have risen with indignation and called him, "Ungrateful wretch." For Ridoux was favoured above all his colleagues; above all his colleagues Divine Providence bad overwhelmed him with its favours. He possessed in his parish, in his very church, at his door, beneath his eyes, beneath his hand, a real blessing from Heaven, a grace of God, a Pactolus always rolling down a mine of Peru, a secret of an alchemist, the veritable philosopher's stone caught sight of by Nicolas Flamel, and vainly sought for till the time of Cagliostro, a marvel which made him at once honoured and envied, which made his name celebrated, which gave him a preponderant voice in the Chapter and a place in the episcopal Council, which swelled his heart with pride and his money-bag with crowns; he had in the choir of his church behind the mother altar, in a splendid glass-case, laid on a bed of blue velvet … an old yellow skeleton! The relics of a saint.

But there are saints and saints; those which do miracles, and those which do them not, those which work and those which rest.

Monsieur Ridoux's saint worked.

LXIII
THE MIRACLES

"Miracles have served for the foundation, and will serve for
the continuation of the Church until Antichrist, until the end."

(Pensées de PASCAL).

The miserable herd of free-thinkers, people who have no faith, those
who are still plunged in the rut of unbelief, are ignorant perhaps that all the
saints have done miracles, that they have all begun in that way, that that is
the condition *sine qua non*, for entrance into the blessed confraternity.

No money, no Swiss; no miracles, no saint. It is in vain that during all
your life you shall have been a model of candour and virtue; it is in vain that
you shall edify the universe by your piety and your good works, that you
shall have resisted like St. Antony the temptations of the flesh, that you shall
have covered yourself with hair-cloth like St. Theresa, with venom like St.
Veuillot, with filth like St. Alacoque or with lice like St. Labre: it is in vain
that you shall have been beaten with rods like St. Roche, been scourged by
your Confessor like St. Elizabeth, that finally you shall have sinned only
six instead of seven times a day; if at your death you should not succeed in
performing some fine miracle, you will never be admitted into the Calendar.

The Pope causes your shade to appear before his sacred tribunal, and
according as the number of the dead whom you have raised to life is judged
sufficient or not, as the touch of your tibia or coccyx has cured the itch or
scrofula or not, you are admitted or excluded.

It is a difficult profession to be a saint, and is not for anyone who wishes
it.

Therefore, the candidates who die in the odour of sanctity hasten to
accomplish their regular total of prodigies, in order that our father the Pope
may be pleased to assign them a place in the highest heaven.

They have hardly closed their eyes before they begin to *operate*. Allured
by the hope of being crowned with a glorious halo, they display infinite
zeal, and we have seen them, from their tooth-stumps to their prepuce,
effecting the most marvellous miracles.

That of Jesus Christ—I speak of the prepuce—is preserved thus in several churches; all of which contend for the honour of possessing the veritable one. It is not yet exactly known which is the best; but all without distinction work wonders, and at certain seasons of the year, are kissed by pious young women.[1]

But this noble zeal of the saints lasts but for a time, and this is a proof of the imperfection of human kind, that our faults and whims follow us even beyond the tomb.

The saints, themselves, fall into all the little meannesses so common with the most ordinary sinners. Like candidates who solicit the votes of the mob in order to gain power, and make the most brilliant promises which they hasten to forget as soon as they have climbed the stairs, so the candidates for canonization perform marvels at first, but once admitted into the seventh heaven, they appear to trouble themselves no more concerning lowly mortals.

Or perhaps miraculous properties are like all other faculties, as they grow old they become worn-out, and an *elect* who has stoutly brought the dead to life when he was only an aspirant for honours, is now only capable of curing the ringworm.

But, as I have said, it was a zealous candidate that the Abbé Ridoux had in his church. His bones had been there for fifty years, and as the longed-for time for his canonization had not yet arrived, and he had as yet only the rank of *blessed*, his zeal had not grown cold.

Each saint, we all know, has his medical speciality, like Ricord, for instance, or Dr. Ollivier.

Suppose you are suffering from ophthalmia, and instead of consulting a physician, you pray to God, in hopes that God will cure you.

You are wrong, that does not concern God. It is the business of St. Claire, who has the principal management of the sight of the faithful.

You are paralyzed, and you commend yourself to your patron saint. "You must not address yourself to me, that one answers. Go to the other office. See St. Marcel (or *Marchel*), to make the impotent walk is entrusted to him."

And so one after another:

> St. Cloud cures the boils; St. Cornet, the deaf; St. Denis,
> anemia; St.Marcou, diseases in the neck; St. Eutropus,
> the dropsy; St. Aignan, the ringworm, and it is generally
> admitted that we ought to pray on All Saints Day to be
> preserved from a cough.[2]

And observe how the good people of France are always the most enlightened and intelligent people in the universe!

The speciality of Monsieur Ridoux's candidate was broken legs, girls in complaints of childhood, and fluxes of the womb. That was what he healed, but he must not be asked for anything else; besides fluxes of the womb, sprains, and girls in complaints of childhood, he did not attend to anything.

That is conceivable; one cannot do everything.

It is quite unnecessary to state that he did not give all his consultations free, and that he did not work for fame alone. No one was constrained to pay, it is true; but it would have been a very unhandsome thing not to make a preliminary contribution to Monsieur le Curé's poor-box.

Little presents have always maintained friendship, and there is nothing like sterling silver to predispose the benevolence of the saints and the love of heaven in our favour.

While on the contrary:

> A poorly furnished niche affronts the saint:
> The God deserts, and when we enter, shows
> His anger from the door of his poor shrine.

He no longer worked every-day, but on fête-days.

All the cripples came from twenty leagues round, and there were miracles then for crutches.

As in the time of Paris the deacon, when Cardinal de Noailles kept a register of the wonders of St. Médard's Cemetery, a churchwarden of the place, assisted by two secretaries and the corporal of Gendarmes, religiously inscribed the miraculous cures of the saint on a magnificent volume.

Credible witnesses attested these prodigies and, if necessary, gave details to the incredulous.

If all were not cured, they had the hope of being so, which was a consolation.

"And then," whispered Monsieur Ridoux in the ear of sceptics, "if the touching of these blessed bones produces no benefit, you are sure it will do no harm, and you cannot say the same of your doctor's drugs."

[Footnote 1: The Holy Prepuce is at Rome in the Church
of St. John Lateran; it is also at St. James of Compostelia
in Spain; at Anvers; in the Abbey of St. Corneille at
Compiègne; at Our Lady of the Dove, in the diocese of

Chartres, in the Cathedral of Puy-en-Velay; and in several other places (Voltaire, Dictionnaire philosophique).

The Able X...., author of *Maudit* also places the holy fragment in the church of Chanoux (Vienné) and asserts that a Bishop of Châlone in the 18th century threw a pattern of it into the river.]

[Footnote 2: Ainsi parchait à Sinay un caphar, qui Sainct Antoine mettoit le feu ès jambes; Sainct Eutrope faisait les hydropiques; Sainct Gildas les fols; Sainct Genou les gouttes. Mais je le punis en tel exemple, quoi qu'il m'appelast hérétique, que dépuis ce temps caphar quiconque n'est ausé entrer en mes terres.

Et m'esbahi si vostre roi les laisse perscher par son royaulme tels scandales. Car plus sont à punir que ceulx qui par art magique ou sultre engin auraient mis la peste par le pays. La peste ne tue que le corps, mais tels imposteurs empoisennent les âmes. (Rabelais).]

LXIV
THE TWO AUGURS

"I am surprised that two augurs can look at one another without laughing."

CATO.

—Ave Marcellus! said the old Curé, giving his nephew a paternal embrace; how are you, my poor boy?

—I am very well, replied Marcel.

—No! your servant has told me that you have been unwell for some time.

—She is really too kind. You have been talking to her then?

—Yes, while waiting for you. She seems to me a worthy and intelligent person, but a little irritated with you. Do you live badly together?

Marcel coloured.

—Come, the blush of holy modesty is covering your face. Don't do so, child, don't we all know what it is, my dear fellow?

—Indeed, much you ought to know what these women are. They are cross-grained and stubborn, and claim to be the mistresses of the house, especially with priests younger than themselves.

—That is the inconvenience of our condition, Monsieur le Curé. What will you? We must pass it over. But, tell me, she is not so *old* as that. Ah, come, the maiden's blush again! I do not want to offend your virtuous feelings any longer, and I am going to talk to you about something else. You know I have centred all my ambition on you, that I occupy myself about you only, and that together with my saint and my salvation, you are the sole object of my care. Therefore, you can explain my indignation and wrath at seeing my pupil buried in this frightful village, at seeing you extinguishing your brilliant qualities, having no other stimulant for your intellect than your Sunday sermons and your stupid peasants, no other emotion than your disputes with your cook. I have therefore asked of the Lord one thing only, only one. *Unam petii a Domino, hanc requiram.* You know what it is—

your promotion. Well, Monsieur le Curé. I come to tell you that everything is going as it were on wheels.

—Really? said Marcel indifferently.

> —Just think. The day before yesterday a letter reached me from the Palace.It was Monseigneur's secretary, little Gaudinet, who wrote to me. You know Gaudinet?

—No, uncle.

He is not a bad fellow, but a devil to intrigue. Well, as he knows the interest I take in you, and as he wants to creep up my sleeve, because he hopes soon to take the place of one of my curates, he wrote to me that Monseigneur had spoken of you with interest, and that he proposed to put an end to your exile. I recognize there the Comtesse de Montluisant's good offices. You see that she has lost no time, and so we will do the same; we most strike the iron while it is hot; you are going to get your bag and baggage, and take yourself off to Nancy.

—Already?

—Why already? Have you any business here which detains you then?

—Nothing ... absolutely nothing; but what shall I do at Nancy?

—That is just why I have come, you impatient young man, to point out to you what line of conduct to follow, and, as I know, you are rather more scrupulous than there is any need for in our profession, to assist you in removing certain scruples which might stand in the way of your promotion.

—Heavens! What scruples?

—We will talk about them at table. Meanwhile, this is the question. I have told you that I will move heaven and earth for you; you, however, must help me a little on your side, for whatever I may do, I can effect nothing without you. In his letter, Gaudinet informs me that the parish of St. Mary, Nancy, is deprived of its pastor. It came into my head directly that you must take the place of the defunct. It is an excellent parish, very prominent, splendid surplice fees, devout ladies, sisters, elderly spinsters to plunge into saintly jubilation, a host of Capuchins, everything indeed which constitutes a *blessing from heaven* for a poor priest. You are young, you are handsome, you are intelligent, you are energetic; while you are waiting for something better, I promise you an existence there, of which the most ambitions of village Curés has never dared to dream. But we most hasten, time presses; Gaudinet tells me that there are already at least a dozen candidates in earnest; and although old Collard's intentions (and he intends to atone for his former injustice) regarding you are favourable, you are well aware that he allows himself to be led by the nose, and generally the last one who talks to him is right. You must be then both the first and the last, and you must not let him slip; not you, but your second, your aide-de-camp, your *fideicommissum*, or rather your protectress, the Comtesse de Montluisant.

—But I do not know this lady.

—It is precisely for that reason that it is indispensable for you to hasten to go and see her, in order to make her acquaintance. You have only to present yourself, and I assure you even if you were not sent by me, she would receive you with the greatest pleasure. For, between ourselves be it said, she is an elderly coquette, but she is good-natured and knows how to remember her old friends. You will have therefore to be amiable, insinuating, respectful, assiduous. You might even tell her that she is charming, and that one sees she has been very pretty; which is true. Old ladies dote on young people, and devout old ladies on young priests, especially on those with a figure and face like yours. "The face is everywhere the first letter of introduction," said Bernardin de Saint-Pierre, and I assure that with Madame de Montluisant, you will not require another. Ah, the Comtesse de Montluisant, my friend, there is a precious soul! What a misfortune that she is a little over-ripe! It is all the same to you, and if you are wise, you will pass over that defect, which she amply atones for by her amiable qualities. She has the complete mastery of Monseigneur. She is the Maintenon of that old Louis XIV. Be to her what she is to him, and have the mastery of her in your turn. I was talking to you a little while ago about scruples; for once you must leave them at home or put them in the bottom of your cassock. *Dixi!* You have understood me I hope.

—No, uncle, I don't understand you.

—Are you talking seriously?

—I declare, uncle, that I don't understand you.

—*O rara avis in terris*, oh phoenix! oh pearl! you don't understand me!!! Well, I am come expressly, however, to make myself understood. Must I put the dots on the i's for you? You don't understand me, you say? Surely, you are making fun of me. Come, look me straight in the face; in the white of my eyes ... yes, like that, and dare to tell me that you have not understood me, and keep serious. Ah, ah, you are laughing, you are laughing. You see you cannot look at me without laughing.

LXV
TABLE TALK

"I allow that it is necessary to be virtuous in order to be happy, but I assert that it is necessary to be happy in order to be virtuous."

CH. LEMESLES (*Tablettes d'un sceptique*).

They sat down to table. It was an excellent meal, and the worthy Ridoux tried to make it cheerful, but a vague feeling of sorrow oppressed Marcel.

That departure, which he had so eagerly desired before, and the hope of which he had clung to as one lays hold of a means of safety, he could not think of without grief, when he saw it near and practicable. Undoubtedly he would leave without regret this village, where his youth was buried, where his abilities were rendered unfruitful, where his sanguine aspirations were slowly killing themselves.... But Suzanne?

That sweet name which he murmured low with love. That sweet young girl the sight of whom was as pleasant as a sun-beam, he was going to leave her for ever.

It was for his good, his honour, his quiet, his future; he knew it, he felt it, but he was full of sorrow.

Meanwhile, he overwhelmed his uncle with marks of attention and friendship; he made every effort to cope with his guest's cheerful discourse, who, after relating the flight of the Grand-Vicar, surprised in criminal conversation with the wife of the Captain of Gendarmerie, acquainted him all the little ecclesiastical scandals. But he gave only a partial attention; his thoughts were absorbed in his inmost preoccupations. Now and again only did he let fall a few observations in reply: "How horrible," or "How shocking," or again: "How abominable!"

Ridoux did not appear at first to pay attention to his nephew's gloomy thoughts. He laughed and joked all alone, but he did not miss a mouthful. Old priests are generally greedy. Good cheer is one of the joys which is left to them.

With no serious preoccupation, with no anxiety for the future, exempt from family cares, they transfer all their solicitude to themselves, and make a divinity of their belly.

But when his appetite, sharpened by his journey, was appeased, he examined Marcel with curiosity, and what he observed, combined with a few indiscreet words of Veronica, confirmed him in his suspicions, that a drama was being enacted in the young man's soul.

—Do you know, he said to him, that you are a pitiable companion. You scarcely eat, you scarcely speak, you do not drink, and you laugh still less. Why, what's the matter with you? Are you not gratified at my visit?

—Forgive me, uncle, but I am rather poorly, said Marcel; that is my excuse.

—That is what the maid-servant told me, but you declared to me that you were quite well.

—How can you suppose that I am not happy to see you? You know my feelings well.

—I know that you have excellent feelings. But I find you quite changed. It is scarcely a year since I saw you, and you bear marks of weariness. You stoop like an old man. Look at me, always the same, firm as a rock. "God smites the wicked with many plagues, but he encompasseth with his help those that hope in him." Second penitential psalm. You are not wicked: what plague consumes you? Ambition? Patience, everything will be changed, since your enemy is vanquished. Is it your conscience which is ill at ease? But conscience should be cheerful; that is its true sign. Is it anything else? Come, tell me. _

—Well yes, uncle, there is something. The same complaint as before, you know, when I hesitated to enter the seminary, when I had doubts about my vocation. You ended my hesitation and silenced my doubts; you have made a priest of me; well, now more than ever, I have moments of lassitude which make me disgusted with my calling.

—Really?

—Yes, there are hours when this priest's robe devours me, like the robe of Nessus; I wish that I could tear it off, but I feel that I should tear off pieces of my flesh at the same time, for it is too late, and it has become a portion of myself. I am ashamed to make this confession to you, but you wished it, and I have opened my heart to you.

—May it not be that the heart is sick? Come. I see that I am come to take you away from here at a seasonable time.

—Do not believe that, uncle.

—So much the better, if I am mistaken. I should be delighted to be mistaken. To be in love, my son, is the greatest act of stupidity which a priest can commit. Make use of women, if you will, for your health and your satisfaction, and not for theirs. Otherwise you are a lost man.

—In truth, uncle, you have singular theories, cried Marcel. Have you not then taken your calling seriously?

—My calling? I have taken it so seriously that you will never see me handling it but in the practical way. Therefore, among those who surround me I enjoy a fine reputation for wisdom. To be wise is to be happy, and I have contrived so as to pass my existence in the most pleasant manner possible. I counsel you to make as much of it, and I am going to tell what I mean by being wise: Make use of the things of life with moderation, discretion, and prudence. Now, what constitutes life? Spirit and matter. Well, I wisely make the enjoyments of matter and spirit march abreast. I obtain the equilibrium: health of body and health of soul. As soon as the equilibrium is broken, the mental faculties are deranged, or the constitution declines. You are in one of these two cases, my dear fellow.

—I!

—Yes, you. And, in spite of all your denials, I wager that you are in love. Ah, ah, ah. It is a good story. He keeps his countenance like a thrashed donkey. Come, drink, cheer up; honour the Lord in his benefits. Your glass is always full. Enjoy yourself, you don't entertain your uncle every day.

Marcel emptied his glass.

—Is she possessed of a husband?

—But uncle, I don't know, what you want to talk about.

—Oh, how well dissimulation is grafted in this young man's heart. I congratulate you on it: it is good for strangers, for the profane.... But I, Marcel, I, am I a stranger?

"Brought up in the Seraglio, I know its windings."

Come, another drop of this wine which could make the dead laugh.

—Listen, uncle, you are my second father, my master, my first director, my only true friend. Yes, I want to ask your advice. I am afraid of soiling one day the robe which I wear, I am afraid of becoming an object of shame and compassion. Ah, I am unhappy.

—Here we are, cried Ridoux. Speak. The only point is to understand one another.

LXVI
GOOD COUNSEL

"Ah, my friend, have not all young people ridiculous passions? My son is enamoured of virtue!... The customs of the word, the need of pleasure, and the facilities of satisfying himself will bring him insensibly to a moderate state of feeling, and at thirty he will be just like any other man; he will enjoy life, and shut his eyes to many things which shock him to-day."

PIGAULT-LEBRUN (*Le Blanc et le Noir*).

At that moment Veronica came in to serve coffee.

In honour of her master's guest, she had put on her black dress of Associate and her silver medal; and on her head she wore coquettishly an embroidered cap, trimmed with tulle of dazzling whiteness.

The old Curé threw himself into his arm-chair with his head back, in order to contemplate her with admiration. She went and came, clearing the table, and he followed her movements with the eye of a connoisseur, estimating the value of an article.

He smiled sanctimoniously, and the smile and attention, which the bashful Veronica noticed, made her blush and cast her eyes modestly down.

-Eh! Eh! he seemed to say, here is a girl who is still fit to adorn a bed.

When the servant had left the room, he rose, drew the screen between the table and the door, and then came and sat down again facing Marcel.

—I don't understand, he said, why a man should go and search away from home, amid perils and obstacles, for a pleasure which he can obtain comfortably, quietly, with no fear or disquietude, at his own fire-side.

—To what are you pleased to allude?

—There is a girl, Ridoux continued, who certainly has merit, and I am convinced that many younger ones are not worth as much as she. She is there, in your hands, at your door, in your home; ready, I am sure, to satisfy all your requirements. Avail yourself of her willingness? No? Make use of this blessing which you possess? Again, no. You throw it aside to run after phantoms. Alas, all the men of your age are the same: like the dog in the fable, they let go their prey to seize the shadow. You are like the fool, who spends his life in vainly following fortune to the four quarters of the world, and who, when he returns to his hearth wearied, worn-out and aged, finds it sitting at his door. But he is too late to be able to enjoy it.

That girl is really very well: handsome, fresh, very well-preserved, with a decent and respectable appearance. Why then do you disdain her? Why? Tell me. Because she is a few years older than you? But that is just what you young priests require. You require women of that age: matrons with more sense than yourselves. She is staid, she is ripe, she is experienced, a mistress of love's science, and above all, she has a great quality, an inestimable quality, she is cautious and will never compromise you.

—Uncle, I implore you.

—Let me finish.

Another thing which is very valuable. She is full of little attentions for her master. Ah, you are not aware with what tender solicitude, with what kindness, with what jealous affection an old mistress surrounds you. She fears more for your health than for her own, she is acquainted with your tastes and knows how to anticipate them, she satisfies all your desires, and lends herself to all your fancies.

—What a conversation! If anyone heard us....

—Be easy. I have drawn the screen.

The young mistress is fickle, egotistical, capricious; she exacts adoration, and most frequently loves you for a whim and for want of occupation.

The old one devotes herself entirely to you and does not ask you (sublime self-denial!), that you should love her, but only that you should let her love you. Balzac extolled the women of thirty; that was because he had not tasted those of forty. Ah! the women of forty!

They are the only women who are of value to the priest, my friend. You have had the good fortune to meet one here, and instead of profiting by it, of thinking yourself fortunate, of thanking heaven and piously and devoutly enjoying the good which God grants you, you cast it away, you disdain, you despise it; and why? For some giddy little thing who will bring upon you every kind of vexation and unpleasantness. *Dixi*. You can speak now.

Marcel made no reply. With his elbows resting on the table and his head in his hands, he stared at his uncle.

He asked himself if he was really awake, if it was really his adopted father, the mentor of his childhood, the wise and virtuous Curé of St. Nicholas, who was talking to him so.

He knew the worthy man's somewhat eccentric character, his coarse witticisms in bad taste, but he never could have believed that he would have stated such theories before him with a cynicism like that. He quite understood that a man might commit faults, he even excused *in petto* certain crimes, and he excused them the more willingly because he himself had been guilty of them; but he did not understand how a man could dare to talk about them.

He was rather of that class of persons who are modest in words, but not in deeds, who are offended at the talk, while they delight in the acts. We hear them utter cries of horror and indignation at the slightest equivocal word, we see them stop their ears at the recital of a racy tale, chastely cover their face before the figure of the Callipygean Venus, treating Molière as obscene and Rabelais as debauched; yet, out of sight, sheltered by the curtains of the alcove, they love to strip in silence some lascivious Maritorne, and cautiously abandon themselves to disgusting orgies with Phrynes whom they chance to encounter.

Therefore the Curé of Althausen was offended and indignant at his uncle's cynicism, who had so crudely broached the chapter about the love of middle-aged women to him, who the evening before had abandoned himself to all the furies of a long-repressed passion, in the arms of a debauched old maid-servant.

At the same he felt that his brain was confused and that he was gradually losing the exact idea of things. The wine he had drunk was more than he was accustomed to; it was rising to his head and he was becoming intoxicated.

—Well, said Ridoux, you give me no answer and you stare at me like an earthen-ware dog.

—What answer do you wish me to give you? except that I believe I am dreaming; in truth, I believe I am dreaming.

—Be more sincere. I do not like hypocrisy.

—You talk of a giddy little thing; I know no giddy thing. As to the rest, I have not quite made out what it is you wanted to tell me. I think that you have intended to make a joke about your old women.

—Ah, you, you never understand anything. Where did you come from?

—Why, from your school, from the seminary, and neither you nor my masters taught me that there.

—To me! to me! to me! you speak in such a manner to me? Oh clever fox! *Alopex, alopex.* Well, you are sharper than I am, cried the old Curé, striking the table and looking at Marcel with astonishment mingled with admiration. Why should I concern myself about your future? You will succeed, my dear fellow, you will succeed. Oh, oh, you are a master. A gray-beard like I cannot teach you anything. Jesus, Mary, Joseph! That is my nephew! My dear old Ridoux, Curé of St. Nicholas, allow me to congratulate you. Monsieur le Curé of Althausen, I swear you will become a bishop. Monseigneur, I drink your health!

LXVII
IN A GLASS

"The fumes of the wine were working in my veins; it was one of those moments of intoxication when everything one sees, everything one hears, speaks to us of the beloved."

A. DE MUSSET (*Confession d'un enfant du Siècle*).

They conversed for a long time still, and they drank too, so much so that Marcel went to his room with his brain charged with the fumes of the wine. He opened his window and breathed with delight the fresh air of night. While he gazed on the stars which were rising slowly in the sky, he tried to analyze the new sensation which he experienced. "How a few mouthfuls of liquor alter a man," he said to himself.

He felt himself to be totally different, and he allowed his thoughts to wander in an ocean of delights. His ardent and ecstatic imagination launched itself into space. Bright unknown worlds rose before him with their atmosphere saturated with warmth, with caresses, and with perfumes. He saw the future, and it appeared to him radiant. There were sons without number and feasts without end; the entire universe belonged to him. He flew from planet to planet without effort or fatigue, borne by a mysterious wing into the fields of the Infinite.

He discovered an unknown audacity, and all obstacles subsided before his powerful will. No more barriers, no more bolts, no more doors, no more pretences, no more social chains, no more terrible father, no more servant-mistress; Suzanne alone remained in all her youthful grace and her chaste nudity. For, after having wandered in boundless space, it was towards her that his hopes, his desires, his aspirations inclined. There was the soul and the body; happiness and life, sacred symbolical wedlock, the chosen vessel, the nubile maid ready for the husband. And he murmured the Song of Songs:

"Let her kiss me with kisses of her mouth,
For her teats are better than wine."

And it was at the very moment when he was about perhaps to be able to taste this exquisite cup, that he must go away. Go away! that is to say, leave her, she who had just cast a ray into his life. Go away, to obey a culpable ambition; to lose for ever this ravishing young girl! And the promises which he had made to himself; and the unsatisfied desires, and the boundless joys, the delicious troubles, the sweet evening talks, the hand sometimes squeezed in a moment of audacity; of all that but the memory would remain. Of all the intoxications of soul, of heart, of sense; of all those joys which should repay him for his wasted youth, for his fair years lost, he would preserve but remorse … remorse for having so senselessly let them go.

And all at once in the whirlwind of his ideas, he seized one as it passed by. He noticed during the day the Captain entering the *diligence* for Vic. It was, in fact, the time at which he drew his pay. He could not return till the following day. Suzanne then was alone with the old maid-servant. She went to bed late, he knew; perhaps she was still awake. He looked at his watch, it was not yet eleven o'clock; he still had a chance of seeing her. He cherished this idea; it pleased him and he was surprised that he had not thought of it before. Yes, certainly, he must see her, in order that she might keep the remembrance of him, as he was bearing away the memory of her.

What would be more delightful than to say to himself: "I hold the thoughts of a beautiful young girl, I hold her simple confidences; I possess the treasure of her sweet secrets."

And although there would never be between her and him but the pure and chaste sympathy of two souls, was not that enough, was not that a compensation, sufficient for the step which he was venturing?

And with the audacity of conception and the temerity of conduct of a man on the border of intoxication, he determined to put his fine project into execution immediately. His sense became inflamed the more he thought of it, and what had at first presented itself to him as a vague desire, soon became firmly fixed in his brain, and, in less than ten seconds, he had conceived the plan and weighed all the chances.

He decided that nothing was more simple, and that the only serious difficulty was to get out of the house without being heard. He still felt a few scruples; he poured himself out a glass of brandy.

—Let me swallow some courage, he said. What a singular piece of machinery is man, who imbibes in a few drops of liquid the dose of bravery which he lacks, and spirit which he needs.

And, in fact, he soon felt a generous warmth which ascended to his head; and his heart became anew surrounded little by little with that triple breast plate of brass, *robur triplex*, without which there is no hero.

He listened inside and out. All sounds were hushed; in the parsonage as in the village, everybody was asleep. He heard only the croaking of a legion of frogs which were sporting in the neighbouring marsh, and, far away, the bark of some farm-dog.

The night was splendid. The moon was rising behind the woods. That was a serious obstacle; but are there any serious obstacles for a man over-excited by drink? He did not even think of it; his mind was cheerful and content. If anyone encountered him in the night, wandering along the roads, what could they say? Had he not a perfect right like anybody else to take, the fresh air of evening? And, besides, might he not have been summoned by a sick person?

On the other hand, no more favourable moment would ever present itself for talking with Suzanne. His uncle was snoring in the next room, and his servant, supposing she was still awake, would she dare, while there was a guest at the parsonage, to come and assure herself if he was in his bed?

He took off his shoes, opened the door noiselessly and glided into the street.

He rapidly went round the parsonage, and he put on his shoes again only when he was at some distance, under the discreet shade of the limes.

Then he walked boldly on, keeping to the middle of the road, on the side, however, where the houses cast their shadow, and advanced with the step of a man who is going to accomplish a duty.

He arrived without any hindrance at the Captain's house. It was fully lighted up by the pale moon-light, and all the shutters were closed. Consequently, the side looking upon the garden was in the shadow, and there was Suzanne's room, the room hung with rose.

So he pursued his way at a rapid pace, entered the little path, bordered with hawthorn, and soon reached the clump of old chestnut-trees.

LXVIII
THE ROSE CHAMBER

"They are women already, they were so when they were born, but one guesses them so still, one reads it in their little thought, one comes across an end of thread here and there, which is like a revelation ... They are ... But forgive me, young ladies, I am afraid of going too far."

G. DROZ (*Entre nous*).

What man is there who has not experienced a delicious emotion on entering for the first time a young girl's room? Who has not breathed with voluptuous delight its sweet and chaste perfumes, and felt his heart soften in its fresh and fragrant atmosphere?

How pretty, neat, and harmonious is everything there. The most insignificant objects, the most common articles of furniture, have a mysterious and secret aspect there which makes one dream; one contemplates with transport all those nothings, all those little trifles, all those trinkets which young girls delight in, and because they have been touched by a white hand, they appear clothed in enchanting colours.

The fairy who lodges in this place has left a *something* of herself on all which surrounds her, and *that something* transforms all into jewels, even the least pin.

But that which above all else arrests the gaze, that which drives the blood to the head and causes the heart to beat, is the bed.

The young girl's bed, the sanctuary, the delicious nest of love.

There is the pillow on which her head reposes ... And then the question comes: What passes in the young head when, softly leaning on the warm down, she lets her thoughts travel into the land of dreams?

When slumber soft on all
Around thee is outpoured;
Oh Pepita, charming maid,
My love, of what think'st thou?

Here is the place of her body. Yes, it is there, beneath the discreet eider-down, that she hides her naked charms. And we begin to dream as well, and we say to ourselves that we would give much to be able to penetrate into this sanctuary at the hour when the divinity is going to bed.

Happy Gyges, lend me your ring that I may assist mutely and invisibly at the sweet mysteries of the night toilette.

She is here! She has given and received the evening kiss. "Sleep well," her father and mother have said, and the child replies: "Oh, yes, I am very sleepy."

Then she quickly shuts the door and breathes a sigh of satisfaction. She is in her own room, she is alone!

Alone! do you believe it? If so, you would be greatly mistaken, for this is the time when she receives her own visitors, and often there is a numerous company.

Oh, be reassured: these guests will not be able to compromise her; they are secret, silent and invisible for all else but her; she alone sees them, talks to them and listens to them.

It is at the summons of her thought that they hasten there, passive and obedient. Then she passes them in review one by one; she examines them from head to foot, she clothes and unclothes them at her will; never has a Captain of infantry, under orders for parade, made a more minute inspection of his conscripts.

Sometimes they come all in a crowd, giving themselves up with her, in the mysterious corners of her imagination, to the wildest frolics. Young people with a stiff collar, beardless sublieutenants, coxcombs with red hands, swells with white cuffs, little heads of wax and little souls of cardboard, run up, ran up, ye pretty puppets.

> Dance my loves
> You are but dolls.

And she makes them dance on every cord and every tune.

But soon the figures are effaced and blend into one. The pomatumed band disappear into space, whence there rises clearly the image of the chosen one.

He is young, he is dark or fair: she has seen him to-day; she looked at him, he smiled at her, he thinks her pretty.

Is she then always pretty? And quickly she goes to her mirror. Heavens! how badly her hair is done. How badly that ribbon sets! If she had put it in another place? And that little wandering lock; decidedly it must set off that. "Perhaps he would like me better if, instead of plaits, I had curls, and if instead of the brown dress, I put on the blue?"

He. Who is he? He is the imaginary lover, the handsome young man whom she has met in the street, he who turned round to look at her, or the one who was so charming at the last ball, or again the one who has just passed the window.

Who is he? Does she know? It is the one she is waiting for. The first who presents himself who is *handsome, young, intelligent and rich*. What does the rest matter provided he possesses all these qualities, and all these qualities he must possess.

Often she has never even seen him, but he is charming, and she feels that she loves him already.

And there are the brilliant displays of the future appearing, the enchanted palaces which are built out of the chapters of novels which never will be finished.

And thus every evening—wild adventures in the young brain, intrigues in embryo, meetings full of mystery, delightful terrors with phantom lovers, until at length a very palpable one presents himself, and comes and knocks at the door of reality.

Sometimes he is very far from the cherished dream. He is neither young, nor handsome, nor rich, nor intelligent. She rather makes a face, but she ends by taking him. It is a man.

And meanwhile mamma has said as she kisses her daughter's forehead, "Sleep well, my daughter," and she murmurs to papa, "What an angel of candour!"

LXIX
THE GUST OF WIND

"I turned my eyes instinctively towards the lighted window, and through the curtains which were drawn, I distinctly caught sight of a woman, dressed in white, with her hair undone, and moving like one who knows that she is alone."

G. DROZ (*Monsieur, Madame, et Bébe*).

Suzanne's room … but why should I describe the room?… let me describe Suzanne to you at this secret hour: I am sure that you would prefer me to do so.

The young people who read this, will do well to skip this chapter, it interests the men alone. Like the preacher who one day turned the women out of church, as he wanted to keep the men only, I warn over-chaste young ladies that these lines may shock….

Suzanne was preparing to go to bed.

To go to bed! That is not done quickly. You have, Mesdames, so many little things to do before going to bed. So Suzanne was going to and fro in her small room, attending to all these little details.

She was in a short petticoat, with her legs and arms bare and her little feet in slippers. I warned you that I had borrowed the ring of Gyges and I can tell you that I saw her calf and right above the knee, and all was like a sculptor's model. Beneath the thin, partly-open cambric her budding bosom rose and fell, marking a voluptuous valley on which, like the Shulamite's lover, one would never be weary to let one's kisses wander.

But on seeing the white plump shoulders, the graceful throat, and the neck on which was twisted a mass of little brown curls, and the back of velvet which had no other covering than the thick rolls of half-loosed hair, and the delicate hips which the little half-revealing petticoat closely pressed, one asked oneself where the kisses would run on for the longest time.

She was delicious like this and under every aspect, and undoubtedly she knew it, for every time she passed before the large glass of her wardrobe, she looked at herself in it and smiled. And she was quite right, for it was indeed the sweetest of sights.

A pretty woman is never insensible to the sight of her own charms. See therefore, what a love they have for mirrors. Habit, which palls in so many things, never palls in this; for her it is a sight always charming and always fresh. Very different to the forgetful lover or the sated husband, whose eyes and senses are so quickly habituated, she never grows weary of finding out that she is pretty, and making herself so; in truth a constant homage, earnest and conscientious.

Suzanne then examined herself full face, in profile, in three-quarters view, and behind, attentively and conscientiously, like an amateur judging a work of art, who cries at length, "Yes, it is all good, it is all perfect, there is nothing amiss." One could have believed that she saw herself again for the first time after many years.

At length, when the survey was completed, and the toilette finished, she let her petticoat slip down, opened her bed, put one knee upon it, and, the upper part of her body leaning forward on her hands, prepared to get in.

The lamp on the night-table, close beside her, threw its light no longer on her face.

But at the same instant a little zephyr taking her astern, caused the white tissue which English-women never mention, to gently undulate.

She noticed then that she had forgotten to shut her window.

"Heavens," cried Marcel to himself, for it was he, who perched on the rise of the road and armed with his good opera-glass, had just been witness of what I have narrated.

LXX
THE AMBUSCADE

"Be not discouraged either before obstacles, or before ill-will. Wait patiently. The sacred hour will sound for you and all the ways will be made smooth."

(Charge of Mgr. de Nancy).

Drawing near to the window, Suzanne distinguished in front of her, behind the open-work palisade, a dark motionless figure.

She immediately recognized the Curé.

Alarmed and trembling, she hastily drew back; but she heard a gentle cough, as if someone was calling and was afraid of being surprised.

"What is happening?" she said to herself, "what is he doing there?"

She covered herself hurriedly with a dressing-gown and drew near the casement again. Marcel, with his hat in his hand, bowed to her, and appeared to invite her by a sign to come down.

Again she drew back. She knew not what to think or what to do. She hesitated to comply with the priest's desire, and, on the other hand, she was afraid lest Marianne, or some neighbour, should happen to wake and catch the Curé of the village making signs, at that unseasonable hour, before her door, during her father's absence. God only knew what a scandal there would be then! and as tongues would wag, her father perhaps might hear of it, and what explanation could she give? already they were beginning to chatter about her absence from the services and their meetings on the road.

She was seized with terror and ran to put out the lamp, calculating that the Curé would withdraw.

But the Curé of Althausen had not undertaken this adventurous expedition to abandon it at the moment when he was attaining his object. Excited by the alcohol, by the dishabille of the charming young girl, and by all that he had just caught a sight of, emboldened by the night and the solitary place, he was waiting with impatience.

Therefore when Suzanne, trembling all over, drew near a second time to see if he was gone, he was at the same place, still bowing to her and calling her by signs. He was not tired, and with perfectly clerical obstinacy, multiplied his salutes and his signs.

She said to herself that there was doubtless some important motive for him to have decided, in spite of dangers and the proprieties, to require an interview with her in the middle of the night "Good God! could some misfortune have happened to my father?" The thought oppressed her mind. She hesitated no longer, put on a light petticoat, threw a shawl over her shoulders, and went downstairs.

LXXI
THE BREACH

"Who art thou, who knockest so loudly. Art thou Great
Love, to whom all must yield, for whom heroes sacrificed
(more than life) their very heart … Ah, if thou art he, let the
door be opened wide."

MICHELET (*L'Amour*).

She saw at once that he was all in a fever.

—What has happened? she said. You have seen my father?

—Nothing has happened, Mademoiselle; as to your father, I saw him
this morning getting into a carriage: I believe that he is well.

—But what is it then? what is it? do not hide anything from me.

—I am hiding nothing from you, Mademoiselle, nothing grievous has
happened. Be comforted. I was passing by in my walk, I saw the light, I
observed you, your window was partly open. I stopped and said to myself:
Perhaps I can make a sign to Mademoiselle Durand that I am going away.

—Oh, Heavens, I am trembling all over.... What! you are going away?
And where? And when?

—To-morrow morning, Mademoiselle, after Mass.

—For ever?

—Perhaps.

—You are leaving Althausen so, without saying good-bye to your
parishioners, to your friends!

—I have no friends, Mademoiselle, I have only you, who are willing to
hear me some … friendship; only you, who have sometimes thought of the
poor solitary at the parsonage, therefore I thank you for it from the bottom
of my heart, and I wanted to bid you … farewell.

—But why this sudden and unexpected departure?

—A more important cure is offered me, Mademoiselle, and I have, like others, a little grain of ambition.

—Oh, I understand, Monsieur, and let me congratulate you on this change in your fortune. Is it far?

—Nancy, Mademoiselle.

—Nancy! I am glad of it on your account. You will have distractions there which you have not here. I almost envy you.

—Do not envy me, Mademoiselle, for I carry away death in my soul. I am sorrowful as Christ at Golgotha. I spoke to you of ambition. It is false, I have no ambition. Other motives than miserable calculations compel me to depart.

—Motives ... serious?

—You will understand them, Mademoiselle, for I must confess it to you, and that I should not do if I was to remain in this parish. But from the day I saw you, I have felt myself drawn towards you by an invincible sympathy. Oh, be not disturbed. Let not my words offend you; it is the fondness which I should have felt for a dearly-loved sister, if God had given me one. Believe it truly, Mademoiselle, the spotless calyx of the lily, the emblem of purity, is not more chaste than my thoughts when they fly towards you, for when I think of you, I think of the queen of angels; that is why I wished to see you again and bid you farewell.

—I thank you, sir.

—I wished to say to you: Farewell! I go away, but tell me, not if I may ask to see you sometimes again—I dare not ask so great a favour—but if I shall have the right to mingle my memory with yours, my thought with your thought; tell me if you wish me to remain your friend though far away. We leave one another, we separate, but is that a reason why all should end? May we not write, give one another advice, follow one another from afar on the arduous road of life?

It is so sweet, when we are alone, when the heart is sad, when the heaven is dark and the tears come slowly to the eyes, to dream that away there, in a little corner behind the horizon, there is a sister-soul to our soul, which perhaps, at that very moment, leaps towards us also and murmurs across space: "Friend, I think of you." We feel less abandoned and less alone.

—Yes, that is true, I understand you.

—It is the communion of souls, dear Suzanne, sweeter than all the pleasures of the body, because it is holy and pure, it is the Ark of the

Covenant, the gate of Heaven. Tell me, will you? Are you willing that we should follow one another thus in life? You do not answer....

—Listen, sir, listen, there is someone in the road.

—There are footsteps, said Marcel, after he had listened. Yes, there are footsteps. Someone comes. I must not be seen here.... Farewell, Mademoiselle, farewell.

—Do not go away. That would be the means of compromising us both, for they must have heard our voices, and your departure would attract suspicions.

—What shall I do? I cannot remain here.

—They cannot have seen us yet: Come in. Under this arbour you will be safe from any gaze.

—What! said Marcel, you wish...?

—I beseech you, come. This village is full of evil-minded people. It is more prudent for both of us.

She turned the key, and Marcel glided like a shadow through the half-open gate, quickly crossed the borders, and threw himself under the arbour.

Suzanne closed the gate again and rejoined him.

LXXII
THE ASSAULT

"Be mine, be my sister, for I am all thine,
And well I deserve thee, for long have I loved."

A. DE VIGNY (*Eloa*).

They were standing up under the dark arbour. One close to the other, excited, panting: they could scarce get their breath again. Does their heart beat so hard because there is someone in the path? Silence!

The cricket, just by their side, sends forth from under the grass his soft monotonous cry, and down there in the neighbouring ditch the toad lifts his harsh voice. Silence!

A noise in the road, faint at first as the murmur of the wind, increases. It comes near. It is the cautious hesitating step of someone listening. It comes nearer and stops. Silence! The philosopher cricket continues his song, the amorous toad his poem.

Behind the branches of honeysuckle they watch attentively, and can see without being seen. A shadow passes slowly by, with its head turned towards the dark arbour. Suzanne made a movement of surprise;—Your servant, she said.

—Silence, murmured Marcel; and he seizes a hand which he keeps within his own.

Veronica slowly walked on.

When she reached the gate, she pushed it as if to assure herself if it was open.

—Well, there is an impertinence, said Suzanne. Who can have made her suspect that you were here?

Marcel, for reply, pressed the hand which he was holding.

Finding the gate closed, the servant continued her road, then all at once returned, stopped for a few seconds facing the arbour, and at length disappeared behind the chestnut-trees.

They followed the sound of her footsteps, which was soon lost in the silence, and found themselves alone, hearing nothing but the beatings of their own heart.

—Let us remain, said Suzanne in a low voice, we must not go out yet. Really, that is the most impertinent creature I have ever seen. By what right does she spy on you thus?

—Dear child, do you not know that these old servants are on the track of every scandal, jealous of all beauty and all virtue. She will have noticed our frequent interviews, and has imagined a world of iniquities. Nevertheless, I bless her, yes, I bless her, since I owe to her the joy of finding myself in this tête-à-tête with you. See, dear child, how strange is destiny, which is none other but the hand of God—for we must be blind not to recognize in all these things the finger of divine Providence—it is precisely the efforts made to put an obstacle between us, to prevent us, me from fulfilling my duties of a pastor, you those of a Christian, which have been the cause of our sweet intimacy. Your father forbids you to assist at the Holy Sacrifice, and you come to me to ask for counsel. This servant pursues us with her envious hate, and obliges us to take refuge like guilty lovers beneath this dark arbour. Almighty God, thanks, thanks. But what a strange situation! If anyone were to surprise us, the whole world would accuse us, and yet what is surer than our conscience? You see plainly, dear child, that we cannot separate thus, and that, whatever happens, we must not remain strangers to one another.

Suzanne did not answer, and he, emboldened by this silence, pressed between his the hand which she abandoned to him.

—I was so much accustomed to see you in our church that, when you ceased to come there, it seemed to me that everything was in mourning. You were the most charming and the chastest ornament of it. When I went up into the pulpit, it was for you that I preached, and when I turned towards my flock to bless them, it was you alone, sweet lamb, that I blessed in the name of the Father. You understand now, why I shall go away enveloped in sorrow.

—But, sir, I do not deserve the honour which you do me, and I am unworthy to occupy your thoughts in this way.

—Do not say that, for since I have seen you, you have become, without my knowing how, the joy of my life, the source from which I draw my sweetest and most holy pleasures. With the memory of you, I lull myself in the Infinite. I see Heaven and the angels, I dream of Seraphims who resemble you, who bear me on their diaphanous wings into the abode where all is joy and love … heavenly love, dear Suzanne, love like that of the angels for the

Virgin, the mother, eternally pure, of our sweet Saviour. You see, you have no reasons to be offended with my dreams. You are not offended at them, are you?

—Why should I be offended at them, said Suzanne softly. Can one be offended with dreams?

—You remember that night, when, alone as we are now, I allowed myself in a moment of pious transport, to bear to my lips your lovely hand. I have often blushed at it.... I have blushed at it, because I thought that you might have mistaken that respectful kiss. I kissed it as I should have kissed the hem of a queen's robe, if that queen had been a saint, as I should have kissed the feet of the Virgin, as Magdalena kissed those of Christ, as I kiss it at this moment, dear, dear Suzanne.

And his lips rested on that little warm, quivering, feverish hand, and they could no more be separated from it.

And, when at length he withdrew his mouth from it, he found that Suzanne was so near to him that he heard the beatings of her heart.

—Leave me, said the imprudent girl, I entreat you, leave me. Oh, why are you doing that?

And she tried with vain efforts to loosen herself from the embrace.

But he murmured softly:

—Leave you, oh, never; you shall be my companion in life as you are my betrothed before the Eternal. Leave you, dear Suzanne, sweet mystic rose, chosen vessel. See, there is something stronger than all the laws and all the proprieties; it is a look from you. Why do you repulse me? I speak to you as to the Virgin, and I kiss your knees. Chaste betrothed of the Levite, let me espouse you before God.

She struggled with all her might, excited and maddened. But what can the dove do in the talons of the hawk! Pressed to his breast by his vigorous arms, it was in vain that she asked for pity. Hell might have opened, ere he would have dropped his prey.

The struggle lasted several minutes, passionate, silent, ardent. Woman is weak. Soon nothing was heard ... a sob ... and all died away in the dense shade.

The startled cricket was silent, and it alone might have counted the sighs, while in the neighbouring ditch the toad unwearied continued its love-song.

LXXIII
AUDACES FORTUNA JUVAT

"If you have done wrong, rebuke yourself sharply:
If you have done well, have satisfaction."

SAINT FRANÇOIS DE SALLES (*Traité de l'Amour Divin*).

Marcel reached the parsonage without hindrance. Veronica had not yet returned. He congratulated himself on that, and went up the stair-case which led to his room with the light step of a happy man, locked his door, and began to laugh like a madman.

Everything was safe; only there was down there in a corner of the village, an honour lost.

—Is it really you, Marcel, is it really you, he said, who have just played so great a game, and won the trick?

And he laughed, and he rubbed his hands, and he would willingly have danced a wild saraband, if he had not been afraid of making a noise.

He listened in the next room where his uncle was in bed, and heard his loud breathing.

—And the hag who is watching still beneath the limes! And the father who is at Vic, and who, I doubt not, is snoring too. Come, all goes well! all goes well!

But he stopped, ashamed of himself.

—Decidedly, he said to himself, I have become in a few days utterly bad. I did not believe that it was possible to make such rapid progress in evil. But nonsense. Is it evil? Has not God made wine to be drunk, flowers to be plucked, and women to be loved? As to that weather-beaten old soldier, why should I feel any pity on his account? He has been insolent, he has detested me without my ever having done anything to him; I have loved his daughter, his daughter has loved me, we are quits. I do not see why I should distress myself about an adventure which would make so many people happy, and for which all my brethren would have very quickly sold the sacred Host and the holy Pyx besides. Ah, my dear uncle, good father Ridoux, sleep, sleep in peace. How greatly am I your debtor for what you have done for me, unwittingly and in spite of yourself; for, have you not, by urging me to drink more than is my custom, in order to draw my secret from me, given me the courage to undertake what I should never have dared to dream of? *Audaces fortuna juvat.* Oh, Providence! Providence! She is mine, the girl with the dark eyes is mine!

He heard a slight noise in the corridor.

—Good never comes alone, he continued, it always has evil for an escort. Behind the sweet form of the angel, the grinning face of Satan. He is coming upstairs and knocks at the door.

He had not lighted his lamp again, and he carefully refrained from answering. He heard Veronica, trying to open the door and calling him in a low voice. But he pretended to be deaf, and quietly got into bed, all the while cursing his accomplice, and thinking of the clumsy trap into which he had fallen like a fool, and of that thick and filthy spider's web where, like an unwary and silly fly, he had daubed his wings.

What a difference between the chaste resistance of Suzanne, her tears and her defeat, and the hideous advances of that old courtesan of the sacristy!

In place of that unclean creature, accomplished in crime, oozing hypocrisy from every pore, he had an adorable, loving, charming mistress, such as he had never dared to dream of. And all this alteration in a few hours! because he had faced it out, because, excited by intoxication, he had taken his courage in both hands, and because he had dared.

Oh, why had he not dared ere this? He would not be under the infamous yoke of his servant. And how many priests, he said to himself, for want of a little boldness, are devoted to a degrading concubinage with faded old spinsters!

He was not without uneasiness. How could he see Suzanne again, situated as he was between the jealous watching of the servant and the vigilance of the father? And above all, how could he discard his uncle's entreaties, and refuse an unexpected promotion, without arousing suspicion in high quarters? For, more than ever, he wished to remain at Althausen and keep the treasure which had just caused him so much anxiety. Yes, he saw them accumulating on his head, swooping from all parts and under all aspects: Veronica, Durand, Ridoux, the Bishop, the gossips, scandal, dishonour.

But, after all, what did it matter to him? The essential is that he was in possession of Suzanne, that Suzanne was his, that he had the most charming of mistresses, and he was indifferent to all the rest.

To see her again readily and without danger, to contrive other interviews, and above all to act prudently, was what he must think of. The chief step was taken, the rest would come of its own accord.

With Suzanne's consent all obstacles could be smoothed away, and clever is he who succeeds in barring the way to two lovers who are determined to see one another again.

The old counsellor Lamblin, who in his capacity of magistrate was aware of that, said long ago:

> "To safely guard a certain fleece,
> In vain is all the watchman's care;
> 'Tis labour lost, if Beauty chance
> To feel a strange sensation there."

It was on this indeed that Marcel calculated; and, smiling, he slept the sleep of the just and dreamed the most rosy dreams.

LXXIV
BEFORE MASS

"You think that we ought not to break in two this puppet which is called Public Opinion, and sit upon it."

EUG. VERMEESCH (*L'Infamie humaine*).

A loud and well-known voice roused him unpleasantly from his dreams.

—Well, well, lazy-bones, still in bed when the sun is risen! You are not thinking then of going away? You go to bed the first, and you get up the last. I, a poor old invalid, am giving you an example of activity. Ah, young people! young people! you are not equal to us. Come, come you can rub your eyes to-morrow. Get up! Get up!

—How early you are, my dear uncle; my Mass has not yet rang.

—Have you no preparations to make for departure?

—For departure. Is it for to-day then?

—Do you wish to put it off to the Greek Kalends?

—To-day! repeated Marcel. I did not think really that it was so soon.

He dressed with the prudent delays of a man who says to himself: Let us see, let us consider carefully what we must do.

—You don't look satisfied, resumed Ridoux; I bring you honour, fortune and success, and you look sulky.

—Honour, fortune and success. Those are very fine words!

—It is with fine words that we do fine things, and one of them is, it appears, to unmoor you from this place.

—The fact is, replied Marcel, that I have reflected to-night; and, after well considering everything, I am perfectly well off, and have no desire to go away to be worse off elsewhere.

—Hey! what do you say?

—My parish, humble as it is, is not so bad as you think. The people are simple, kind and affable. I love peace and tranquillity, and I tell you, between ourselves, that to be Curé in a large town has no attractions for me.

—What stuff are you telling me now?

—Your town Curés are full of meanness and intrigues. The little I have seen of them has disgusted me for ever. They spy one upon another. It is who shall prejudice a fellow-priest in order to supplant him, or play the zealot in Monseigneur's presence. When I was the Bishop's secretary, hardly a day passed without my being witness to some shameful piece of tale bearing. You must weigh all your words, cover your looks and have a care even of your gestures. The slightest imprudence is immediately commented on, exaggerated, embellished and retailed at head-quarters. The Vicar General is the spy in general.

Marcel uttered the truth.

The position of the priest is a difficult one; he is surrounded with the malevolence of enemies. But the priest's chief enemy, is the priest. As a body, they march together, close, compact, disciplined, defending their rights and the honour of the flag, resenting individually the insults offered to all, and all rejoicing at the success of each. As individuals, they spy on one another, are jealous of one another, fight, accuse and judge one another; and they do all this hypocritically and by occult ways. These hatreds and intrigues do not go outside the sanctuary domains. It is a strange world which stirs within our world, a society within a society, a state within the State. It is the behind-the-scenes of the temple, and it stretches from the sacristy to the parsonage, from the parsonage to the Palace. The profane world suspects nothing; it passes unconcernedly by without dreaming that tempests are rumbling by its side. But, like the revolutions raised by the eunuchs of the Seraglio, the intrigues of the sacristy have been known to change the face of nations.

The priest is the spy upon the priest.

Misfortune to the cassock which unbuttons itself before another cassock. The old priests are aware of this, and when they are among themselves, they draw the folds of their black robe close, carefully hiding the least tell-tale opening. But the young ones, simple and unreserved, often let themselves be taken. They sound them and turn them up, and soon know what they have underneath. In order to please Monseigneur and to deserve the good graces of the Palace, there are few priests who resist the temptation to sell their brother-priest, and are not ready to deny Jesus like Peter the good apostle, the first and the model of the Roman pontiffs, three times before cock-crow, that is to say before Monseigneur gets up.

—No, that will not do for me, added Marcel; if I am poor here, at least I am free.

—Pshaw! You did not raise all those objections to me yesterday.

—I have reflected, my dear uncle, as I have had the honour of telling you.

—Your reflections are fine. Well, whether you have reflected or not, is all the same to me. I have taken it into my head that you should go, and you shall go. I will make you happy in spite of yourself, for I have reflected also, and more than ever I said to myself that you most go. Do you want me to enumerate the reasons?

—The same as yesterday I have no doubt.

—No, there is one more, and that is worth all the rest.

—I know what you are going to say to me, but I have my answer all ready. Speak.

—What! at your age! in your position! Are you not ashamed to fall into errors which would scarcely be pardonable in a seminarist? Ah! you want the dots on the i's, well I am going to place them.

—Place them, uncle, place them.

—Had you not enough girls then in the village without going to lay a claim on the one yonder? On a well-educated young lady, whose fall will cause a scandal, the daughter of an enemy, of a Voltairian, almost a radical, a gaol-bird in fine who will be happy to seize the occasion to raise a terrible outcry, and to proclaim your conduct to the four quarters of the horizon. You see I know all.

—And who has informed you so correctly?

—I know all, I tell you. You can therefore keep your temper. Will you act like the Curé of Larriques?

—What is there in common between the Curé of Larriques and me?

—You ought to humble yourself before God. If you wanted a young girl, if your immoderate appetites were not satisfied with what you had under your nose, is there no cautious person in the village who would have been proud and happy to be of service to you, and whom you could have married to some clodhopper or to some Chrysostom ready for the opportunity; whilst that one, whom will you give her to? There will be an uproar, I tell you, and that will be abomination.

—Really, uncle, said Marcel pale with anger, if anyone heard us, would they believe that they were listening to the conversation of two ecclesiastics? you talk of these shameful things as if you were talking of the Gospel. In fact, I do not know which to be the more astonished at, the freedom of your talk or the sad opinion which you have of me. But I see whence all this emanates. Do you take me then for a bad priest?

—What is that? Do you take me for a simpleton? for one of Molière's uncles?... Enough of playing a farce. You do not take me in, my good fellow. I told you yesterday that you were cleverer than I; you did not see then that I was joking? Your mask is still too transparent. One sees the tears behind the grinning face. No tragic aim. Come down from this stage on which you strut in such a ridiculous manner, and let us talk seriously like plain citizens.

—Or bad priests!

—Be silent. The bad priests, that is to say the clumsy priests, which is all the same, are in your cassock; and the clumsy ones are those who allow themselves to be caught. You have been caught, my son; and caught by whom? by your cook. Ha! Ha!

—Are you not ashamed to listen to the tale-bearing and calumny of that horrible woman?

—Horrible! Be quiet, you are blind. It is your conduct which is horrible. To concoct such intrigues!

—I concoct no intrigue. And when that does occur; when my feelings of respect, of esteem, of friendship for a young person endowed with virtues and graces, change into a sweeter feeling: at all events, if my position compels me to conceal my inclinations from the world, I shall have no need to blush for them when face to face with myself, that is to say: with my dignity as a man. While your allusions, your instigation to certain intimacies, which in order to be more closely hidden are only the more abominable and degrading, inspire me only with disgust.

—Oh, Holy Spirit, enlighten him. He is wandering, he is a triple fool. When I suspected, when I discovered, when I saw that you were entering on a perilous path, I gave you yesterday the advice which a priest of my age has the right to give to one of yours, especially when he is, as I am, regardful of his future.

—I am as regardful of it as you.

—Cease your idle words. Have you decided to go?

—No, uncle, I am well off here, and I stay here.

—Well off! Mouldy in your vices and obscurity. Wallowing, like Job, on your dung-heap. Roll yourself in your filth: for my part I know what course remains for me to take.

—You will do what you think proper.

—I am sure of it. But you, instead of having the excellent cure which was destined for you, you shall have one lower still than this where you can wallow at your ease in your idleness, your nothingness and your vices, for, I swear to you by my blessed patron, that if I go away without you, you shall not remain here for forty-eight hours. I will have you recalled by the Bishop. You laugh. You know me all the same; you know when I say *yes* it is *yes*. A word is enough for Monseigneur, you know. *Magister dixit.*

Marcel knew the character of the old Curé well enough to know that he was capable of keeping his word. Fearing to irritate him more by his obstinacy, he thought it better to appear to yield.

—It is time for Mass, he said. We will talk about that again.

—Go, my son, and pray to the Holy Spirit.

LXXV
DURING MASS

"I have my rights of love and portion of the sun;
Let us together flee ..."

A. DE VIGNY (*La Prison*).

It will easily be credited that Marcel's thoughts had little in common with the Holy Eucharist. He would have been a very ungrateful lover, if his whole soul had not flown towards Suzanne. This was then his chief preoccupation, while he murmured the long *Credo*, partook of Christ, and recited his prayers.

What should he decide? that was his second. Should he go away? That meant fortune, reconciliation with the Bishop, putting his foot in the stirrup of honours. Young, intelligent, learned, what was there to stop him?

But that meant separation from Suzanne: saying farewell to all those divine delights which he had just tasted. He had hardly time to moisten his parched lips in the cup, before the cup was shattered. He was truly in love, for he should have said to himself: "There are other cups." But for him there was but one. Uncle Ridoux, the Bishop and greatness might go to the devil. The promised cure and the episcopal mitre might go to the devil too. Did he not possess the most precious of treasures, the most enviable blessing, the supplement and complement of everything, the ambition of every young man, the desire of every old man, of every man who has a heart: a young, lovely, modest, loving, intelligent and adored mistress. But what might not be the result of that love? What drama, what tragedy, and perhaps what ludicrous comedy, in which he, the priest, would play the odious and ridiculous character?

This love, which plunged him into an ocean of delights, would it not plunge him also into an abyss of misfortunes?

Could it proceed for long without being known and remarked?

Scandal, shame, and death perhaps, a terrible trinity, were they waiting not at his door?

For the viper which harboured at his hearth, had its piercing glassy eye fixed unweariedly on him; and how could he crush the viper?

What could he do? What could he venture? He remembered hearing of priests who had fled away with young girls whom they had seduced, and he thought for an instant that he would carry off Suzanne and fly.

Willingly would he have left behind him his honour and his reputation, willingly would he have torn his priestly robe on the sharp points of infamy and scandal, willingly would he have quitted for ever that cursed parsonage where shame and humiliation, vice and remorse were henceforth installed; but Suzanne, would she follow him?

Then, had he well weighed the mortifications which await the apostate priest!

To be nameless in society, with no future, repulsed, despised, scoffed at by all!

Should he, like the Père Hyacinth, go and found a free church in some corner of the republic, and rove through Europe, like him, to confer about morality, the rights of women and virtue?

Would not poverty come and knock at his door? Poverty with a beloved wife! It would appear a hideous and terrifying spectre, chilling in its livid approach and in its kisses of love.

To struggle against these obstacles he would need high energy and high courage, and he felt that courage and energy were lacking in him, the miserable coward, who had shamefully succumbed to the clumsy artifices of a lascivious woman, who had allowed the first fruits of his virginity and his youth to be lost in shameful debauch; while close by there was an adorable maiden whose heart was beating in unison with his own.

Thus did his reflection lead him till the end of the Gospel, and when he said the *Deo gratias* he had as yet decided nothing.

LXXVI
AWAKENING

"We never permit with impunity the mind to analyze the liberty to indulge in certain loves; once begin to reflect on those deep and troublesome matters which are called *passion* and *duty*, the soul which naturally delights in the investigation of every truth, is unable to stop in its exploration."

ERNEST FRYDEAU (*La Comtesse de Chalis*).

When Marcel had gone away, Suzanne, when she had quietly shut the street-door, by which she had gone out, went upstairs to her room and sat down on the side of her bed.

She asked herself if she had not just been the sport of an hallucination, if it was really true that a man had gone out of the house, who had held her in his arms, to whom she had yielded herself.

Everything had happened so rapidly, that she had had no time to think, to reflect, to say to herself: "What does he want with me?" no time even to recover herself.

A kiss, a violent emotion, a transient indignation, a struggle for a few seconds, a sharp pain, and that was all; the crime was consummated, she had lost her honour, and that was love!

She wished not to believe it, but her disordered corsage, her dishevelled hair upon her bare shoulders, her crumpled dressing-gown, and more than all that, the violent leaping of her heart, told her that she was not dreaming.

He was gone, the priest; he had fled away into the night, happy and light of heart, leaving her alone with her shame, and the ulcer of remorse in her soul.

And then big tears rolled down her cheeks and fell upon her breasts, still burning with his feverish caresses. "It is all over! it is all over. Where is my virginity?"

Weep, poor girl, weep, for that virginity is already far away, and nothing, it is said, flees faster than the illusion which departs, if it be not a virginity which flies away.

And a vague terror was mingled with her remorse.

The first apprehension which strikes brutally against the edifice of illusions of the woman who has committed a fault, is the anxiety regarding the opinion of the man who has incited her to that fault; I am speaking, be it understood, of one in whom there remains the feeling of modesty, without which she is not a woman, but an unclean female.

When she awakes from her short delirium, she says to herself:

—What will he think of me? What will he believe? Will he not despise me?

And she has good grounds for apprehension; for often (I believe I have said so already) the contempt of her accomplice is all that remains to her.

And then, what man is there who, after having at length possessed *illegitimately* the wife or the maiden so long pursued and desired, does not say to himself in the morning, when his fever is dissipated, when the bandage which hitherto has covered the eyes of love *suppliant*, is unbound from the eyes of love *satisfied*, when the *unknown* which has so many charms, has become the *known* that we despise, when of the rosy, inflated illusion there remains but a yellow skeleton: "She has given herself to me trustingly and artlessly; but might she not have given herself with equal facility to another, if I had not been there? for in fact … what devil…?"

A strange question, but one which unavoidably takes up its abode in the heart, and waits to come forth and be present one day on the lips, at the time when Satiety gives the last kick to the last house of cards erected by Pleasure.

And it is thus that after doing everything to draw a woman into our own fall, we are discontented with her for her sacrifice and for her love.

For there comes a moment when the *angel* for whom one would have given one's life, the *divinity* for whom one would have sacrificed country, family, fortune, future, is no more than a common mistress, ranked in the ordinary lot with the rest, and for whom one would hesitate to spend half-a-sovereign.

Have you not chanced sometimes to follow with an envious eye, on some fresh morning in spring or on a lovely autumn evening, the solitary walk of a loving couple? They go slowly, hand in hand, avoiding notice, selecting the shady and secret paths, or the darkest walks in the woods. He is handsome, young and strong; she is pretty and charming, pale with emotion, or blushing with modesty. What things they murmur as they lean one towards another, what sweet projects of an endless future, what oaths which ought to be eternal, sworn untiringly, lip on lip.

"One of those noble loves which have no end."

Happy egotists. They think but of themselves; all, except themselves, is insupportable to them, all but themselves wearies and weighs upon them. The universe is themselves, life is the present which glides along, and in order to delay the present and enjoy it at their ease, they have no scruple in mortgaging the future. And they go on, listening to the divine harmony, the mysterious poem which sings in their own heart, of youth and love.

You have envied them; who would not envy them? It is happiness which passes by. Make way respectfully. What! you smiled sorrowfully! Ah, it is because like me, you have seen behind these poor trustful children, following them as the *insultores* used to follow the triumphal chariot of old, a demon with sinister countenance who with his brutal hands will soon roughly tear the veil woven of fancies; the Reality, who is there with his rags, getting ready to cast them upon their bright tinsels of gauze and spangles.

Wait a few years, a few months, perhaps only a few weeks. What has become of those handsome lovers so tenderly entwined? They swore mouth to mouth an endless love. Where are they? Where are their loves?

As well would it be worth to ask where are the leaves of autumn which the evening breeze carried away last year.

"But where are the snows of yester-year?"

What! already, it is finished! And yet he had sworn to love her always. Yes, but she also had sworn to be always amiable. Which of the two first forfeited the oath?

There has been then a tragedy, a drama, despair, tears? Nonsense! Those who had sworn to die one for the other, one fine day parted as strangers.

The charming young girl whom you saw passing by, proud and radiant on the arm of that artless stripling, see, here she comes, a little weary, a little faded, but still charming, on the arm of that cynical Bohemian.

That poetical school-girl, who smiled and scattered daisies on the head of her lover, as he knelt before her, has become the adored wife of a dull tallow-chandler; and the other one, who took the ivy for her emblem, and who said to her sweetheart: "I cling till death!" has clung to and separated from half-a-dozen others without dying, and has finished by fastening herself to a rheumatical old churchwarden, peevish but substantial.

And the lover? He is no better: he has loved twenty since; the deep sea of oblivion has passed between them, and among so many vanished mistresses, can he precisely remember her name?

Suzanne did not say all this to herself, she was ignorant of the whirlpools of life, but she felt instinctively that she was about to be precipated into an abyss.

She was not perverse, she was merely frivolous and coquettish, but she had received a vicious education. Her imagination only had been corrupted, her heart had remained till then untainted. It was a good ear of corn which somehow or another had made its way into the field of tares.

She reproached herself bitterly therefore for the shameful facility with which she had yielded herself to the priest, and she sought for an excuse to try and palliate her fault in her own eyes.

But she was unable to discover any genuine excuses. A young girl is pardoned for yielding herself to her lover in a moment of forgetfulness and excitement, because she hopes that marriage will atone for her fault.

But what had she to claim? What could she expect from this Curé?

Again a young wife is pardoned for deceiving an old husband, or a husband who is worthless, debauched and brutal, and for seeking a friend abroad whom she cannot find at her fire-side; but she? Whom had she deceived? Her father, who though severe, adored her. Whom had she dishonoured? The white hairs of that worthy, brave old man.

She saw clearly that she could find no excuse, and she was compelled to confess that she ought to feel ashamed of herself; but what affected her most was the thought that her lover, the priest, must have been extremely surprised at his victory himself, and that if he too were to attempt to find an excuse for her conduct, he could discover none either. But in proportion as she felt astonished at her shame, as she saw into what a corner she had been driven, as she dreaded the man's scorn, for whom she had fallen so low, did she feel her love grow greater.

LXXVII
CONSOLATIONS

"Every fault finds its excuse in itself. This is the sophistry in which we are richest. The struggle of good and evil is serious, and really painful, only in the case of a man who has been brought up in a position where actions, deeds and thoughts have had the power of self-examination."

EMILE LECLERCQ (*Une fille du peuple*).

Before her fault, or if you prefer it, her fall, this was but the odd caprice of an ardent, amorous, passionate young girl whose feelings are exhilarated and excited by a licentious imagination, continually nourished by the senseless reading of the adventures of heroes, who have existed nowhere but in the brain of novelists.

Therefore, eager for the unknown, she hastens to lay hold of the first rascal who comes forward, having a little self-assurance, talkativeness and good looks, and who will be for one day the ideal she has dreamed of, if he knows how to brazen it out.

"Every woman is at heart a rake," said the great poet Alexander Pope.

And as for those who, in spite of the heat of an ungovernable temperament, remain virtuous and chaste, we must scarcely be pleased at them on that account.

It is simply because they have not had the opportunity to sin. The opportunity, which makes the thief, is also the touchstone of women's virtue. Therefore, when this blessed opportunity presents itself, although it is said to be bald, they well know how to find other hairs on it by which they seize and do not let it go again.

Certainly there are exceptions, and I am far from saying *Ab una disce omnes*.

You, Madame, for instance, who read me, I am convinced that you are not in that category of women of whom the Englishman Pope made this wicked remark.

Suzanne felt now possessed by a wild infatuation for the man to whom she had yielded herself almost without love; and do not young girls frequently yield themselves in this manner? She felt herself attracted towards him by the purely physical and magnetic phenomenon which impels the female towards the male; for we shall try in vain and talk in vain, raise ourselves on our dwarfish heels, talk of the ethereal essence of our soul and the quintessence of our feelings, idealize woman and deify love, there always comes a moment when we become like the brute, and when the passion of seraphims cannot be distinguished in anything from that of man.

........who goes by night In some street obscure, to a lodging
low and dark.

Suzanne certainly had not taken note of her impressions.

Attracted towards Marcel by his sympathetic beauty, by his sweet and unctuous voice, and especially by the vague sorrow displayed on his countenance, perhaps still more by the opposition and slanders of her father, she had allowed herself to be won, before she know where she was going.

She was far from any carnal thought, and she would have been considerably surprised if anyone had told her that the priest loved her otherwise than as a sister is loved.

But that is not what we men understand by love.

The Werthers who regard their mistress as a sacred divinity whom we ought to touch with trembling, are rare. They are not met again after eighteen. Marcel was more than eighteen; therefore he had found his desires become more inflamed than ever in the presence of his mistress.

If he had been hesitating and timid, like Charlotte's lover, I do not doubt that she would have found time to gather within herself the force necessary to resist him, but she felt herself mastered before even she had recovered from her terror and confusion.

I do not wish to try and excuse her, but she repented; and how far more worthy of respect is the repentance of certain fallen women than the haughty virtue of certain others.

And, perceiving that she found no excuse for her fault, Suzanne tried to deceive herself by exalting above measure the worth of the man who had ruined her.

—He is no ordinary man after all, she said to herself, and we do not love the man we wish. It does honour to the heart to repose its love rightly. It is natural then that I should say, that I should confess to myself, since I cannot confess it to others. Yes, I love him; who would not love him? Yes, I have given myself to him; but who in my place would have had the power to resist him?

Is it not a fact that everybody here loves him? Have I not observed the looks of all these village girls fixed on him with eager desire? It would have been easy for him to make his choice among the prettiest, but he has seen me only.

He is a priest, but what does that matter? is he not a man? And this man as handsome as a god, I feel that I love him much more than a lover ought to be loved; for I love not only for the happiness of loving him and being loved by him, but also from pride, because I am proud of him, because I admire his fine and noble nature, so open, so sweet, so charming, so audacious, which, led astray into this false and thankless position, must find itself so unhappy. Then, I was so affected the first time that my look met his, I felt that all my being was his, but especially my inward feelings, my spirit, my soul, and my sentiments.

And in this way there is a great difference in man and in woman in their love.

In man, possession most frequently causes passion to disappear; the reality kills the ideal; the awakening, the dream; in woman on the other hand, it nearly always enhances, for the first time at any rate, the fascination of being loved, for she attaches herself to him in proportion to the trouble, the shame, the sacrifice.

For with man, love is but an episode, while with woman it is her whole life.

LXXVIII
FALSE ALARM

"She's there, say'st thou? What, can that be the maid
Whose pure, fresh face attracted me but now,
When I beheld her in her home; alas,
And can the flower so quickly fade?"...

DELPHINE GAY.

Suzanne, who had passed a sleepless night, was fast asleep in the morning, when her father burst into her room like a hurricane.

She woke with a start, all pale and trembling; she tried nevertheless to assume the most innocent and the calmest air.

—What is the matter, papa?

But Durand did not answer. He surveyed the room with a scrutinizing eye, apparently, interrogating the furniture and the walls, as if he were asking them if they had not been witnesses of some unusual event.

But if walls at times have eyes and ears, they have no tongue; they cannot relate the things they have seen. Then he turned towards his daughter in such a singular way that Suzanne dropped her eyes and felt she was going to faint.

—Suzanne, he demanded of her abruptly, did you hear anything in the night?

—I! she said with the most profound astonishment.

—Yes, you, Suzanne. It seems to me that I am speaking to you. Did you hear anything in the night?

She thought she saw at first that her father knew nothing, and, in spite of herself, a long sigh of relief escaped her breast; therefore she replied with the most natural air in the world:

—What do you mean that I have heard, father?

—Something has happened, my daughter, this very night, in the garden, said Durand, scanning his words, something extraordinary.

This time Suzanne was terrified.

Nevertheless she collected all her courage; fully determined to lie to the last extremity.

—Well?

—Well, father? you puzzle me.

And leaning her pretty pale head on her plump arm, she looked at her father with perfect assurance.

She was charming thus. Her black hair, long and curling, partly covered her round, polished shoulders, and her velvety eye was frankly fixed on Durand's.

The old soldier was moved; he looked at his daughter with admiration, and reproached himself doubtlessly for his wrongful suspicions, for he said gently:

—Do not lie to me, Suzanne, and answer my questions frankly. I know very well that you are not guilty, that you cannot be guilty, that you have nothing to reproach yourself with; you quite see then that I am not angry. But sometimes young girls allow themselves to be led into acts of thoughtlessness which they believe to be of no consequence, and which yet have a gravity which they do not foresee. Last night a man entered the garden.

—The garden? said Suzanne, alarmed afresh, and ever feeling the fixed and scrutinizing look dwelling upon her. No doubt, it is a thief. No, father, no, I have heard nothing.

—I have several reasons for believing that it is not a thief; thieves take more precautions; this one walked heavily in my asparagus-bed.

—Ah, what a pity! In the asparagus-bed! He has crushed some, no doubt...

—Yes, in the asparagus-bed. The mark of his feet is distinctly visible.

Suzanne could contain herself no longer. Her self-possession deserted her, and she felt that her strength was going also. She believed that her father knew all, she saw herself lost, and, to conceal her shame and hide her terror, she buried herself under the bed-clothes, sobbing, and saying:

—Ah, papa! Ah, papa!

The old soldier mistook her terror, her despair and her tears.

—Come, he cried, confound it, Suzanne, are you mad? Don't cry like this, little girl, don't cry like this, like a fool: I only wanted to know if you had heard anything.

—No, father, sobbed Suzanne under her bed-clothes.

—You did not hear him? Well! very good. That is all, confound it. Another time we will keep our eyes open, that is all.

But the shock had been too great, and Suzanne continued to utter sobs; she decided, however, to show her face all bathed in tears, and said to her father in a reproachful tone:

—And besides I did not know what you meant with your night-robber and your asparagus-bed; I was fast asleep, and you woke me up with a start to tell me that.

—True, I have been rather abrupt, I was wrong; well, don't let us talk about it any more, hang it.

But Suzanne, having recovered herself, wanted to enjoy her triumph to the end.

—I don't know what you could have meant, she added still in tears, by coming and telling me in an angry tone that a man had been walking in your asparagus, as if it were my fault.

—It is true nevertheless, Suzanne. It is quite plain. I arrived this morning quite dusty from my journey, and went down into the garden very quietly as I usually do, thinking of nothing, when all at once I stopped. What did I behold? ... footsteps, child, a man's footsteps, right in the middle of my borders. "Hang it," I cried, "here is a blackguard who makes himself at home." I followed their track, which led me to the wall of the house and right up to the stair-case. That was rather bad, you know. There was still some fresh soil on the steps. Good Heavens! I asked myself then what it meant, and I came to you to learn.

—To me, father. But I know no more about it than you do. Why do you suppose that I know more about it than you?

Durand had great confidence in his daughter: he knew her to be giddy and frivolous, but he did not suppose for an instant her giddiness and frivolity amounted to the forgetfulness of duty.

Many fathers in this manner allow themselves to be deceived by their children with the same blindness and meekness as foolish husbands are deceived by their wives, till the day, when the bandage which covered their eyes, falls at length, and they discover to their amazement that the *cherub* which they had brought up with so much care and love, and whose long roll of good qualities, talents and virtues they loved to recount before strangers, is nothing but a little being saturated with vice and hide-bound in overweening vanity.

He embraced her with a father's tender and affectionate look, and for some time gazed upon Suzanne's clear eyes:

—No, he said to himself, there can be no vice in this young soul; is not this calm brow and these pure eyes the evidence of the purity of her soul?

And, taking one of her hands in his, he remained near her bed and said to her gently:

—It is a fact, I say again, my child, that I know young people sometimes, without thinking or intending any evil, commit imprudent acts, which are nothing at first, but which often have dangerous consequences. Sometimes carelessly they fasten their eyes on a young man whom they meet at church, at a ball, during a walk, or no matter where ... well! that is enough for him to construe the look as an advance which is made to him, or at least as an encouragement, and to believe himself authorized then to undertake some enterprise. Good Heavens, all seductions begin in the same way. We men are for the most part very infatuated with ourselves. I, my dearest child, can make that confession without any shame, for I have long since passed the age of self-conceit, although we still come across some old rascals who want to gobble up chickens, and forget that they have lost their teeth. Men are very foolish, young men particularly, and willingly imagine that all the ladies are dying of love for their little persons. A young woman passes by, and happens to look at them, as one looks at a dog or a pig; good, they say directly, "Stop, stop, that woman wants me." And immediately they try the knot of their tie, arrange their collar, and, assuming a triumphant air, begin to follow her and consider themselves authorized to address her impertinently.

—Ah, ah, said Suzanne, I can see that now, father. There were some young fellows who used to follow us always at school, with their moustaches well waxed and a fine parting in their hair behind. Heavens, how they have amused us.

—At other times, said Durand, a young girl is at her window. A gentleman, passing by, all at once lifts his nose. The young girl sees him, their eyes meet: "Eh, eh," says the gentleman, "there is a little thing who is rather nice; 'pon my word, she is not bad, not bad at all, and I believe that it would not be difficult … the devil, it would be charming! What a look she gave me! let us have a try." And the rogue commences to walk up and down under the windows, doing all he can to compromise the girl.

And all these young fellows, my dear, are like that; they have the most deplorable opinion of women, that one would say that their mothers had all been very easy-going ladies. And now, that is enough.

Together they passed in minute review all the young village *beaux*, but Durand's suspicion did not rest on any.

LXXIX
IN THE DILIGENCE

"Hydras and apes. Triboulet puts on the mitre, and Bobêche the crown, Crispin plays Lycurgus, and Pasquin parades as Solon. Scapin is heard calling himself Sire, Mascarillo is My Lord ... Cheeks made for slaps, are titles for honours. The more they are branded on the shoulder, the more they are bedisened on the back. Trestallion is radiant, and Pancrace resplendent."

CAMILLE LEMONNIERE (*Paris-Berlin*).

During this time, the *diligence* for Nancy was carrying away Marcel and Ridoux at full trot. Marcel had appeared to yield to his uncle's exhortations, and said to himself: "Let us go; that does not bind me to anything. In a couple of days at the latest, I shall be on my way back;" and this had made the worthy Ridoux quite happy.

They were alone in the *coupé*, and could converse at their ease.

—Look at this lovely country, that valley, those little hills, and away there the large woods, and do you not think that I shall feel some regret at leaving this part?

—And that little white house at the foot of the hill?... Is it there?

—Ah! so Veronica has pointed it out to you.

—Reluctantly, my son. But I wanted to know all. She is a cautious and trustworthy person who is entirely devoted to you.

—Not a word more about that cautious woman, uncle, I pray.

—Let us rather talk about your promotion.

—My promotion. I assure you, uncle, that I am no longer ambitious.

—What are you saying there? You are no longer ambitious! You are going perhaps to make me believe that you are happy in your shell. Come, rouse yourself. Has a moral torpor already seized you? You are no longer ambitious. Well, I will be so for you, and I intend, yes, I intend, do you hear, that you should make your way. What happiness for a poor old man, like me, when I hear them say: "Monsieur Ridoux, I have just seen your nephew, Monseigneur Marcel, go by." I shall answer then: "It is I, however, who have made him, who have formed him, his Right-Reverence." You will give me your patronage, will you not?

—Dear uncle, said Marcel softened, pressing the old Curé's hands, you still have those ideas then, you always think then that I shall become a Bishop?

—What? yes I think so; I do more than that, I am sure of it. Are you not of the stuff of which they make them? Why should not you become one as well as another?

—A bishopric is not for the first-comer.

—Don't worry me. Are you the first-comer? See, my dear fellow, you really must get this into your head, that in order to succeed in our profession, evangelical virtues are more detrimental than useful, and that there are two things indispensable: first to have a good outside show, to stir yourself and to know how to intrigue to the utmost. As for talent, that is an accessory which can do no harm, but after all, it is merely an accessory. Now, you have a good outside show; you have more talent than is necessary, there is only one thing in which you are faulty, you are not sufficiently intriguing. Well, I will be so for you, and I will stir myself up for you. Success wholly lies in that.

You say that a bishopric is not for the first-comer. You make me laugh. Look at ours, Monseigneur Collard; what transcendant genius does he possess? Is not his morality somewhat elastic, and his virtues very doubtful? But he has a magnificent head, and that from all time has pleased the world in general and the women in particular. Ah, the women, my dear friend, the women! you do not know what a weight they are in the scales of our destinies, and in the choice of our superiors. I know something about it, and if I had had a smaller nose and a better-made mouth, I should not be now Curé of St. Nicholas. But I am ugly and they despise me. How many I know who owe their cross and their mitre to the way in which they say in the pulpit, "my sisters", and to the amiable manner in which they receive the confessions of influential sheep.

—You confess, uncle, that it is abominable.

—I confess that it is in human nature, that is all I confess. Is it not logical to befriend people whose appearance pleases you, rather than those whose face is disagreeable to you? Good Heavens, it has always been the case since the commencement of the world. All that you could say on the subject would not make the slightest change. Let us therefore profit by our advantages when we have advantages, and leave fruitless jeremiads to the foolish and envious.

—Birth also counts for much in our fortune.

—Often, but not always. Look at Collard again, who is the son of a journeyman baker.

—He has that in common with Pope Benedict XII.

—Yes, but he has that only. Therefore, since it is neither his birth, nor his genius, nor his virtues which have helped him on, it is then something else.

—In fact, ecclesiastical history abounds in similar instances. Men, starting from the most humble condition, have attained the supreme dignity: Benedict XI had tended sheep, the great Sixtus V was a swineherd, Urban VI was the son of a cobbler, Alexander V had been a beggar.

—And a host of others of the same feather. Well, that ought to encourage you who are the son neither of a cobbler, or of a pig-seller.

—Would to heaven that I were a cobbler or a shepherd myself; I could have married according to my taste and have become the worthy father of a family, an honest artisan rather than a bad Curé.

—Yes, but Mademoiselle Durand would not have wanted you.

—Oh, uncle, do not speak of that young person with whom you are not acquainted, and regarding whom you are strangely mistaken, for you see her through the dirty spectacles of my servant. You want to take me away on her account, but are there not young persons everywhere? You know, as well as I, to what dangers young priests are exposed; shall I be safe from those dangers by going away? No. And since it is agreed between us that, no more than others, can we avoid certain necessities of nature....

-Alas, alas, human infirmity!

Omnia vincit amor, et nos cadamus amori.

—Then....

—Then, we choose our company; for instance, that pretty girl there.

And Ridoux leant his head out of the door. They had just reached Vic, where they changed horses.

LXXX
AN OLD ACQUAINTANCE

"Methinks Queen Mab upon your cheek
Doth blend the tints of cream and rose.
And lends the pearls which deck her hat
And rubies too from off her gown,
To be your own fit ornament."

E. DARIO (*Strophes*).

Before the *Hôtel des Messageries*, a young girl, modestly dressed, was waiting for the *diligence*, with an old band-box in her hand.

Marcel, who had also put his head out of the coach-door, looked at her with surprise. He had seen this girl somewhere. Yes, he remembered her. He had seen that charming countenance, he had already admired that fair hair and those blue eyes. But the face had grown pale; the cheeks had lost their freshness with the sun-burn, and the bosom its opulence. Marcel thought her prettier and more delicate like this. For it was really she, the mountebank's daughter, whom he had seen a few weeks before, dancing in the market-place of Althausen.

By what chance was she still in the neighbourhood, this travelling swallow?

Was the house on wheels then in the vicinity with its two broken-winded horses, and the clown with the cracked voice, and the big woman with the red face, and the thin and hungry little children?

He looked if he could not see them all, but he saw only the pretty fair girl, who had recognized him also, and made him a friendly bow.

—Mademoiselle Zulma! called the conductor.

—It is I, she said.

—This way, this way, my little dear, said the conductor with a good-natured familiarity which disgusted Marcel; there is no room inside. And, to the priest's great delight, he opened the coupé.

The young girl seemed surprised, for she hesitated a little and said:

—What, in the coupé?

—Yes, my imp of Satan, in the coupé, and in good hands too. Do you complain? If you are not converted yet, here are two gentlemen who will undertake your conversion.

—Well, I ask for nothing better, she answered laughing; and addressing herself to Marcel: Will you take my band-box for me?

He took the box, and at the same time offered his hand to help her to get up. She leant on it prettily; and bowing to him, and to Ridoux also, she sat down beside Marcel.

—You have come back then into the country, Mademoiselle.

—I have not left it, sir; I have been ill. I am coming out of the hospital.

—Oh, really. And what has been the matter with you?

—'Pon my word, I don't know. I caught a chill after an evening performance, and when I woke up the next morning, I could not move arm or leg. My father was obliged to leave me here in the hospital. They have been very kind to me, and an old gentleman has even paid my coach-fare. Oh, there are good people everywhere.

—And you are going to Nancy?

—To Nancy first, then I shall rejoin the company, which ought to be at Epinal.

Ridoux was listening in his corner.

—You know this young person then? he said.

—I know her through having seen her once at Althausen.

—Twice, the young girl corrected him: when I arrived and when I went away. You remember, we were both of us at our window?

Marcel remembered it very well; he remembered still better the fantastic sight in the market-place, and the lascivious dance, and the theatrical low-cut dress of the mountebank, which had awakened all at once the passion of his feelings. But as he was afraid of allowing the young girl to suspect that the memory of her had left too deep a mark upon him, he answered.

—I don't remember.

Meanwhile, a throng of beggars besieged the *diligence*; allured by the sight of the two cassocks, they recited all at the same time *litanies, paters* and *aves* in undefinable accents and in lamentable voices. Ridoux and Marcel with much ostentation distributed a few *sous* among the most bare-faced and importunate, that is to say among the most expert beggars and consequently those who least deserved attention, then they threw themselves back into the carriage and shut their ears.

—I have nothing more, said Ridoux, I have nothing more; go and work, you set of idlers.

—Poor things, murmured the player; no doubt, among the number there are some who cannot work.

—There, said Ridoux, is where the old order of things is ever to be lamented. Formerly there were convents which fed all the beggars, while now these starving creatures will soon eat us all up. Ah, it makes the heart bleed to see such misery.

And he took a pinch of snuff.

A poor woman, pale and sickly, with a child on her arm, kept timidly behind the greedy crowd. Zulma perceived her, and made her a sign. Then, taking a pie out of her hat-box, she cut it into two and gave her one half.

—You are giving away your breakfast, said Marcel.

—Yes, sir, it is a present from the kind Sisters. I should have eaten it yesterday, but I preferred to keep it for to-day; you see I have done a good action, she added laughing.

—I see that the Sisters were very kind to you.

—Yes, sir, they have converted me, they made me confess and take the Communion, which I had not done for a long time.

—That is well, said Ridoux.

The *diligence* had started again. A tiny child, emaciated, in rags and with bare feet was running, cap in hand.

He was quite out of breath, and with a little panting, plaintive voice, he cried:

—Charity, kind Monsieur le Curé; charity, if you please.

—Go away, said Ridoux, go away, little rascal.

-My mother is very ill, said the little one: there is no bread at home.

—Wait, wait, I am going to point you out to the *gendarmes*.

The child stopped short, and sadly put on his cap again.

—Poor little fellow, said the dancer.

And she threw him the other half of the pie.

Ridoux thought he saw an offensive meaning in this quite spontaneous action, for he cried angrily:

—Would you tell us then, Mademoiselle, that you have taken the Communion?

No doubt it was with that piece of meat.

—Why, sir?

—In what religion have you been brought up?

—In the Catholic religion.

—Is it possible? Really! you are a Catholic and you keep some pie for your meals on a fast-day, on a Friday! A Friday! he repeated with an accent of the deepest indignation: has not your Curé then taught that it is forbidden to eat meat the day on which Our Lord Jesus Christ died to redeem you from your sins?

—I know it, answered the young girl colouring, but we are not able to attend to religion much. We do not belong to any parish.

—What do you mean by "we?" What is your calling?

—I am a travelling artiste, sir.

—A travelling artiste. What is that?

—I dance character dances, and I appear in *tableaux vivants* and *poses plastiques*.

—*Poses plastiques*! at your age? Are you not ashamed to follow that calling?

—That is the calling which I was taught, sir; I know no other, replied the young girl, whose eyes filled with tears. I have always heard it said that when we gain our living honourably, we have nothing to reproach ourselves with.

—Honourably! that's a fine word!

—I mean to say, without wronging our neighbour.

—And you are talking nonsense. Can you think your life is honourable, when you do not discharge even the most elementary duty of a good Catholic, which is to keep the Friday as a fast-day? And not only that, you encourage others in your vices; in short, that wretched woman, to whom you have given that piece of meat, you incite her to disobey the Church....

—I did not think of that.

—And that little child, he continued with growing anger, that little child to whom you have given this bad example, whom you lead into a disorderly life by throwing him, before two ecclesiastics, some pie on a Friday.... You have caused this little child to offend. Do you not know then what Our Lord Jesus Christ has said about those who cause the little children to offend? But you know nothing about it. Do you take heed of the Divine Master's words, you who, at the beginning of your life, display your youth in sinful dances for the lewd pleasure of passers-by?

—I make my living as I can, replied Zulma, wounded by the rebuke.

—A fine way of making your living! You would do better to pray to the Holy Virgin.

—Will the Holy Virgin give me what I want to eat?

—Ah, they are all like that. Eating! Eating! They only think of eating! It appeals that they have said everything when they have said: "Who will give me to eat?" That is the great argument to excuse the lowest callings, and work on Sundays. Eating? Eating? Eh, unhappy child, and your soul? You must not think only of your body, which will be one day eaten by worms. Your soul also requires to eat.

Marcel interrupted.

—Uncle, I ask you to excuse this young person. She is ignorant of the duties of a Christian, and it is not her fault. This is a soul to guide.

—I do not say that it is not; I wish then that she may find someone to guide her.

Thereupon he opened his breviary; but he had not finished the second page of that potent narcotic before he was sound asleep.

LXXXI
A LITTLE CONFESSION

"Let us not ask of the tree what fruit it bears."

CAMILLE LEMONNIER (*Mes Medailles*).

—Monsieur le Curé is a trifle abrupt, said Marcel, bat he has an excellent heart.

—Yes, he seems to be quickly offended. It is quite different with the old gentleman who came to see me at the Hospital. There is a good sort of a man!

—The Chaplain, no doubt.

—No, he is a judge. When I knew it, I was quite alarmed at it. A judge, that makes one think of the *gendarmes*. I was quite in order, fortunately. Besides, he is the president of a great Society, which enters everywhere, and knows what is going on everywhere. Ah, he is a man who frightened me very much the first time I saw him. But he is as kind as can be.

—You are talking, no doubt, of Monsieur Tibulle, President of the Society of St. Vincent de Paul, and Judge of the Court at Vic.

—Monsieur Tibulle, that is he. A benevolent man, but who does good only to people who are religious and honest and right-minded—as he says. As I am an artiste, the Sister was afraid that he would not trouble himself about me, but he saw plainly that I was an honest girl.

—What do you mean by honest girl?

She looked at him attentively:

—You know very well, she said.

—But it is not enough to receive the Communion once, by chance, to be honest.

—Was I not obliged to go to confession before?

—Ah, I can explain it all now. You have been washed from your sins. That is well, my daughter, but you must not fall into them again.

—Fall where?

—Into your sins.

—That will be very hard, said Zulma with a sigh, for I commit so many of them.

—Many! so young! How old are you?

—Sixteen.

—Sixteen; and so grown-up already. But what are the sins that you can commit at sixteen?

—Many. The Curé of the Hospital has assured me so. He said to me that I was a cup of iniquity.

—Oh, he has exaggerated; I feel sure that he has exaggerated. What sins do you commit then?

—I do not say my prayers, I do not fast on Friday, I do not go to Mass.

—What then?

—Others besides.

—What are they?

—I do not know; there are so many.

—Which are those that you commit by preference? The sins which you have just related to me are infractions of the Church's laws. But the others ... you do not know what are the sins which you take pleasure in committing?

—They all give me pleasure. If I sin, it is because it gives me pleasure, is it not? If it did not give me pleasure, I should not sin.

—But, after all, there are pleasures which you love more than others.

—Assuredly. Are not all pleasures sins?

—All those which are not innocent, yes.

—How can I distinguish innocent pleasures from those which are not so?

—Your conscience is the best judge.

—And when my conscience says nothing?

—That is not a sin.

—Well, Monsieur le Curé of the Hospital has accused me of a heap of sins for which my conscience does not reproach me at all.

—My child, habit sometimes hardens the heart, but you are not of an age to have a hardened heart. I feel certain that your heart, on the contrary, is kind and tender, and that if you commit faults, it is through ignorance. What are then those great faults?

—Must I tell you them in order to be an honest girl?

—Yes, I should like to hear them; I might be able to give you some good advice. Advice is not to be despised, particularly in your condition, exposed as you are, young and pretty as you are.

—Pretty! you think me pretty?

—Yes, said Marcel smiling; am I the first to tell you so, and don't you know it?

—Oh, no, you are not the first. When I am passing by somewhere, or when I am taking part in the outside show, I often hear them say: Eh, the pretty girl! But you are the first from whom it has given me so much pleasure to hear it. Is that a sin too?

—A little sin of vanity, but extremely pardonable. If you have no greater ones than that, you are really an honest girl.

He looked at her and smiled. Zulma caught his look, and blushed.

—Where are you going to stay at Nancy?

—The gentleman who paid my fare, gave me also the address of a house where I can rest for a day or two while I am waiting for news from my company: the *Hôtel du Cygne de la Croix*.

—I know it, said Ridoux who had just woke up, it is a respectable house, the best which a young person like you could meet with. I have no doubt but that you will be welcomed there and at a moderate price, being recommended by the worthy Monsieur Tibulle. The mistress of the establishment is a conscientious lady, well-disposed and observing her religious duties. She is not one who will give you meat on a Friday. Monsieur Tibulle takes a great interest in you then?

—Yes, sir. He has even said that if I wished, he would find a more suitable position for me; but what position could he give me?

—He might find you some … he is an influential man. I invite you to follow his advice. He is a member of the *Society for the protection of poor young girls*.

—But, no doubt, I shall not see him again.

—Then, said Marcel, I, for my part, would wish to be useful to you; but unfortunately, you are only passing through, and I also am not here for long. Nevertheless, if for one cause or another you should have need of anyone ... you understand ... a young girl might find herself at a loss in a huge town ... you will enquire for the Abbé Marcel at this address.

-Many thanks, sir.

They had arrived. The travellers separated. The young girl with her small amount of luggage directed her steps in all confidence towards the inn which the old member of the Society of St. Vincent de Paul had acquainted her with, while Ridoux and Marcel took their way to the Place d'Alliance, where resided the Comtesse de Montluisant.

LXXXII
THE CHURCH-WOMAN

"Devotion is the sole resource of coquettes: when they are
become old, God becomes the last resource of all women
who know not aught else to do."

MME. DE REUX.

As *his uncle* had foreseen, the young Curé pleased the old lady greatly.
She examined him with satisfaction and predicted that he would make his
way.

—You have not deceived me, she said to Ridoux, here is a priest such as
we require. We are encumbered with awkward, ridiculous, red-raced men,
who bring religion into disrepute. Why not send all those peasants back to
their village, and select men like Monsieur l'Abbé? It is a shame, an absolute
shame to allow you to stagnate in this way. I shall reproach Monseigneur
severely for it.

—It is the fault of the Grand-Vicar Gobin, said Ridoux; he had taken a
dislike to my nephew.

—I have known that. He was a very harsh and a very tiresome man.
Too frozen virtue which has melted, I am told. I do not want to believe it.
He is the talk of the town. It is abominable, but I do not pity him. That is
what comes of not making religion amiable. Although we are old, Monsieur
Marcel, we are of the new school; we firmly believe that religion and
agreeable gaiety ought to proceed in harmony. We want conciliatory and
amiable priests. In this way the women let themselves be won over. I may
confess it to you, I who am double your age; and in so far as we shall have
the women, the world is ours.

While asking himself, what influence this more than middle-aged
lady could exercise over the Bishop's decisions, Marcel quickly perceived
that in order to be successful, he had only to be in the good graces of this
estimable dowager, and, in spite of the remembrance of Suzanne, he tried to
be amiable and witty.

But soon his ideas of ambition returned to him in this sumptuous drawing-room, surrounded with comfort and luxury: he thought that he had only to wish it, in order to become himself too, one of the great of the earth, and it appeared to him that the Comtesse do Montluisant ought to be the instrument of a rapid fortune.

The old lady was one of those women, very numerous in the world, who make of religion a convenient chaperone for their intrigues and their affairs of gallantry. When they are old, and can scarcely *venture* any longer on their own account, they generously place their experience and their small talents at another's service, and willingly assist the intrigues of others. That is called *lending the hand*, and more than once the old lady had countenanced, through perfectly Christian charity, the secret interviews of sweet sheep with their tender pastor.

The deduction must not be made from this that all the devout are courtesans when they are young and procuresses in their ripened age.

Whatever may be said, all are not hypocritical and vicious. Vice usually comes in the long run, and hypocrisy, which oozes from the old arches of the temples, and from the antique wainscoting of the sacristies, falls at length upon their shoulders like an unwholesome drizzling rain, but for the most part they begin with conviction and good faith.

They attend church frequently, not only because it is *good form*, not only through want of occupation and through habit, but from inclination.

The melodies of the organ, the odour of incense, the singing of the choir, the meditation and silence, the flowers, the wax-tapers, the gilding, the pictures, the mysterious light which filters through the stained-glass windows, the radiant face of the Virgin, the sweet and pale countenance of Christ, the statues of the saints, the niches, the old pillars, the small chapels, all this mystic poetry pleases them, everything enchants and intoxicates them, even to the sanctimonious and hypocritical face of the beadle and the sacristan.

It is their element, their centre, their world. They attach themselves to the old nave as sailors attach themselves to their ship.

They know all the little corners and recesses of the temple. They have knelt at all the chapels and burnt tapers before all the saints. But there is always one place which they have an affection for, and where they are invariably to be found. Why? Mystery! What do they do there? Mystery again. They remain there for whole hours, motionless, dreaming, their eyes fixed on vacancy, their thoughts one knows not where, and in their hands a book of prayers which they open from time to time as if to recall themselves to reality.

A young priest passes by. He recognizes them. He bows and smiles to them like old acquaintances. In fact, he sees them there every day at the same place. Godly sheep! They look at him passing by, and, while pretending to read their psalms, they follow him with that deep, undefinable, mysterious look, which inspires fear.

What connection is there between their prayers and reveries, and the lively behaviour of this red-faced Abbé?

How he must laugh, and how he must inwardly despise these women, who can find no better employment for the day than to mutter *Paternosters*, devoid of meaning, before an image of wood or stone, or to remain in the vague sanctimonious contemplation of a *mysterious unknown*.

Poor women! who, better led, better instructed in their duties and mission in life, would have become excellent mothers, might have been the light and joy of some hearth which now remains deserted, and who, lost and misled by a false education and a detestable system of morality, fall into wasting mysticism, hysterical ecstasies, a contemplative and useless existence, into degrading practices and shameful superstitions, and instead of being the fruitful animating springs of moral and social progress, become the passive instruments, the unfruitful *things* of the priest, that is to say the agents of reaction.

It is they who have caused thinkers to doubt the noble part which woman is called to fulfil; who have compelled Proudhon to say: "Woman is the desolation of the just," and that other apostle of socialism, Bebel, that she is incapable of helping in the reconstitution of Society:

"Slave of every prejudice, affected by every moral and physical malady, she will be the stumbling-block of progress. With her must be used, morally certainly, perhaps physically, the peremptory reason to the slaves of the old race: The Stick!" We are far from the divine book of Michelet, *Love*.

No, do not let us beat woman, even with a rose, as the Arab proverb says. She is a sick child, foolishly spoiled, who requires only to be cured and reformed by another education. The Comtesse was not like this. Skilful and intelligent, she knew *what talking meant*, and how to read in wise men's eyes and between the lines of letters. Therefore, she had learnt in good time, how to bring together two things which the profane suppose to be so opposed to one another, and which form the secret of the Temple: *Religion and pleasure*.

"And she was quite right," Veronica would have said, "for how can pleasure hurt God."

LXXXIII
CONVENTICLE

"Je, dist Panurge, me trouve bien du conseil des femmes, et mesmement de vieilles."

RABELAIS (Panurge).

They took a light repast, and it was decided that Marcel should repair to the Palace that very day.

—There is no time to lose, said the Comtesse. The Curé of St. Marie is much coveted, and we have competitors in earnest. There is firstly the Abbé Matou, who is supported by all the fraternity of the Sacred Heart; he is young, active, wheedling and honey-tongued. He is the man I should choose myself, if I did not know you. He has had certainly a funny little story formerly with some communicants, but that is passed and gone, and as, after all, he is an intelligent priest and very Ultramontane, Monseigneur would he desirous of nominating him in order to rehabilitate him in public esteem. He is dangerous.

Now we have little Kock. He has rendered important services. But he is the son of an inn-keeper, and he has common manners. Let us pass him by. There is yet the *Sweet Jesus*. Do you know the sweet Jesus, Abbé Ridoux?

—Yes, it is the Abbé Simonet.

—The Abbé Simonet, said Marcel, I know him; we were together at the Seminary. Do they call him the sweet Jesus? He was a terrible lazy fellow.

—Well, he is not so among the ladies, I assure you They all are madly in love with him. He confesses the wives of the large and small shop-keepers, and he has enough to do. The gentry used to go to the Abbé Gobin. Now he has gone away, what will become of all the sinners of the Old-Town? Supposing they were all to fall upon that poor Simonet! It is enough to make one shudder. Dear *Sweet Jesus!* When I see him wandering in the Cathedral with his long fair hair, and his down-cast eyes, I understand the infatuation of the women. He is nice enough to eat; yes, gentlemen, to eat. Ah, you do not know as well as we do, how religion gains by young and handsome pastors for its interpreters, and with what rapidity the holy flock increases. It is an astonishing thing. I fear that we must strive very hard against the *Sweet Jesus*.

—We will strive, said Ridoux.

—And we will employ every means. Go, dear Abbé, hasten to Monseigneur's, he is warned of your visit, and before entering on the struggle, it is well to reconnoitre the ground. Go, I have good hopes that we shall have St. Marie.

Thus Marcel found himself enlisted, in spite of himself. The Curé of St. Marie was, to tell the truth, perfectly indifferent to him. That one or another mattered to him but little. He had considered that it was perhaps indispensable that he should quit Althausen for the sake of his reputation and the tranquillity of his heart. His heart? Was it then no longer Suzanne's? More than ever: but he thought by this time that if there are reconciliations with heaven, there were none such with his maid-servant, and that to rid himself of her, he must first quit Althausen. Suzanne from time to time could come to Nancy, and it was much more easy and less perilous for him to contrive interviews with her there, than in that village where they were spied upon by all. Afterwards they would see....

LXXXIV
AT THE PALACE

"This world is a great ball where fools, disguised
Under the laughable names of Eminence and Highness
Think to swell out their being and exalt their baseness
    In vain does the equipage of vanity amaze us;
Mortals are equal: 'tis but their mark is different."

VOLTAIRE (*Discourse sur l'Homme*).

Marcel felt oppressed at heart, when he put his foot again, for the first time after five years, within the episcopal Palace.

It was there formerly—five years ago, quite an abyss—he had dreamed of a future embroidered with gold and silk, but it was there also that he had seen his first illusions and his inmost beliefs flee away.

Nothing had changed; the Palace was always the same; there were the same faces, the same porter with the wan complexion, the same attendants, at once haughty and servile. Nevertheless, nobody recognized him. This priest, browned by the sun, old before his years through disappointment, almost bent beneath the load of his secret troubles, was different from the young and brilliant curate, who, full of hope had launched himself formerly into the illimitable future.

The lacqueys of the episcopal palace saluted him respectfully for his good looks; but when he gave his name, they eyed from head to foot with disdain and insolence this obscure country Curé, of whose disgrace they were aware.

—Monseigneur is much engaged, said a kind of *valet de chambre* with a sneaking look; I don't think he can receive you. You will call again to-morrow. Monseigneur has given orders not to be disturbed.

—Then I will wait.

—Wait if you wish to, replied the lacquey, but you run the risk of waiting a long time.

If it had not been for the valet's insolence, Marcel would no doubt have gone away, and perhaps, would have abandoned the affair; but, humiliated at hearing himself addressed in that tone, he became obstinate.

—Can you not then inform Monseigneur that the Curé of Althausen desires to speak with him?

—Althausen! Ah, well! I believe that the Curé of Mattaincourt and Monsieur le Curé of the Cathedral have called and not been received, replied the valet; consequently, he added *in petto*, we shall not disturb ourselves for a junior like you.

—Can I speak with *Monseigneur* the Secretary?

—Monsieur l'Abbé Gaudinet does not like to be disturbed, and I believe besides that he is in conference with his Lordship.

Marcel was aware that in the episcopal Palace the village Curés are treated with less regard than the dogs in the back-yard; therefore he took his own part, and he had just sat down on a bench without saying a word, deliberating with himself whether be ought to wait or to go away, when a little priest with a busy and important air, with spectacles on his nose and a pen behind his ear, quickly crossed the anteroom.

—Is it not Monsieur l'Abbé Gaudinet? said Marcel rising.

—Ah, cried the former, Monsieur le Curé of Althausen, I think?

It was the Secretary, and he aspired, as may be remembered, to the envied post of curate at St. Nicholas. He thought to obtain the good graces of Ridoux by rendering a service to Marcel.

—Monseigneur is really too much engaged, said he, but I will obtain admittance for you anyhow.

And he made him go into a small apartment next to the Bishop's private cabinet.

—I will call you when it is time, he said to him and went out.

Marcel, left alone, heard the sound of a voice in Monseigneur's cabinet, and he recognized perfectly old Collard's.

He would have been failing in good clerical traditions, if he had not gently drawn near the door and listened with all his ears; struck with amazement, he heard the singular conversation which follows.

LXXXV
LITTLE PASTIMES

"One thing which it is necessary to take into account, is that they are very precocious. A French girl of fifteen is as much developed as regards the sex and love, as an English girl of eighteen. This is accounted for essentially by Catholic education and by the Confessional, which brings forward young girls to so great an extent."

MICHELET (*L'Amour*).

—Let us see, little one; look me right in the face. Madame de Montinisant has assured me that you were very nice, very sweet, very submissive, very modest, in fact ail the good qualities in the superlative, and that you were worthy of entering into the sisterhood of the Holy Virgin, in spite of your youth; is that quite true?

—Yes, Monseigneur.

—Ah, ah! It is true, do you say? I am going to know exactly, I am going to know if you are truthful or not. God has bestowed on Bishops the gift of divining everything. Did you know that?

—No, Monseigneur.

—Ah, ah! You are smiling; you believe perhaps that it is not true; wait, wait, you shall see indeed. Is it long since she made her first communion?

—Nearly two years, Monseigneur.

—Two years, ah, ah! Then the little girl is fourteen.

—Only thirteen, Monseigneur.

—Thirteen! thirteen! that is very nice. At thirteen one is already a grown-up girl. Are you already a grown-up girl, little rogue?

—I don't know.

—You don't know, ah, ah. We are going to see first, if you are modest. Come close to me; see, little girl, give me your chin, and this pretty little dimple.... Oh, oh! you are laughing, stay, stay ... she has some pretty little dimples on her cheeks too, the little naughty thing. We are going to make a little confession.... Ah, you are blushing. Why are you blushing? You have then some great sins on your conscience? Come, you are going to tell me all that ... quite low ... in my ear.

—But, Monseigneur....

—There is no *but, Monseigneur.* It is the condition *sine qua non* of entering the sisterhood. You understand that in order to admit a sheep into his flock, the shepherd must be completely edified regarding that fresh sheep.... The sheep then must relate all her wicked sins to her Bishop. It is God who wills it, it is not I, little girl. What enters by one ear, goes out directly by the other. I should be much puzzled, after the confession to repeat a single word of what you have told me. You know what a speaking-tube is.

—Yes, Monseigneur.

—Well, the Confessor's ear is the speaking-tube of the ear of God. Has not your Confessor taught you that?

—Oh, yes, Monseigneur.

—Well, then, we have nothing to be afraid of, and she must not hesitate to confide to us her little faults. Even were there very great sins, I shall hear them without making any remonstrance, for that will prove to me that you have confidence in your Bishop. Come, place yourself there, near me, on your knees. You have no need to recite your *Confiteor*; it is only an examination of conscience that we are both going to make. There! very well, put this little cushion under your knees, you will be less tired. See, where are we going to begin?

—One God only thou shalt adore...

No, no, that is unnecessary; I am fully persuaded that you love God and your parents with all your heart.

—The goods of others thou shalt not take...

Ta, ta, ta, I am quite aware that you are not a thief—a thief has not a pretty little face like that; let us go on at once to the sixth commandment:

The works of the flesh thou shalt not desire
But in marriage only.

There, that is what moat concerns little girls. Do you know what are the works of the flesh?

—No, Monseigneur.

—Oh, it is something very abominable, and I do not know how to explain it to you. Nevertheless, in order to know if you have sinned against this commandment, I must make myself understood. Has not your Confessor already spoken to you about it?

—No, Monseigneur.

—Ah, do not tell a falsehood. It is a mortal sin to tell a falsehood in confession. Who is your Confessor?

—He is Monsieur Matou.

—Ah, Matou! the Abbé Matou. Yes, yes, he has spoken to you about it, I know him; he must have spoken to you about it. Come, tell me all about that.

—Well, once he asked me....

—Ah, ah! well, well! do not stop. What is it he asked you?

—He asked me ... ah! it is a long time ago, before my first communion.

—Well?

—He asked me, if I did not go and play with the little boys.

—And then?

—If I had not culpable relations with them.

—Culpable relations with little boys, well! And what did you answer him?

—I answered him that I had not.

—That you had not! Was that quite true? Do not blush, and do not tell a falsehood. I shall see if you are going to tell a falsehood.

—Yes, Monseigneur, it was quite true; I did not even know what Monsieur Matou meant.

—And you know it now?

—Yes, he explained it to me.

—Oh, oh! he explained it to you. And how did he explain that to you?

—He told me....

—Let us see what he told you. Come, come, you most not hang down your head: see, lift up this pretty face and show me this little dimple; what did the Abbé Matou say to you?... Eh, eh! who is there! who is knocking at the door? Is it you, Gaudinet? Rise up, my little daughter, and go and sit down there, in the corner. Come in, Gaudinet, come in then.

Gaudinet put his head discreetly inside.

—Monseigneur, I came to inform you that the Curé of Althausen has been there for some time.

—There? where is that?

—In the cabinet.

—What! in the cabinet? Ah, are you mad, Gaudinet, to send people in this way into my cabinet? I do not approve of that, I do not approve of that at all. What does that Curé of Althausen want with me?

LXXXVI
SERIOUS TALK

"Such were the words of the man of the Rock; his authority was too great, his wisdom too deep, not to obey him."

CHATEAUBRIAND (*Atala*).

Marcel had not heard these last words. At Gaudinet's first word, he had quickly vanished, foreseeing that a terrible tempest would burst upon his head, if the Bishop should suspect that he had been a witness of his way of hearing little girls' confessions, the usual way however of nearly all priests; I appeal to the memories of the Lord's sheep.

—Monsieur le Curé!... cried Gaudinet, opening the door. Ah, he is no longer there. He has gone away, Monseigneur. I had told him, in fact, that your Lordship was very busy, and, no doubt, he wished not to trouble you.

—I was, in fact, expecting him. He will return to-morrow. But, for God's sake, Gaudinet, never let anybody enter that room without warning me beforehand.

Marcel was already at the bottom of the stairs. A valet called him back, and Gaudinet, after bringing out the little girl, introduced him to Monseigneur's presence.

—Ah, there you are, said the latter in a harsh tone, looking him straight in the face. Why did you go away?

—I was told that Monseigneur was engaged, and I feared to disturb your Lordship.

—Who told you that?

—The Abbé Gaudinet.

—You are much changed. I should not have recognized you. I have received a letter from Monsieur le Curé of St. Nicholas, he added, searching on his desk. Here it is. He says that you have returned to better sentiments ... that you are amended, humbled before God ... that you wish henceforth to follow the good way ... Is that so?

—That is my desire, Monseigneur.

—It is not enough to desire, sir, you must intend, firmly intend.

—I intend also.

—I intend to believe it. I ask nothing better than to oblige my old friend Ridoux by doing something for you. Sit down. We are in want of priests, that is to say, intelligent, hard-working, active priests, on whom we can absolutely rely. Times are becoming difficult. Evil doctrines are spreading. Faith is passing away. Infamous writers, wretched pamphleteers are spreading everywhere, at so much a line, the seeds of doubt and perversity. And to crown the evil, imprudent and maladroit priests are indulging their vices and creating scandal. But we are not discouraged. Is the holy arch in danger because a few nails are rusty, because a few cords are rotten? Other nails and cords are supplied in their place, and the rottenness is cast away. But we must not hide from ourselves that we are passing through a melancholy period. This is what priests for the greater part do not clearly see. They slumber in their priesthood, take their emoluments, grow fat, go their small way, and believe they have discharged their duty. That is not the case. When a man has the honour to be a priest, he must be active. It is necessary, as in the time of the persecutions, to make proselytes and win souls; to confront the irreligious propaganda with our propaganda; lampoons, with lampoons; speeches, with sermons; acts, with acts. In short, we must struggle. Can we remain still and idle, when our Holy Father is imprisoned in a den of thieves?

The time has come. We are fighting for our very existence, we must close the ranks, take count of ourselves, and above all see on what and on whom we can count. Let us see what we can expect from you? What do you ask? You wish to come to the town? I warn you that it will be hard, if you intend to do what I expect of you.

—The trouble does not frighten me, Monseigneur.

—You will have a difficult parish. You will have to run foul of a thousand different interests, and not give the slightest pretext for slander. You understand me? There are five or six influential Liberals whose wives or daughters you must win over adroitly, and at any cost—at any cost, you understand. Do you feel yourself qualified for this work? Are you the man we need?

—I will try, Monseigneur.

—You will try. That is not on answer. It is not enough to try; you most succeed. We are surrounded with men who commit nothing but follies, while intending to do well. Hell, you know, is paved with good intentions.

He looked at Marcel attentively, and the latter asked himself if this were really the man he had heard, only a few moments before, talking lightly with a little girl.

—You have good manners, continued the Bishop; you are intelligent, I know. You will succeed therefore, if you intend it seriously. Our misfortune is, that we are encumbered with dull and stupid peasants, whom the Seminary has been able only partly to refine, and who render us ridiculous. You must certainly have gone to sleep in your village?

—No, Monseigneur, I have worked.

—We shall see that. And what sort of people are they? Do they perform their religious duties?

—A good and hard-working population.

—Do they perform their religious duties?

—Yes. Monseigneur, I was satisfied with them.

—What society?

—Very little. The lawyer, the doctor....

—Right-thinking?

—Tolerably so.

—And the women?

—Much the same as all country-folk, ignorant and narrow-minded.

—No, you were not the man needed there. You would lose your time and your powers. I will send one of those brutes of whom I have just been speaking. Well, go; you can tell the Abbé Ridoux that you will have the cure. Come again to-morrow. I even think it will be useless for you to return to Althausen.

LXXXVII
THE SEMINARY

"I turned my head and I saw a number of the dead in living bodies. These are the worst spectres, because they must be subdued: you touch them, they touch you, and, in order to drag you away to their tomb, they seize you with an arm of flesh which is no better than the marble hand of the Commendatore."

EUGENE PELLETAN (ÉLISÉE, *Voyage d'un homme à la recherche de lui-même*).

Marcel went away disconsolate. So it was done. He was changed, another put in his place at Althausen. He had hoped for opposition, he had counted on objections from the Bishop, he thought, in short, that he would remain in suspense for some weeks, perhaps for some months, during which he would have the time to look before him and reflect; but no, all at once: "Go and tell the Abbé Ridoux that you have the cure." Well, and Suzanne? Could he leave Suzanne in this way? He had, it is true, informed her of his departure the day before; but had not everything changed since the day before? Could be abandon thus his heart which he had left behind there? More than his heart, his whole soul, his life, the maiden who had yielded herself.

Strange contradictions. When he had believed his change far distant and still but slightly probable, he had thought he could leave Suzanne easily, arrange far away from her for secret interviews, and await events; now that this change was certain and had just become an accomplished fact, he looked upon it as a catastrophe. Instead of hastening to announce *the good news* to Ridoux, he proceeded to roam through the streets, assailed by his thoughts.

"And I shall be obliged to live in this world which I have just caught a glimpse of, to elbow these men at every hour, to mingle in their intrigues, to blend myself in their life. That unscrupulous old Comtesse, that insolent prelate, Gaudinet, Matou, Simonet and the rest, all oozing forth hypocrisy, intrigue and vice; dreaming of one thing alone, to satisfy their ambition, their passions, and their appetites. And these are the ministers of God! Veronica was quite right:

"'All the same, we are all the same, all.' And I am one of the least bad. I was blind and idiotic not to have cast my gaze earlier into this filthy sewer.—Blind, idiotic and deaf."

He passed near a lofty, gloomy building. It was the Seminary. The desire came upon him to go in. Some of his old fellow-pupils had remained there, as masters or professors. But he altered his mind. What was the good? What would he do? What would he say to them? There was henceforth an abyss between him and these men who remained encrusted in the vessel of clericalism, the most uncrossable of all abysses, that which divides the thoughts. They were perhaps happy. He recalled to mind the long hours he had passed beneath the Sacred Heart in the little chapel of an evening, amidst the wax-lights, the incense and the flowers, mingling his voice in exaltation with the voices of the young Levites, and singing senseless hymns, with his heart melting with love of God.

And he began to envy those young fanatics whose blind and unintelligent faith killed every rising thought, and who were ready to suffer martyrdom to support the ridiculous beliefs which they had been taught and which they were called upon to teach. Blind, idiotic and deaf.

"Why am I not so still!" he said; "I should believe myself the only guilty one, the only wicked and perverse one among all those apostles; I should curse my weaknesses and myself; but at least I should have faith, I should walk onward with a star upon my brow, the star of sublime follies which gives light and life, whereas I see nought around me but desolation and death. I should humble myself before the Almighty, and I should cry to him like the poet:

"'Oh Lord, oh Lord my God, thou art our Father:
Pity, for thou art kind! pity for thou art great!'

"And instead of that, I am obliged to humble myself before that Bishop whom I despise, to endure the scorn of his lacqueys, and the offensive patronage of his secretary, to have the opportunity of saying:

"'A little place in your good graces, Monseigneur!' No, a thousand times no. My village, my poor belfry, my humble parsonage, my liberty, and my Suzanne!"

By his dejected look, his uncle and the Comtesse believed he had not succeeded.

—Too late! they cried. The cure is given away.

—Yes, he answered.

—To whom? To the *Sweet Jesus*, I wager. Ah, the Tartuffe.

—To me.

—And that is why you have a funereal expression?

—Yes, uncle, for I am burying for ever my tranquillity and my happiness.

—Is it only that? Madame la Comtesse, I present to you the oddest and the most extraordinary man you have ever met. Judge him yourself. He has just carried off at the first onset what he was eagerly desiring, and there he is as cheerful as a flogged donkey. Ah, my dear Madame, how difficult it is to benefit people in spite of themselves.

—That is my opinion also, said the Comtesse, looking tenderly with her little eyes, still brilliant in spite of their long service, at the young priest, for whom she felt that vague unfruitful passion which old courtesans have for every young and handsome man; and she made him relate minutely all the details of the interview.

—Bravo! bravo, she cried. It is more than I hoped. But do not alarm yourself at the difficulties of the task. Monseigneur wishes to prove you. I am acquainted with the parish. The Radicals have no influence there. One of them the other day took it into his head to die *civilly* and, in spite of the protestations of some low scoundrels, he has been buried in the early morning without drum or trumpet in the criminals' hole. Two primary schools are in our hands, and with a little skill we shall have the third.

—How?

—By taking away all the means of work from the workmen who send their children there. It is a task, Monsieur le Curé, which is incumbent upon you.

—And so, said Marcel bitterly, I must try to take away their bread from the fathers.

—I suppose, said Ridoux severely, that when the interest of religion is in question, there is no reason to hesitate. Madame la Comtesse, pardon this young priest, he comes out from his village and he is still imbued with certain prejudices.

—Which we will root out, said the old lady smiling; that shall be the task for us women.

LXXXVIII
THE FAIR ONE

"Pretty to paint! as graceful as an ear of corn, slender and yet robust, never was seen a morsel of flesh so delicate, or better rounded. Her hair, a wonderful fleece, smelt as sweet and fresh as the grass, and shone red like the sun."

LÉON CLADEL (*L'Homme de la Croix-aux-Boeufs*).

It was with a great feeling of relief that, in the evening, after supper, Marcel retired to the room which, in spite of his protests, the Countess had caused to be made ready for him.

He had need to be alone. Events had hurried on in such an astounding and rapid manner, and he had had no time to think about them.

His resolution was fully taken. He would refuse the new core. The odious part which he was called upon to play there, decided him. He was about to shatter his future. It meant a disagreement with his uncle, the hatred of this influential woman, the formidable persecution of the Bishop; but what was all that? He saw Suzanne again, amiable, gracious, smiling, looking at him with her soft, dark eyes; Suzanne approving of his conduct and saying to him: "You are a man of courage. Let us go away together; cast your frock into the ditch."

And he wrote three letters: one to his uncle, the other to the Comtesse, and the third to the Bishop, entreating them to excuse him, and telling them that he did not feel qualified to perform his ministry in a large town. He implored Monseigneur to leave him at Althausen and to think no more about him.

But the night brings counsel. And when he woke up the next morning and saw his three letters on the table, he thought that he could not do a more awkward thing.

He threw them in the fire, dressed and went out. The idea came to him of going to see the parish which was destined for him. He followed the streets, drawn in a straight line, of that too regular city, and when he arrived at the corner of the *Rue des Carmes*, he heard his name pronounced.

Be turned round and saw the landlord of the inn where he was accustomed to stay, when he came to Nancy.

—What, you are passing before my door without coming in, Monsieur le Curé;
I was expecting you, however. I had prepared your room.

—You were expecting me, Monsieur Patin? And who told you that I was here?

—Who told me that? It was a young person who is very pretty, upon my word. She came to ask for you yesterday evening, and we expected you up to ten o'clock.

—Dark? said Marcel much disturbed.

—No, fair, the prettiest fair complexion which I have ever seen.

Marcel remembered immediately the little mountebank, whom he had altogether forgotten, and to whom he had given the address of Monsieur Patin's hotel, where he had expected to stay.

—It is a young girl who is recommended to me, he said; I regret that I did not see her.

—You are not coming in?

—No, for perhaps I am going to set out again for Althausen.

—For Althausen. That is impossible to-day. I have just seen the *diligence* go by. Come, you will sleep once more at my house, Monsieur Marcel; your room is quite ready, and my wife, who has a fancy for you, will not let you go away. Stay, here she comes; she has recognized your voice.

The little Madame Patin, plump, brown, active and pretty, hastened up, indeed, and compelled Marcel to come in, almost in spite of himself.

—You shall remain, you shall remain! she said to him, relieving him of his hat.

—No, he answered smiling, I shall not remain, and I will tell you the reason. I came with my uncle, and I have my room at Madame de Montluisant's.

Before that declaration Monsieur and Madame Patin bowed.

—Ah, that is not right, said Madame Patin; Madame de Montluisant is opposing us, she is drawing our clients to her house…. My dear, have you told Monsieur Marcel that a young person has come?…

—Your husband has told me, Madame, and that proves to you that I certainly had the intention of staying with you, since I showed her your address. It had escaped my memory, otherwise I should have called to ask you to send the young person to Madame de Montluisant's.

—She will certainly come back again, for she seemed very desirous of seeing you. Must I send her to you at that lady's?

—No, but tell her to come again this evening late. I have a thousand things to do, and I can scarcely see any moment but that when I shall be free.

That evening at eight o'clock, he was at Monsieur Patin's, where he found a good fire in a small sitting-room well closed, with the newspapers and a cup of coffee. The young girl had called again during the day, and would return. Marcel installed himself comfortably in an arm-chair and waited for her.

He had seen the Bishop again, who had flashed before his eyes a future, full of golden rays. The visit of Ridoux and the Comtesse had preceded his own, and in the sudden change of manner of the prelate towards him, he recognized the good offices of his new friend.

A good dinner had completed the happy day, and life appeared to him, after all, to have some sweetness.

LXXXIX
LOVE AGAIN

"Oh Folly, which we call love, what dost thou make of us?
Out of free-men thou dost make us slaves; thou dost breathe
into us all the vices. It is thou who dost supply the altars of
disloyalty and fear! It is thou who dost extract from thought
the rhetorician's art, and from enthusiasm a vile profession.
How many young people have you blighted! all the fairest.
Ah, siren, thy voice is sweet. Thou speakest to us the
language of the gods, but thou are only an impure beast."

JEAN LAROQUE (*Niobe*).

A kind of emotion seized him. He was almost ashamed of it, and tried
to give an account of it to himself. It seemed to him that he was affected as
if at the approach of sin. He restrained his feelings and enquired of himself
what this young girl could want with him.

Perhaps she was but a common courtesan who, attracted by the
handsome appearance and tender look of the priest, counted on speculating
profitably in a clandestine intrigue.

Nevertheless, he was not terrified at the prospect, and he recalled
complacently the scene in the open air in the market-place at Althausen.
With his eyes closed, he saw her again playing the castanets, rounding her
hips and shooting forward her little foot, in order to make the enraptured
rustics admire the sculptural beauty of her leg. He saw again that bosom,
free from all covering, which had plunged him into such confusion.

Ah, if instead of his love for Suzanne, so full of fever and danger, he
had picked up on his way some pretty girl like this Bohemian, who, while
calming his feelings, would have left his heart in peace.

With a common peasant girl, vigorous and sensual, like this dancer at
the fair, he would have gratified the only low permissible to a priest; for it
was the most unpardonable folly, he recognized now, to surrender his heart.

The Curé of St. Nicholas was a thousand times right! Let the priest make use of woman, nothing is more proper, as an instrument, as a pastime, hygienic and aperient; but let him stop there.

At certain periods, when the brain is heavy, the digestion is inactive, and the bowels are confined, when dizziness occurs, when the blood becoming too plentiful, grows thick and congested in the veins and rises to the head, then it is that nature needs to accomplish her work. Then one seeks for a woman, one throws oneself on her who happens to be there, and is willing to lend herself to this hygienic and benevolent part. Servant or mistress, girl or wife, lady or work-girl, young or old, courtesan from a drawing-room or the pavement, one takes her, has one's pleasure of her, and goes away.

But to love long, to make of the woman the aim of our life, the spring of our actions, the ideal of our existence; to believe in happiness together, to put faith in these fragile, vain and ignorant dolls!... What trickery!

To believe in happiness through love! Dream of the school-boy! It is permissible to the neophyte who puts on for the first time the white surplice and the golden chasuble with so much joy and pride. The sweet young girls, the youthful wives, the grave matrons regard you with softened eyes. Then you have faith, you have confidence, you see the future illumined by angels with virgin bodies who murmur mysterious words in your ear, which melt your heart. You dare hardly lift your eyes, and you say to yourself: "Which one shall I love in this legion of seraphims? Oh, I will love them all, all!" Presumptuous youth which doubts of nothing!

But when you have loved one, two, three of them ... afterwards, afterwards?

After having experienced the nothingness of all these trifles, of all these follies of the heart, of all these caprices of the imagination, of all these abortions of the thought, of all these voids of the soul, of all these impurities of the body, of all the uncleanness of the woman with whom you are satiated, and whose couch you are leaving, then go and speak of eternal love.

Oh, how right Diogenes was to call love a short epilepsy.

How right that Imperial sophist of the Decline to call it a convulsion! and the first Bonaparte, an affair of the sopha.

Thus Marcel moralized, like an old prelate, coming out from a closed room when some filthy scene has been enacted.

The fact is, that for some time he had been the hero of a comedy and of a drama; the grotesque comedy which he had unrolled with his servant, the terrible drama in which he saw himself involved with Suzanne Durand.

And he was wearied and satiated. The satisfaction of his senses left him by way of retaliation, shame, trouble and fear.

Daniel Defoe has written in his admirable book:

"From how many mysterious sources, opposed one to the other, do not different circumstances cause our passions to proceed? We hate in the evening what we cherished in the morning; we avoid to-day what we sought for yesterday; we desire an object passionately, and a few moments after, we shall not know how to endure the idea of it."

Thus Marcel was cursing love, when Zulma came and knocked at his door.

XC
LE CYGNE DE LA CROIX

"As soon as she comes
The Hostess looks hard:
—My beauty no ceremony,
The supper is ready;
Come in, come in, my beauty
Come in, and no more noise
With three gallant captains
You shall spend the night."

(*Popular Songs of France*).

Madame Connard, a widow, and the landlady of the Cygne de la Croix, a godly and right-thinking person, made a significant grimace when she saw a young girl, quietly dressed, entering her house, with no other luggage than an old band-box.

But when she handed her the card of Monsieur Tibulle, judge of the Court at Vic, president of the Society of St. Vincent de Paul, and member of the Committee for the protection of poor Young Girls, her grimace changed into a gracious smile.

She soon gave her a room and asked her what she wanted to eat, informing her, however, that it was a fast-day and that, consequently, she had not much choice.

—Whatever you like, said the dancer; I am convalescent; I have a good appetite, and I accommodate myself to everything: don't give then the best which you have, but the cheapest.

—The little thing is sharp, thought Madame Connard; and she added aloud: A young lady, recommended by Monsieur Tibulle, need not fear that she will want for anything. Consider what you would like, my little dear, and don't disturb yourself about the rest. And since you are ill, the Church allows us to give you meat to eat.

She went out in the meantime, and an hour afterwards she herself served a dinner which would have made the most greedy of curates envious, and washed down with that light wine, acrid but heady, which the slopes of the Meurthe produce.

The dancer, like a true child of Bohemia, dined heartily, and without needing to be asked. She was at her coffee, when she heard a whispering in the corridor, and a little cracked voice, which said:

—I am a little late, dear Madame, but I have been kept by Monseigneur. Has the little one behaved well?

—Like an angel, Monsieur Tibulle, and a demon for beauty.

—Yes, yes. This will be a fine acquisition for the Church. A soul snatched from Satan, dear Madame, snatched from Satan. We shall make something of her.

—Ah, how happy you gentlemen are to snatch in this way pretty little souls from hell. We, poor women, have not that power.

—But you prepare the ways. You open them, dear Madame Connard; everything has its purpose, its purpose, its purpose.

—Well, Monsieur Tibulle, proceed to yours. It is number 10. I leave you.

And she quietly half-opened the door of No. 10, into which Monsieur glided like a shadow, saying in his tremulous voice:

—Eh! Eh! it is I, I, I, my little dear. How happy I am to see you again, to find you here, comfortably installed like a little queen. Eh, eh.

Madame Connard put her head in for an instant, smiled, and cautiously closed the door; "He is still pretty young for his age," she said to herself. "Ah, these men! these men! that goes on to the very end."

XCI
THE CALVES

"Non formosus erat sed erat facundus Ulixes."

OVID.

Zulma had run forward to meet him. He took hold of both her hands and made her sit down close beside him on the sofa.

—Well, what is the news? How have they received you here? Are you satisfied? Have you had a good dinner?

—Too good, replied Zulma: I am afraid I have spent a deal of money.

—A deal of money! Eh, eh! the good little girl! But you have nothing to pay here, my little puss. Nothing at all to pay, nothing at all. All the expense is my concern, and the more you spend, the better pleased I shall be. Have they not told you that, told you that, told you that?

—You are too kind, Monsieur; but I, what shall I do then for you?

—She is heavenly, eh, eh! But I want nothing, darling, nothing, nothing … except to see your pretty eyes. When we see them once, we have only one wish, and that is to see them again, again, again. I am well paid for the little I have done for you, since I have that pleasure. Yes, yes, yes. We are only too happy for what we can do for a charming little face like yours, and when we have obliged it, we say thank you! That is what I do, my little duck; thank-you, thank-you, thank-you.

—I am very grateful to you….

—That is what I was thinking. I want to kiss you for that kind word. Alas, we come across so many ungrateful people in the world…. What a fine and velvety skin; how soft it is under the lips … again, again…. I could eat it … again…. Ah, you do not want to again. What are you afraid of? I might be your father…. Come, another little kiss for poor papa.

Zulma let him kiss her again.

[PLATE V: THE CALVES. "I want to see them again, again, again."

—Well, there they are, but do not touch.

—Oh, oh, you are cheating. That is only half, I want to see them all ... up to the knees.]

—Ah, what a pretty girl! Look how strong and well made she is! continued the old President passing his trembling hand over the young girl's waist: have not these breasts grown a little thin? Yes, I believe, a little, a little, but how firm they are! like a rock, like a rock; hard as a rock, heavenly girl.... Eh, eh! you are drawing back, you are afraid of me ... of me who might be your papa.

—And perhaps my grandpapa, said Zulma.

—Grandpapa! Ah, the little girl is not flattering. Grandfather! you think then that I am quite old? I am going to pinch her calves for that naughty word, those big calves which I saw at Vic, and which have turned my head. Have they grown smaller too? Let us see, let us see.

Zulma held back the too presumptuous hand.

—What, said the worthy man astonished, you will not show your calves?

—What is the good, since you have seen them at Vic?

—I want to see them again, again, again.

—Well, there they are, but do not touch.

—Oh, oh, you are cheating. That is only half, I want to see them all ... up to the knees; at the least what I saw in the market-place.

—No, sir.

—Ah, you must not say *no* to me.... I do not like *no*. Let me help you, my pretty. Women always have a lot of strings under their petticoats and sometimes there are knots, knots, knots. I know that, so let me do it.

—But I don't want to, I tell you.

—Nevertheless, just to show me your calves, your fine big calves.

—You have seen them enough.

—What, cried Monsieur Tibulle, indignant at length at such obstinacy, you refuse to show to me what you exhibit in public, to everybody, in the market-places, in the streets, to the first who comes along; you refuse me when I am all alone, in this little room where nobody sees us. Ah, it is very wrong, wrong, wrong. I intend to punish you for that naughty act.

—In public, that is my profession, and besides I have a costume.

—She is nice enough to eat! A costume! If you only want that, it is very easy to find. I know of a little costume, very nice and not dear; and if you like, we will both of us put it on.

—What is it?

—That which God gave us. It is the best of all, and besides it is that which will become you the best. Ah, my little dear, nothing is equal to the gifts of God, and all the fripperies of women will never serve them as well as the simple attire of our first mother. We are going then to try the costume of Adam and Eve. Does that suit you, little one? You will no longer be afraid then of showing your calves. Come, come, Sophie, my dear, enough of these affectations.

—My name is not Sophie.

—Your name is Zulma, and also Aspasia, and Phryne, and again it is Eve. For it is long since you ate of the forbidden fruit, is it not, you little rogue?

—Let me alone, I ask you.

—Leave you alone! you would think I was very silly. Come, heavenly Eve, be quick into the costume of your part; I will play Adam and you shall see what a fine apple we will eat.

—Sir, a man of your age!

—Old men are always more amorous than the young ones, you will see, you will see.

—I don't want to see anything, let me go.

—Go! and where do you want to go to? A man does not let a little duck like you go away when he has hold of her, for I have you, you little rogue, yes, yes, I have you. Listen. We will go away to-morrow morning, each our own way, neither seen, nor known. And I assure you that you will be satisfied. My wife does not expect me till to-morrow.

—Your wife? What, you are married?...

—Does that surprise you? My wife is an old she-goat who is good for nothing more. Therefore I make no more use of her. Come, let us be quick; into the costume of Eve, and if you absolutely keep to it, I will fasten a fig-leaf on to you.

But Zulma was not the girl to allow herself to be forced in this way; and the worthy old man, who wanted to add deeds to words, received a vigorous slap on the face.

He stopped, quite confused, and rubbed his cheek.

—She has a strong wrist, he said. Who would suspect that such a little hand could hit so hard? But the ice is broken now, and you are going to pay me for it.

XCII
THE SCAPULAR

"And the old bearded fellow rubbed away, pushed with his hips, embracing her in front: clasped with his arms embracing her behind; stuffing at the chancellery, throwing her gently and collecting his strength, labouring with his chest, and even tripping her up: he made use of all."

LÉON CLADEL (*Ompdrailles*).

—I shall scream, said Zulma, who was defending herself valiantly; I shall scream if you do not loose me.

—Scream as much as you will, said the holy man as he recovered breath: here the walls are deaf, and you will have to deal with me.

—I just laugh at you. You old Punch!

—Old Punch! Punch!

—You ought to be ashamed.

—You insult me; take care.

—Let me go directly, or I shall know whom to complain to.

—Ah, you assume that tone! You want to make a complaint do you? And to whom, you little wretch?

—To whom it may concern.

—Ah, what a fine expression you have learnt by heart. Who is *whom it may concern*? I do not know him. Whoever he may be, *whom it may concern* will laugh in your face. You, a daughter of the streets, a rope-dancer, a clown, a ragged slut, you would lodge a complaint against me! Surely you do not know who I am. I am an honourable man; known everywhere, respected everywhere. Come, you see clearly that you are talking nonsense; be more reasonable again. What! it pleases me to cast my eyes upon you, to want to pass a little while with you agreeably; I honour you by stooping myself to a girl of your kind, and you refuse, and are fastidious. Has one ever seen such a thing? It is enough to make God laugh. Come, come now, not so many affectations: for the lost time, how much do you want? A hundred francs?

—You horrify me. Let me go away.

He cast a fearful look upon her, and said, with a laugh which chilled her blood:

—Oh, you want to go away. Well, how about the money I have spent on you, and on your journey?

—Your money! I did not ask you for it. But I will let you have it back again, be assured; when I have worked and earned it.

—And you believe that I shall be satisfied with this fine promise? You will let me have my money back immediately, or I shall certainly accuse you of being a thief … an adventuress.

—I will say what happened. It was you who compelled me to take the money for the coach-fare.

—I make you a present of that, but you will have to pay all that you have spent here; if not, you will be put in prison, you understand, little good-for-nothing? Do you think people are going to keep you and let you enjoy yourself for nothing?

—And who has told you that I shall not pay, replied Zulma, struck by the logic of this objection.

—Then you will pay immediately, said the worthy man, for I have been answerable for you, and it is on my recommendation that they have received a trollop like you into this respectable house. Madame Connard, he cried at the door, dear Madame Connard, will you bring up the bill, the little bill?

Madame Connard appeared at once:

—What, Mademoiselle is going away, is she not sleeping here?

—No, Mademoiselle is going to try her fortune elsewhere.

Madame Connard handed the bill to Monsieur Tibulle.

—No, no. It is Mademoiselle who is going to settle it; this young lady.

Zulma glanced at it and grew pale. She had hardly 10 francs, and the bill amounted to 19 francs, 75 centimes.

—And besides, it is so little because it is you. Everything is so dear here, and one does not know what to do for a living.

The poor girl remained silent; she looked at the bill without seeing it, for her eyes were full of tears.

—Well, said Monsieur Tibulle in a wheedling tone. Is there some little hindrance to your settling that?

—Madame, said Zulma, I have not enough money with me; no, I do not believe I have enough money ... but I can find it, I know where to find it ... and in an hour or two....

—Oh, oh, cried Madame Connard, in an hour or two, that is a very fine tale. But I know it, my girl, and people don't tell me that sort of thing.

—Well, dear Madame, I leave you, said Monsieur Tibulle, making her a knowing sign; I am going to see if my horse is put to, for I am setting off directly. Good-bye, little one, good-bye. No malice.

—Well, Mademoiselle, said Madame Connard, what do you decide?

—I have told you, Madame, I can give you five or six francs, and, although it is a downright robbery, I will find you the rest.

-What! a robbery? you little thief, you little hussy, you dare to call me a thief, you little street-walker. You are going to pay me immediately, or I will hand you over to the police.

—Very well, call the police, if you wish; I ask for nothing better; I will relate what has occurred.

She considered no doubt that she was wrong, for she cried:

—Look, that is not all, pay me immediately and take yourself off somewhere else. Has one ever seen anything like? You believed perhaps that I was going to lodge you and keep you for your pretty face? No, my dear. I have been done already in that way, and you don't catch me any more. There was a respectable gentleman, very polite, rich, and wearing a red ribbon, who was answerable for you, if you had been willing to make an arrangement with him; but instead of making an arrangement with him, you have a dispute; so much the worse for you, your family quarrels don't concern me. What I want is the money, that is all that I know; pay me my bill and get out, you little prostitute.

—Come, dear Madame, I will try and arrange this little matter, said Monsieur Tibulle, appearing again; the little one is going to think better of it, I feel sure. Let me reason with her.

Madame Connard withdrew complacently.

—You see, you see in what a position you are placing yourself, said the excellent old gentleman, crossing his arms and looking at the young girl with all the dignity and sorrow of a father who has detected his child in some shameful act.

—Say rather into what an ambush you have driven me, you old scoundrel.

—Oh, oh, oh! no bad word, my girl. Bad words are no use. I am going away to pay the bill.

—A fig for you and your money.

—What! a fig for me and my money! In the first place you should never despise money, my girl; we can do nothing without money in this world. And then you are wrong to despise me, who only wish you well, my dear; yes, yes, wish you well.

—I tell you to leave me alone.

—Look now, don't be naughty, for I am going to settle the matter.

—I don't want you. Don't touch me....

—And how are you going to get yourself out of this scrape, if you will not let me get you out. You rebuff me again, though I only want to make you happy.

—I tell you not to come near me.

—Come, be pacified, you little angry cat; only a kiss and that shall be all.

He wanted to take hold of her waist, but she pushed him back. But he had gone too far to believe that he ought to beat a retreat, and he retained to the charge with renewed vigour. In the struggle she seized him by the neck, his waistcoat came undone, and a little square bit of painted canvas, of a dubious colour, remained in her hand. She threw it back in his face in disgust.

—My scapular! he cried. You throw my scapular about in this way. Stay, you are a little wretch, a street-walker, a hussy, a reprobate. You will perish miserably, and I leave you to your fate. Ah, you throw away my scapular!

When he had said this, the good gentleman piously recovered his scapular, buttoned up his overcoat, and retired full of dignity.

XCIII
FROM THE DARK TO THE FAIR

"Moderation should preside over pleasure: let us seek in
new pleasures a refuge against the satiety of our souls."

KALVOS DE ZANTE (*Odes nouvelles*).

Zulma had remembered Marcel and had gone to him boldly.

—You have been crying then, my child? said the priest who noticed her
red eyes.

The young girl in a few words informed him of her adventure.

—Who would ever have believed that? she said. Such a kind man! Such
an obliging lady! The old gentleman said to me at Vic: "I shall not concern
myself about you if you do not go to Confession, if you do not receive the
Communion, if you do not say your prayers." Whom can one trust?

And that Madame Connard: "Eat what you like, and don't stand on
ceremony. Monsieur Tibulle wishes it so. Old men are made to pay." And
with all these fine words, I owe her ten *francs*.

Marcel could not help laughing at the girl's artlessness.

—Then you have come to ask me for them.

—Yes, said Zulma blushing; have I not done right? She has kept my
band-box, the old thief; what it contains is not worth ten *francs*, but I don't
want to leave it with her.

—And what will you give me in exchange?

—Everything you want.

—That is a great deal to promise; but you have nothing.

—It is true, I have nothing, she said piteously. Well, I will kiss you and
will love you very much. One may kiss a Curé, may one not?

Marcel thought she was getting to business very quickly.

—Priests do not receive kisses from anybody, he replied.

—From nobody? not even from a sister?

—But you are not my sister.

—Well, I will be your comrade.

—No more do they have a comrade.

—Oh, well, if I were a man I should not like to be in your position; one must get awfully tired of being all alone. What are you able to do all the blessed day? For my part, in the first place I must have a lover.

—Ha, ha! and who is your lover?

—A rider at the Loyal Circus. A handsome boy too. A tall dark fellow like you. He is a little too proud, but I like that in a man.

—And for how long has he been your lover?

—Ever since I have seen him. It is nearly two years ago at the fête at Mirecourt. Our booth was beside the Circus.

—Two years! cried Marcel: but at what age did you begin?

—Begin what? to dance on the tight-rope?

—To have lovers.

—But I have only had one, and that is he.

—Well, how old were you when you had him?

—I have never had him.

—Look, dear child, you have told me that you are sixteen.

—Yes, sir.

—Then you began at fourteen.

—Began what?

—With your lover.

—We never began anything. I have told you that he was too proud. I wanted to speak to him once, and he answered, "Go along."

—But he is not your lover.

—But he is, because I love him.

—And you have not had others.

—No, because I love him.

—Well, you are a good girl, and if what you have said is true, you are worth your weight in gold.

—My weight in gold! cried Zulma laughing; then buy me, for it is true, and I shall be rich.

—But how shall I know if what you say is true?

—Ah, that is embarrassing, she said thoughtfully. What can I do to prove it?

—I believe you without proof. But I am not rich enough to pay you.

—It doesn't matter, to you I give myself for nothing.

Marcel was bewildered and hurriedly gave her the ten *francs*.

—How kind you are; I should like all the same to do something for you.

—You wish to please me? Well, remain good.

—Only that! And till when?

—Until I give you permission not to be so any longer.

—I will certainly.

She took a few steps towards the door, opened it, then turning back suddenly, she advanced her bust, as though she were making a bow to the crowd, and placing the tips of her fingers on her lips, she wafted a gracious kiss to the priest.

—There is pleasant and easy love-making, said Marcel to himself. Why did I not know it sooner?

He ran to the door.

—Wait, my child. Where are you going to sleep to-night? It is late. Have you a lodging?

—Stay, my word no, I had forgotten it.

—This is what you will do. First, settle your account with this landlady, without making allusion to anything. A scandal must always be avoided. Monsieur Tibulle is a man, highly esteemed, with a considerable position in the world, and anything you might say against him, would only turn against you. Do not tell this story then to anybody; and do not tell anybody that you know me. Now take these two *louis*, my dear child, and buy yourself a few little articles of dress. You must be dressed properly. Go, and come back here. Monsieur Patin!

The landlord appeared.

—Monsieur Patin, said Marcel, I confide this young person to you, or rather, to Madame Patin here. She has been recommended specially to me by some ladies of high rank. She is going to fetch her small articles of luggage, and will soon be back again. Be careful of her. Give her a room and her meals; I am answerable for her. Mademoiselle, I shall see you again to-morrow.

What were Marcel's intentions?

Had he felt the appetite for the unknown awakening?

He who had just poured forth his bitterness upon woman and upon love, had be come to the conclusion in the presence of this stranger that he could not do without woman or without love!

But the other?

The other was not there, and the absent are in the wrong.

Could this one make him forget the other? Could a new fancy destroy the strong love which bound him and was ruining him? Could a love facile and without risk soothe the hidden mischief and diminish the fury of a dangerous passion? She had all that was required for that, this little fair girl with the tempting lips.

Like Suzanne she was young and charming, like Suzanne she would be loving, and unlike Suzanne, she would be submissive.

Her eyes swimming in their azure, her aquiline nose with its mobile nostrils, her scarlet fleshly lips, her golden hair like ripened corn, her rosy cheeks in which coursed health and life, the slimness of her waist, the delicacy and whiteness of her hand; it all said: Love me.

And she was a fresh woman … a fresh woman, eternal temptation.

When he returned to the hotel, he found the Comtesse anxiously waiting for him.

With a smile she handed a large packet, sealed with the episcopal arms.

It was his nomination to the Curé of St. Marie. He would have to take possession of it immediately.

XCIV
THE CHANGE

"Prayer on that day is said within the gothic church,
The old men mourn beneath the ancient oak.
Resisted are the games but just begun.
The village maidens will no longer dance."

MME. DE GIRARDIN (Elgire).

The worshippers at Althausen were much surprised the next day to see a priest whom they did not know, officiating without ceremony in the place of their Curé. He was stout and plain, with an inflamed face, bloated lips, a cynical look, and a thundering voice: he said Mass in such a hasty and indecorous manner that they went away scandalized. The handsome Marcel certainly was no longer there, with his sweet and unctuous voice, his evangelic piety, and his eyes which stirred their hearts.

The report spread through the village that the handsome Curé had gone away, and all the gossips at bay grouped in the market-place and watched for Veronica to assail her with questions. But the old maid-servant to her mortification knew no more about it than the gossips. She ventured to interrogate her new master, but he slapped her on the back and sent her away to her kitchen-stove.

—He is disgusting, this old fellow, she said. For my part I am not going to remain here. I prefer the Corporal.

Durand had just sat down at table with his daughter, when Marianne with a scared air, looked at Suzanne in a mysterious way, and said to the Captain:

—Do you know? Monsieur le Curé has gone away.

—Pleasant journey, said Durand.

—There is a new Curé already in his place. He said Mass this morning.

—A new Curé, cried Suzanne; then he has gone away not to return again?

—Gone away without hope of coming back, said the Captain, that is discouraging! It surprises you then, little girl, that the handsome priest has disappeared with neither drum nor trumpet, and with no touching farewells to his flock. For my part, I am not surprised at it, and I wager that he has committed some act of blackguardism, and has absconded.

—Oh, father!

—He has not absconded, Marianne said quickly; he went away on Friday very quietly with another Curé.

—Let him go to the devil!

Suzanne had difficulty in hiding her palor and her distress. She pretended to have a head-ache, left the table, ran to her room and burst into tears. Why this decisive departure? Why had she not received a single warning from Marcel? No doubt, he had done it for the best, but that best was incomprehensible to her; her heart was broken, and her self-love received a cruel wound.

Soon the news arrived. The new Curé announced Marcel's change in the sermon, and said farewell for him to his parishioners. Everybody was in consternation. He might have announced the seven plagues of Egypt.

For her part Marianne received a mysterious packet which was intended for Suzanne. The priest, in cautious terms informed her of his change, and said it was necessary to wait. Wait for what? Suzanne waited.

But one morning she awoke full of dismay; she had felt something give a start in her entrails. She wrote a long letter to Marcel, and Marcel answered: Wait.

Wait for what? She waited again.

XCV
THE CURÉ OF ST. MARIE

"The white ground and the gloomy sky
Blended their heads sepulchral;
The rough north winds of winter
Breathed to the heart despair."

CAMILLE DELTHIL (*Poèmes parisiens*).

Weeks and then months passed away. One rainy winter's evening a young woman, in deep mourning, with her face covered with a thick veil, stopped at the Curé of St. Marie's door.

She had hesitated for a long time; several times she had passed in front of the tall gray house, casting a furtive glance on the lofty windows, slackening her walk and seeming to say: "Ought I to go in? Yes, I must go in." But each time she pursued her way again. At length, as the rain kept falling ever colder as night came on, she controlled herself by en effort, slowly retraced her step and rang gently.

The door was opened at once, and an old woman with a face the colour of leather, invited her in mysteriously, "Whom shall I announce?" she asked.—"Do not announce me. I am expected."

The old woman smiled discreetly and showed her into a large parlour, the door of which she closed upon her.

It was a bare wainscoted room, gloomy, lighted by two candle-ends.

A *prie-Dieu*, a table, some straw chairs, a few rows of old books on shelves painted black, composed all the furniture.

A large crucifix of wood which stretched its thin arms from one window to the other, contributed no little to give a sorrowful and monastic look to the room.

The young girl approached the chimney-piece, where a few brands were burning at the bottom of a huge grate. She shivered, perhaps more from emotion than from cold, for she remained there, thoughtful, forgetting even to warm her feet, soaked by the rain.

A door opened soon at the other end of the room and Marcel entered.

He had greatly changed during these few months.

His eye shot forth a gloomy fire, his cheeks were hollow, and numerous threads of silver showed themselves in his dark locks. It was evident that anxiety, watchings and cares, contended on his wrinkled brow.

At the sight of the young woman he assumed a livid palor.

—You, he murmured in a stifled voice, you here, Mademoiselle?

—I am, replied Suzanne; did you not reckon then on seeing me again?

—Not now, dear child, I confess to you. I had said to you: Wait.

—And I have waited. And weary of waiting, I decided to come and to know finally from your own mouth what I must wait for, and on what I most count. But ... sir.... I am tired: will you allow me to sit down?

—Pardon me, Mademoiselle, I mean to say, dear Suzanne, but your coming has filled me with such confusion....

He handed her a chair, and sat down facing her.

—Ah! dear child, you do not know with what cares I am overwhelmed.

—They must indeed be very serious, sir, since they have made you forgetful of your duties, even to the care of your honour and of mine ... for the moment is approaching when I shall no longer he able to hide the consequences of your....

—Of our fault, dear Suzanne, of both our faults. Do not overwhelm me alone, for it was your pretty face which made me mad. But is it really possible? Can it be true? what, you are....

—I have let you know it, sir, a long time ago, and you have not deigned to give any answer on that subject. I have read and read again your letters many times, seeking for a word which might console me, for a hope, for a light, but there was nothing. You have told me to wait; you have tried, like a coward, to gain time, you have reckoned on something unforeseen occurring, which might settle the question without your aid ... and you would have washed your hands of it in peace in your broad conscience. But the time has gone on, the unexpected has not come, and now here I am, and I come to ask you: What do you intend to do with me?

—In truth, dear Suzanne, I had not believed ... Ah, you are more beautiful than ever ... No, I had not believed that the case was so desperate.

—You have not believed. No doubt, amidst your life of lies, surrounded by hypocrites and criminals, you have included me charitably in the number, and supposed that I lied.

—Suzanne, dear Suzanne, do not be offended … I believed that you wished to terrify me … Ah, how lovely you are like this … Ah, it is a terrible misfortune. We must guard against it. And your father, does he suspect?

—Not yet, sir, but the moment is approaching when I shall no longer be able to hide the truth.

—It is true then. What is to be done? What is to be done?

—Stop; you would make me laugh, if I did not pity you. I am come to ask you, for the last time, if I ought to count upon you.

—Count upon me? But, my dear child, upon whom would you count if not upon me? There is no doubt but that you have only me to count on. I am your friend, your only friend. Always the same, dear Suzanne. I am ready for anything, in order to get you out of this scrape. But judge yourself. I am observed by all here, the slightest report would re-echo terribly and would ruin me. I am surrounded by those who envy me and consequently are my enemies. In a year or two, perhaps, I may be Grand-Vicar. You see how careful I have to be of my position. I will do everything, be well assured of it, it is my interest as well as yours, but I cannot do the impossible. What do you ask?

—You have a short memory, sir, but I remember, I remember with what infernal art you induced me, not to yield to you—for you well know, and God is witness to it, that I yielded only to violence—but to listen to you with a too trustful ear. No, I see you do not remember it: you have forgotten so many things that it would be lost time to try and refresh your memory. You do not answer? For in truth, sir, the parts are strangely altered, and if I am ashamed of it for myself, I blush still more for your sake. But since you are so careful of your future and of your fortune, I am come to tell you this: I am rich, sir, do not then fear anything, do not dread poverty; I have inherited from an aunt, who leaves me enough to provide me with a husband. But what I want is a father for my child….

—Mademoiselle, dear and fondly-loved Suzanne, yes, ever fondly-loved Suzanne, I am full of confusion and remorse; I thank you from the bottom of my heart for your generous offer … but … can I accept it? I make you the judge of it yourself. Do I belong to myself? I am the Church's, bound from head to foot, body and soul; not a thought belongs to myself, I am but the infinitesimal portion of an immense wheel which carries me away in spite of myself. How can I loosen myself from the gear? Can I do it? Can I defy such a scandal? My honour, my dignity as a man….

—Ah, you are appealing to your honour now … but, sir, your duty, is not that your honour? And what is your duty? Stay, you are a wretch….

As she uttered these words, a young girl's head, fair, charming, rosy looked inquisitively through the half-open door. Suzanne saw it and grew pale. Her brows contracted and a bitter smile passed across her lips.

—I understand, she said, I understand your hesitation, your honour and your scruples. Farewell, sir....

And she went out, without turning her head, stifling her sobs.

Marcel followed her with his eyes, and ran to the door:

—Suzanne, Mademoiselle, to-morrow you shall have an answer. Another word...

She made no reply and he heard the street-door close.

A tear rolled to the edge of his eyelid.

He rushed to the window to call her back, but a hand laid hold of his and the fair girl stood before him.

—Well, Monsieur my uncle, well! And who is that handsome dark girl?

—Ah, my poor Zulma, do not be jealous of her.

—I am jealous of everything, and I want to know.

XCVI
FINIS CORONAT OPUS

"No mortal can foresee his fate
Let none despair. Comrades, good night."

BYRON (*Mazeppa*).

The following evening, the canal toll-collector on the Malzeville road discerned a black shadow which, despite the icy rain, remained for a long time leaning on the parapet of the turn-bridge, then all at once disappeared. He called for help and, a few minutes afterwards, they drew out of the water the body of a young girl of remarkable beauty.

A portion of a letter was found upon her which at first aroused a thousand comments.

This is what was written:

"I have just celebrated the Holy Sacrifice of the Mass, and during the Elevation, I prayed God to inspire me with a good idea. I likewise asked of the Queen of Angels what I could do for this unfortunate one. The All-pitying God and the Mother chaste and pure hearkened to me. Let my sister in Jesus Christ whose image will never be effaced from the heart of her spiritual friend, go and knock at the gate of the Convent of Our Lady of the Seven Sorrows, in the parish of St. Marie; there, the cares which her interesting condition demand, will be afforded her. It will be easy to explain her temporary absence, and, in case of need, to obtain the permission of a parent who wished to place an obstacle in the way of this pious necessity. Divine Providence will assist in this as it assists all those who have recourse to it. The ladies of the Seven Sorrows are informed, and they await the new sheep with mothers' and sisters' hearts.

"Let it be thus done in the Name of the Father and of the Son and of the Holy Ghost:

"Jesus, Mary, Joseph."

On applying at the Convent of the Seven Sorrows, the good sisters said that in fact they had received a letter, sealed with the episcopal arms, announcing the arrival of a young lady. They were unable to say more.

Monseigneur, when questioned, summoned the Abbé Marcel who gave the examining magistrate the most satisfactory explanations, acknowledging that he was the author of the letter, and that she was a young girl whose honour he desired to save.

This event did the greatest good to the reputation of the former Curé of Althausen. His discretion, his wisdom and his virtue were lauded more than ever.